Praise for *Mixedbloods*

"A compelling and stunning debut novel, *Mixedbloods* tells the story of Exley DeGroat, a Ramapough Lenape teenager. Joseph Rathgeber takes us back and forth in time in order to explore the history of a persecuted people. Through vivid language and relentlessly musical yet gritty prose, Rathgeber describes a polluted land, underneath which exists a warren of abandoned mines. This is a tragic and gripping tale of prejudice, precarity, and how heartless corporations view indigenous peoples as disposable. This book is both terrifying and beautiful."
—Maria Mazziotti Gillan, American Book Award-winning author of *All That Lies Between Us*

"*Mixedbloods* is brilliant. The style is intense and unrelenting, and the narrative is powerful, moving, heartbreaking, and important. The devastation of a community and their struggle to find some way to get justice is beautiful and vital. It is the kind of book we need right now."
—Nathan Oates, author of *The Empty House*

"A writer of unnerving originality, harrowing precision, and searing conscience, Joseph Rathgeber captures in a heart-quaking minuteness of detail the rages and graces of two generations of Ramapough Lenape Indians surviving at the margins of twenty-first-century northern New Jersey. *Mixedbloods* will enthrall and consume you."
—Gary Lutz, author of *Stories in the Worst Way* and *Divorcer*

Also by Joseph Rathgeber

The Abridged Autobiography of Yousef R. and Other Stories

MJ

MIXEDBLOODS

JOSEPH RATHGEBER

Billy—
thanks for the support.
_Joe

6-5/10

Fomite

Burlington, VT

The pure products of America

go crazy—

—William Carlos Williams, "To Elsie"

I am curious about one thing. In all the years the mine people—those Jackson Whites—have been in this community, what have they really achieved? I would submit, over a hundred years to accomplish something and they blew it. This is except ride the welfare rolls.

—Winston J. Reed, Mahwah Councilman

Always in summer
Stand the seven trees;
ash and oak and all along
   past they cannot proceed.
What are they standing on?
—a Negro/Lenape charm

VERSIONS & VARIANTS

They have no name for themselves. *They are Jackson Whites. They are Jacks and Whites. They are colored. They are non-white. They are hybrids. They are mongrels. They don't meet the blood quantum standard. They are wild renegades. They are Hessian mercenaries. They are deserters. They are the offspring of English and West Indian prostitutes. They are runaway slaves, fugitive slaves, freed slaves. They are half-breeds. They are a folk legend. They are mestizos. They are negroes. They are mixed Indian and negro blood. They are reticent, indolent, improvident. They are outcasts. They are vagabond white men. They are an amalgamation. They are albinos. They are piebald. They are mulattoes. They are zwaart. They are Aethiopes. They are burnt-faces. They are Injuns. They are human hunters, cannibals. They are not federally recognized. They are blue-eyed niggers. They are a separate little race. They are unbelievers in soap. They are endogamous marriages. They are polydactyl. They are webbed toes.*

They are fecund. They are sub-normal intelligence. They are mutants. They are woodpile relations. They are sacrifice zones. They are separate areas of existence. They are the exoticism of poverty. They are a disaster area. They are pollutants themselves. They are a proliferation of stories. They are cousins in the bush. They sure as hell don't look like Indians to me.

1

MAY 1996.
Norval DeGroat walked, wending through the woods. He hugged a tarp to his chest. His boots crunched the understory as he passed a boulder wall of gneiss. He traced the banding of the rock and fingered the mossy fissures and held his wrist to it. His compass needle spun off north. Figuring the time, he hurried along, arriving at Peters Mine sooner than he'd imagined: the sky hadn't yet begun to gloam.

He climbed over rocks and corrosive scrap and wiped his brow. His skin was weathered and the chalkiest taupe in color. Norval's great-grandda ran slush in the mines century last. His grandda was a castings grinder. His da was a woodcutter. Norval never worked the mines like them. He wasn't nothing but the wearer of that plaited lanyard compass, passed onto him. He noised a common flicker pecking for beetle larvae. He saw the sky blackening. He began to strip.

Norval unbuttoned his plaid shortsleeve and lifted off his wife-beater, mindful of the carbuncles on his neck. He pulled down his ripstop cargos, his drawers, and pried off his hiking boots and socks. He gave a hacking cough so hard it caused wingbeats. He folded and piled the clothes like a cairn—socks balled on top—at the crotch of a white oak. He dragged a pallet to the mouth of the mine and flapped open the tarp.

Prior to taking his place—on the pallet, within the tarp, in the adit of the mine—he scrawled a note on a yellow sheet. He creased it, bedaubed the ends with saliva, and sandwiched the paper between his clothes.

He sat—cross-legged and uncovered—in the center of the pallet. He centered himself. Now he held the blued handgun that had been enveloped in the tarp, the blued handgun that could jump a deer back five yards. He gathered the tarp around and tented his whole body. He didn't want to defile nature. No one wanted that. He suffered the oppressive heat, breathing heavy. He brought the muzzle to the center of his forehead, imprinting a third eye on his bald noggin. The tarp filtered his vision. Everywhere he looked was azure. The ribbed mountains or the valley-cleft or the branches of the white oak could not be discerned. What he heard was the crosscurrents of the riverbed or the rustle of the tarp—there was no knowing for sure. Everything was chaos. Norval committed to it in that moment, to killing himself. His body blustered backward and crumpled into the tarp.

2

ZIKE AND ELSIE LIVED in a 1960s Rollohome ten-wide trailer with broad, horizontal stripes on the exterior—pastel pink, blue, and white. A giveaway NY Jets flag was roped to the hitch, and a slide-out awning provided some cover for the steps where Elsie grew thyme, spearmint, and basil in buckets. Zike's roached out, 4-stroke Honda dirt bike was leaned against the rear of the trailer. Its chain and sprockets were oxidized orange, and the seat fairing had a graphic of the Blessed Virgin aureoled with blue acetylene flames. She was crowned with a Wu-Tang "W" decal, and the Misfits' crimson ghost skull logo was stuck where her mons pubis would be.

Exley DeGroat made a rattly knock on the door but pulled it open to let himself in. The TV was on—a game show rerun—and, aside from the shrieks of a winning contestant, the place was silent.

The bedroom was full of light; there were no window treatments. Zike was asleep in bed, sheeted toes to chin. The sheet was tucked under his sides like a mummy. An issue of *X-Force* the family-size Listerine. He plopped down into an armchair. "Unky Orrin's been on me about taking the teetotal pledge. Like he's one to talk, right?"

Exley sat across from him on the sofa. Zike kept guzzling, wincing after each draft. He raised his arm and sniffed his pit. Ex got a clear view of the tawny carbuncles.

"So where's Elsie?"

"She was in A.C. for the weekend. Now she's visiting with Sandra."

"Where's she live?"

"Neptune." Zike sniffed himself again. "I stink."

Exley inventoried the items on the top shelf of the entertainment center: a semicircle of picture frames, an air freshener, a stack of CD jewel cases, a gaudy bowl of potpourri, a pedestaled crucifix.

Zike leaned forward. Exley watched the colostomy bag crease.

"Alright, let's do this, heh?"

Zike finished off the Listerine and flung the bottle into the kitchen.

He staggered to the shower stall so full of ire that Exley had to do the undressing. He tried to be gentle, stretching the elastic as wide as would allow, careful not to graze his brother's maculate flesh. There were wens and boils and striated strips—he was a body full of pus. Whole sections seemed flakily scalded. He'd been cut, excised, whittled down. His body was the rough draft of a horror story, and there was more to be deleted, *but*—Exley thought—*with so much gone, what's left to take?*

It was ablution by sponge bath. Exley pointed the shower-head away from Zike's body and the weak water pressure cascaded down the tiles. Exley ragged him down, tentatively. Zike groaned and braced himself with both hands on the frame of the shower door. His sweat glands were prone to infection, and that accounted for most of his surgeries. Exley gently went over the grafts with the washrag. He skimmed over wrinkly tissue.

"I'm sorry, bro," Zike said, beginning to cry.

The smell was overpowering. Exley had to turn his face away from the shower stall every few seconds.

"I'm good, bro. Don't worry about it," Exley said, closing his mouth and pushing the air out his nostrils.

The pus running out of Zike's body was a slurry spiraling down the drain, like the Freon, the battery acid, the radiator fluids streaming through the valleys of the Ramapos. Zike began to sob.

"I stink, bro. I fucking stink." Zike's chest heaved, and Exley rinsed the soap off him. "Elsie can't sleep with me in the same bed, man. My wife—*my own wife*—won't even fuck me. I ooze, Ex. I'm feest of myself. I disgust her. I disgust me. I reek, bro. I'm fucking gross. She's afraid to even touch me."

Exley remembered when they were kids—the shared tub, bathing in the same basin of grime and skin cells as his elder brother. He remembered how Zike's long legs lined the tub, his knees slightly bent and emerging from the surface, the wet hairs:

wooded hilltops. Exley—always a shorter version of his brother—would sit between those legs, meditatively folding the washrag into a smaller and smaller square until Zike held up his shriveled fingers, retching in a hoarse and trembling voice—a monster.

Exley would clamber out of the tub—afraid as he ever was—and run into his parents' bedroom, leaving a trail of bubbly water behind him. "Stop scaring your brother!" Hannah would holler. Their da would hear the rapid footsteps, the splashing, and call from the living room: "That wood's gonna get waterlogged and rot, Hanny!" She'd answer, "Get off your keister and come clean it then, Norval."

And then they'd hear Exley slip and crash into the wall and they'd all roar.

"LET'S GET OUT OF HERE," Ex said, turning off the water, grabbing a ratty towel. He held Zike's elbow. "C'mon. Step."

Exley patted him dry. *Pat pat pat* around the puckering fistulas. The craterous moonscape of his broad back—*pat pat.* Zike was sterile. He was unmanned. Exley moved him into the bedroom and searched through a hamper for clean clothes.

There was a cheval-glass facing the corner wall. Zike approached it, mother-naked, and turned the mirror around. He wanted to behold his body in full. He assessed the totality of the damage done unto him. The geology of his body—the way the skin grafts bulged or depressed in thrust faults: he marveled at it. How couldn't he? What other way was there to interpret the quicksilver pus that pushed through his body and pooled in a surface abscess? He tilted back the cheval-glass and leaned forward, filled with a naïve hope of falling inward—into another dimension or an alternate universe or even into a shattered oval of reflective glass that would cut open his veins and drain him completely. He stood there before his own image and held it in the hollow of his hands.

"C'mon, Zike. Sit down."

Zike followed his brother's lead and sat on the edge of the bed. Exley began dressing him, stretching and applying gauze. Zike opened the nightstand drawer for a prescription bottle and tapped out morphine tablets. Exley pinched the ends of a thin paper pouch and smoothed a fentanyl patch onto Zike's meaty arm, completing the rite.

Falling back onto the bed, Zike said something.

"What?" Exley asked.

"You been ballin'?" Zike mumbled.

Sometimes it was a struggle for him to speak. The surplus of cankersores lining the interior of his mouth—his fleshy cheeks, his geographic tongue, not to mention the booze—made for a muddled talk. A court transcript would indicate *garbled* in square brackets. It was nothing short of speaking in tongues, at times. But Zike was beyond religion and beyond saving.

"Here and there," Ex answered.

"*Here and there?* Why? Is your knee still injured?"

"It's feeling better lately, stronger. I don't know if I'm gonna go out next year, though."

Across the street from the shopping plaza a curtain blew out a second-story window and lapped against the stucco.

Exley stubbed out his cigarette on the wall, lolled, and reentered his workplace through the sensor doors like a lesser god.

Exley nodded to Sue who propped her face in the heel of her hand, an elbow on the cash register. She wore a forearm splint with overhanging velcro tags.

"Where's Aaron?"

"You know where."

Aaron, the manager, was perpetually stationed next to the dumpster in the back lot. He wrangled with his girlfriend over the phone for hours.

Exley busied himself by replacing shelf strips and mylars in Vitamins & Supplements.

Sue paged IC3, and Exley started in the direction of checkout to help. But he turned when a synthesized bell ding sounded over the intercom. A woman's voice—automated and saccharine—announced: ASSISTANCE NEEDED IN THE BABY AISLE.

A young father in mesh shorts, a jordy blue Mahwah Thunderbirds t-shirt, and flip-flops, tapped the locking case on the formula shelf as Exley approached. "That one," he said, pointing to an Enfamil tub of powdered formula. Exley fumbled with sliding the key into the cylinder lock. He huddled his body close to the shelf as if he were shanking someone, turned the key, and lifted the plexiglass lid.

"Nah, *that* one," the customer said.

"Soy?"

"Yeah, the soy one."

Exley passed the tub to the customer and cradled another in his arm. He went straight to the employee locker room.

He opened the door of his cubby and removed a large ziploc. He sliced the seal on the formula tub with his fingernail and dumped the powder into the bag. He buried the empty plastic tub in the garbage bin under paper towels, granola bar wrappers, and styrofoam cups. He shoved the ziploc down his khakis, clasped it with his hand in his pocket, and strolled into the parking lot.

There was a wrinkled black trash bag flat in the trunk of the Ford Escort, license plate H4NN4H. Merchandise was spread throughout the trunk—rolls of gauze, Depends, air tubing, a carton of Virginia Slims, and other ziplocs bellied with powdered formula. Exley returned to the store, went to Sexual Health, and began facing the disordered condom boxes.

Exley never got nervoused up when he stole. To steal was nothing to him. He did it on the regular, a routine operation. And besides, Aaron hadn't done a locker sweep in months and the CCTV was unreliable.

His shift ended. The soured light of the setting sun glared off the pane glass windows. He swaggered to the locker room, peeled off his polo, and swapped his khakis for cargo shorts. Exley was rangy but built—a dented chest and ribs like chair rungs. His head was side-shaved, a thatch of crimped, red hair flopped forward. He reached for the rake comb and nearly grabbed the boxcutter. He hackled back his hair with a beeswax gel. He remarked himself, the shimmer blue eyes recessed behind bone. So full of displeasure, he could almost carve himself up.

"You going to the party in Cragmere?" Sue asked, searching for a barcode on a box of skin numbing cream.

"Heading there from here."

"Okay. I'll probably see you there then."

"Bet."

4

B Y THE TIME EXLEY ARRIVED in Cragmere, the skies were dark-ish—the avenues illumined only by the flowers of Callery pear trees, smelling not so much semen-sweet this late in June as poison. His car stalled out at the LED-fringed stop sign, flashing red. As he pumped the gas pedal, turning over the ignition, he stared out the window at the cobblestoned curbs.

The address of the party was on a tear of paper on the dash—*83 Masonicus Road* flickered against the odometer. Exley was halt-ing, iffy as he gathered a backpack of over-the-counter medicines out of the trunk. He was only welcome at the party because of the tangible items he could provide to his peers.

The paver walkway leading to the side gate was trimmed with artificial flowers—asters and freesias. Pesticide flags poked up from the lawn. A Slomin's Shield placard was conspicuously positioned below a bay window. The gate opened onto a vast yard.

Brash music blared from a small stereo on the deck rail. Nobody was letting a song finish. Kids were just pecs and breasts and necks and arms and heads and mist-damp hair in and—thanks to the raised-relief landmasses—did. He made a show of it. Hitch worked on a blunt with the slow delicacy of an entomologist dissecting a chrysalis with a scalpel.

"Hitch, what the fuck—," Adams said, "let DeGroat, my Injun, roll that shit and light it up. Your people make them good fires, am I right?"

Aubrey, whose house it was, staggered through the screen door, freaking.

"No smoking in the solarium!" she clamored. "What the fuck is wrong with you people?" She ran into the house.

"Fuck's a solarium?" Womack said.

THEY RECONVENED BY THE STORAGE SHED. Kids were stacked on shoulders, splashing, fully-clothed in the pool. The reek of chlorine was still strong. Someone had killed a koi. Exley flame-sealed the blunt with a white lighter. "Check that!" Adams snatched the lighter and tossed it into the pool.

"What gives, Nelson?"

"Bad luck, DeGroat—white lighter. You should know that shit."

Exley stared at Adams as though he could see the pink under his eyelids.

The cypher proceeded but with Adams speaking ceaselessly on all matters of bullshit. About assist-to-turnover ratios. About copping feels. About—as Adams put it—*Exley's people in the hills.* Ex tried to toke and to ignore.

"What you pulling on, DeGroat? That a calumet?" Adams doubled over, stomped his feet. Exley passed the blunt to Womack.

"Your shit ain't even funny, dude."

"Relax, DeGroat," Adams coughed and smiled through it. "Don't get all big brother on me." Adams smacked Hitch in the chest again. "You know about DeGroat's brother back in the day, right? Big goth-looking motherfucker. Dude went off the fucking reservation at school. Some dude called DeGroat's brother a fucking ogre or Grendel or Swamp Thing or some shit like that, and this guy pulls the fucking porcelain water fountain from the wall and smashes it over dude's head, nearly kills him. Fucking brains leaking out. DeGroat's brother got expelled a week before graduation."

Exley's eyes burned like he'd been swimming underwater.

"Retard strength, yo."

The crowd gathered just as fast as Exley stepped to Adams. Womack was as quick to split them apart, stretching Exley's t-shirt collar in the process. A siren bleeped and the side of the house lit up red.

Aubrey came running out of the solarium, bawling: "*Hitch! Can you come?*"

Hitch's father was Mahwah police captain; his uncle was a municipal judge. He headed to the side gate with the blunt still in his hand.

Haggard and reasonably high, Exley parted the privet hedges, hopped a composite split-rail, and circled back toward his car.

Sue was just arriving, still in her CVS polo, albeit untucked. She waved stiffly with her sprained wrist.

"Party over already, Ex?"

"Maybe not," Exley pointed to the cop cars parked pell-mell a few houses down. "Hitch is talking to them. But I gotta be out."

He reversed down Masonicus Road until he hit the intersection he'd stalled at earlier. Then he headed for home.

5

THE COLLAR OF EXLEY'S T-SHIRT was badly stretched. The rearview mirror showed it to be a stroke mouth. Exley stared off while he sat in accident traffic on 287. He saw the Sunoco station and thought about the times his da brought him there to refill jerrycans. His da would let him sit shotgun in the truck, unbuckled, on the short drive down from the mountains, despite the broken up asphalt on Geiger Road. He bounced in the bucket seat as his da drummed to fiddle music on the steering wheel.

While his da plugged the fuel nozzle into a jerrycan, Exley stomped on the black hose stretched across the lot, trying to apply enough pressure to it to make it *ding-ding*. "Traffic, Exley!" his da shouted over the din of the highway. The gasoline fumes he breathed were as familiar as the grease smears on his da's forearms. He moseyed into the convenience store and scanned the snack racks for Yodels.

Exley liked to remove the massive road atlas from the spinny magazine rack and skim its pages. He'd feel the laminate cover and its spiral-bound spine. He'd open it and glean what he could—the

Erik's pit was on a choke chain, asleep, leashed to a pile of mortared cinderblocks. Exley spied Rhetta's wire-meshed chicken ark beyond a rust-gutted junker. Pallets were stacked next door. A moldy, plaid loveseat was hoisted onto the bed of a gooseneck trailer. The trailer had a set of flats and had sunk into soft earth. Gussie and Ora had weeds growing out of their rain gutters and a milk crate hinged onto their meter box and nobody knew why.

Exley pulled into his moeder's driveway. He grabbed a ziploc from the trunk and walked across the road to Lib's house. Her stoop included a steel-latch cooler for mail and a plastic bucket brimming with shovels and water pistols. The wrought-iron railing was stickered with smiley faces. She, too, had chimes— hers were assembled of brake shims and galvanized shank nails. They hung from the zinc awning. Exley set the ziploc inside the screen door and ambled back to his ma's.

Their home was an old company house, a frame dwelling with its windows still plasticked from the raw winter. The roof was, purportedly, shingled with the scales of a legendary catch—an alligator gar wangled into a fyke net in Cupsaw Lake by his great-grandda. Exley moved a stack of *Good Housekeeping* back issues to another corner of the porch and sat in a wicker chair. His moeder was always referring to the porch as the narthex, imbuing it with dirt-poor holiness. The home—a family home—was holy, she insisted.

He leaned forward, folded his hands, and knuckled the tip of his nose. The gravelly grunt of a turkey vulture could be heard in the beeches. His ma's gourd birdfeeder was first in his line-of-sight. But he could, he felt, follow that line through the woodlot, off Stag Hill, down Cannon Mine Road, to the superfund site—the landfill created, Genesis-like, by Ford.

He could see the chain-linked fences chained and padlocked, protecting the dreck and waste that had been dumped there for decades. The EPA signs were mounted at the gate—KEEP OUT and NO TRESPASSING. The fenceposts were weighted down with sandbags. He could see EPA officials drilling monitoring wells in a swale beside the Wanaque Reservoir. They wore yellow knee-high boots and muttered to each other. He could see a contracted toxicologist from the college wandering beyond the Tenax orange mesh fence and toeing a mud puddle, sleeving the sweat from her brow, and tightening her ponytail.

Beyond that, Peters Mine—a deep, multileveled shaft shoveled full of Ford's paint sludge—strippers, lacquers, and thinners. Barrels upon barrels upon barrels. All that O'Connor Disposal had hauled and illegally dumped: the dross and the heavy metals and the benzene and the xylene and the dioxane.

An otherworldly ether emanated from Peters Mine like a mouth belching. Exley and his extended family used to picnic there on aluminum beach chairs—the breezes were blessings. Oxidized Ford parts were strewn about the entranceway. Unky Orrin would be fossicking through the ruins of the ironworks, looking for usable scrap. He'd stumble on a split switch and then a manganese frog, too heavy to haul at once.

But there were also the lakefront money mansions, the Rio Vista palaces, and the newbuilt subdivisions. Exley could envision them, too. There were the high-voltage power lines. And there was always the Manhattan skyline with its highrises and skyscrapers, the tips like metal plectrums raking at the troposphere. Manhattan, which was *Manna-hata*, which was *Mannahattanink*, which is the Munsee and Unami word for *the place of general intoxication*. That's not to say there was a lack of the swigging of mash swill on Stag Hill. Cases of bending elbow filled his moeder's death ledger. Here was Exley, helpless—on his side of the Hudson—a youngblood in a wicker chair, haggling with revenants about his family history, the history of the hills.

6

THE WHIRR OF THE NEBULIZER could be heard throughout the first floor. The house was dark except for the dimmed track lighting coming from the kitchen. Exley's moeder, Hannah, was sedentary at the table in the alcove, deep breathing an aerosol mist. He removed a glass from the cupboard, fetched ice from the freezer, and ran the tap. He approximated two minutes, filled the glass, and guzzled.

Hannah used to be strict—astringent even—but had softened since Norval's death. She looked mellowed, crocheting an afghan that already blanketed much of her body. She rubbed her palms together as though working a hand-warmer, and then extended her arms, inviting Exley over to the table.

She'd been woken by a coughing fit, which wasn't uncommon. Hannah would lift the primitive nebulizer from the pantry shelf—it was encased like a sewing machine—and stabilize it on a dishtowel. The contraption was oldfangled, antiquated, what with its bones stress fractured, crazing at the corners, and the compressor ready to crap-out. She'd forsaken the mouthpiece in favor of a facemask, freeing up her hands for her crocheting, for her crosswords.

Exley set his glass in the sink and walked over to his moeder's receiving hands. She took his hands in hers, squeezed, and said, *My son*—the sentiment reverberated and her smile distorted behind the mask.

The kitchen table was cluttered: orange rinds on a tissue, coupons and a pair of nail scissors, an expanding file open like an accordion, weeks-old church bulletins. Hannah shuffled the clipped coupons and hooked the elastic closure on the expanding file. She adjusted the ravel of tubes on her lap.

Exley flicked the albuterol boxflap, waiting for his moeder to finish her treatment. Exley knew Janet in pharmacy—knew her role with inventory—and was able to secure ampules of the stuff.

He eyeballed the death ledger, yawning open beside the Kleenexes. The death ledger was a logbook. Page after page, it was his ma's looping script, detailing the deaths and causes of death of the community. Her handwriting smelled of the woods. She maintained the ledger so that when all was said and done they wouldn't be unlettered. Hannah was a ruthful woman, a remembrancer. She recited her nightly prayers.

Hannah rubbed her face. She was light-skinned enough to be damned with rosacea, and the rubber mask only exaggerated the redness. She clicked off the nebulizer and sighed.

"Why you getting in so late, Exley?" He sat back in his seat, scratched his neck. "You been drinking."

"No, Ma."

"Smoking then."

Exley stood up and gathered the valve cap, cup, facemask—all the component parts of the nebulizer. He filled a bowl with water, squirted in Palmolive, added a jigger of white vinegar, and soaked the pieces in the suds.

The peeling laminate countertops were papered with medical bills, and there was also the propped up corkboard with push-pinned Medicaid statements. The edges of the papers flittered in the bluster of the oscillating fan.

Hannah billowed the afghan and folded it. Her nightgown was raised to her knees and her compression stockings were rolled down to her ankles. Her legs were varicosed, marmorate with blue bolts of dammed bloodflow. She swiveled on a sandwich of motley seat cushions.

"Did you drop off some formula to Libby?"

"I did."

Libby was Lib Van Dunk, his brother's ex before he met Elsie. Hannah always had a fondness for her. Lib was spending the unbearable summer afternoons dragging an inflatable kiddie pool from her yard down the hatch steps into her cellar. It was cooler there. The hose followed the pool, spritzing leaks from kinks. Lib's twin toddlers *duck-duck-goosed*, their feet-bottoms flecked with the sediment of the cellar floor, while she hipped her colicky ten-month-old.

Exley walked over to the hutch—which was more like a

museum vitrine—housing his moeder's Indian gewgaws and doodads, not an artifact among them. Most of the collection was flea market finds. He hooked his fingers through the eyeholes of a synthetic buffalo skull festooned with colorful beads and feathers.

"Libby's child been wailing longer than I wish to tell you. The mewl of that infant, Lord help it."

"I put the bag between her doors," Exley reassured her.

Hannah parted the curtains to look to the sky.

"*Halve maen* tonight," she said, as though it were an explanation for the baby's crying.

Exley replaced the buffalo skull and picked up a pair of miniature moccasins. There were also pennants, dreamcatchers with fake horsehair nets, toy balsa wood canoes, and headbands with the requisite featherwork.

"Why do you fill the house with this shit, Ma?"

Hannah shambled to the fridge and retrieved a cutting board. She sat back at the table and gnawed on chilled rhizomes and fennel stalks. She pried open a Tupperware of Russian dressing.

"I want you to visit your brother tomorrow. Elsie's been out of town all weekend. I don't like him alone for that long," Hannah said. "I worry."

Hannah was born with a veil. The story goes that her da thought she was faceless—just a scummy gossamer—until the midwife ordered somebody to summon him back so she could make proof of the child and skim off the membrane with him as a witness. It happened to her and her sister both. So Hannah and Black Mag had always been weird together, and they had long claimed they could predict deaths. Exley admired his ma's hoodoo—found it endearing, especially as a kid—but as of late thought her a simpleton when it came to this auguring nonsense.

"He can take care of himself, Ma."

"This is what I'm asking of you, Exley. And bring him some gauze."

Exley ended the charade. He didn't want to be cruel. His ma didn't deserve that, even if she was a nag.

"I already went, Ma. He's good."

"Oh," Hannah beamed, "that's my good boy. And the gauze?"

"That too, Ma."

"Did you spend some time with him? He hates being alone."

"Yeap. I did, Ma. Quality time."

"That's my good boy."

IN THE HALF BATH, EXLEY WASHED UP in the hush following the cascade of the columned sinkwater. He wrung the rag and watched it unravel. He draped the rag over the faucet and shut the light.

Exley heard the *pock pock pock* of compressed air, of a paintball gun, as he headed down the hall. He startled and ran to the front door. He saw a tinted-out Audi hang a U-ey and peel, speeding down Stag Hill. He heard howls but couldn't make any faces through the cloudburst of dirt dust. He stepped off the stoop and saw the house had been hit—the shutters, the siding, and a direct hit on the door hasp of the skinning shed. Radioactive green and hot pink splats.

Hannah was waiting for him in the kitchen.

"That's why I fill the house with *this shit*," she said, gesturing to the hutch. "Now pass me the goshdarn phone."

"*Why?* You know they won't do nothing."

"Irregardless," his moeder said, her voice raised. "I'm filing a report, a complaint. They gonna know we're still here even if they don't want to believe it." Exley soughed. "I don't want to hear it, Exley. I'm concerned with the wellbeing of our people. We'll all be whilomed if we just let be, if we take your attitude. We can't afford to just let be."

Exley stared off, through the buffalo skull and through the dreamcatchers.

"I need to sleep," he said. "I gotta be up early tomorrow."

"Why's that? You working a morning shift?"

"Summer school starts tomorrow."

"*Exley!*" Hannah shouted. "And you out this late."

She started coughing, dry and coarse. She smothered her face in her elbow.

"I need to borrow the car when you get back, Exley."

He kissed her on the cheek, but it was really only his face brushing against the hair covering her ear.

LINGUISTICS

Jersey Dutch is a dead language. The lowest Dutch. Language extinction. It is an argot of the hillfolk. The vulgate—the vulgar tongue—of the mountain people. The mountains have been dispeopled. Their language has been killed. And kill *is the Dutch for* creek. *And, as H.L. Mencken wrote, "in the Jersey counties of Bergen and Passaic it still survives, though apparently obsolescent, and is spoken by many persons who are not of Dutch blood, including a few negroes." And* kop *is* head, *and* bloot *is* bald, *and* oog *is* eye *as* oogen *is* eyes. *But nearly nobody has that facial composition anymore. Jersey Dutch is* Negro Dutch, *which is* nexer däuts *or* neger däuts. Ma *is* mom. Da *is* dad. Moeder *is* mother *is* mother *is* MOTHER. *These words are rarely spoken, but—when they are—they leave a stranger listener with an* orek (earache). *Most are* feest *of it (disgusted by it). A language in its decomposing state would be, wouldn't it? Repulsive. Rotten Pond was Roten Pond before it was corrupted,* roten *being Dutch for* muskrat. *On a* heit (hot) *day. Under a* halve maen *(half moon). Skin so swollen and black and* blauw *(blue). The language is the land and the land is the language.* Kloof *is gap (in a range, not a row of teeth). The word* don[c]k—*as in, Van Dunk—means a slight elevation or hill in a depression or hollow. And* hollow *is always gwine be* holler. Mahwah *is formerly* mawewi, *meaning: "meeting place or assembly." Location, location, location. If you slip on* ramapo—*"slanting rock" or "formed of round ponds"—your dislocation does not guarantee you a doctor's visit. Act like* gentry *(gentlemen). Count to* twalf *(twelve). Nothing is* tabu *(taboo). Walk with a* hunt *(dog). And employ what slang and alternate spellings you can when you need it. Don't be* scairt *(scared) of the* spook *(ghost). Nod and affirm with* yeap *and* yea-up *until your mouth clots dry. Know that* Houvenkopf Mountain *breaks down to "hooge kop" and translates to "high head." Know* Milligan *shapeshifted from* Milliken *and* Mulligan *and* Millican. *From the Gaelic* Maolagán, *derivative of* máel *or* maol, *meaning* bald *[bloot] or tonsured. Like the head of a monk. Like the clear-cut hillock. Know* DeGroat *is the man who grew oats.* DeGroat *is de (the)* groat, *the* groot, *the* grote, *the greatest man in size and shape. And* whilom *is dead death dying deceased.* DEAD. *A tombstone in the colored folk burial plot inscribed with words you can't even begin to understand. So don't try, youngblood. Language death.*

7

GUSSIE AND ORA MILLIGAN LIVED with their daughter Emilia through an alley of elms. Their off-kilter bungalow was raised on a cement foundation, and the home was situated along a ravine flanked by bracken ferns. It was an inheritance from Ora's side. Well within walking distance, Exley made frequent visits and did so on Monday morning.

There was wash on the line, and Gussie still had coffee can cloches over his seedlings even though there hadn't been a frost warning for months. The Milligans maintained a riot of a vegetable garden and crated produce to a biweekly farmers' market in Fardale. They grew in raised beds with untainted topsoil and advertised as such. Otherwise nobody would buy.

Gussie was pitchforking a compost pile. Exley snuck up, brushing back a tousle of spoonwood, and pelted Gussie with an infant chestnut still in its spiky seedpod. Gussie turned and mimed a stabbing motion.

"You punk-ass."

"What's the word?" Exley greeted.

mped his Virginia Slims and offered one to Gussie. "I'm good," he said. "What's with the bitch cigs?"

"I take what I can get, Gussie."

Gussie's pants and V-neck looked like scrubs, but they were DOC blues gotten from Goodwill. The shrilling of cicadas could be heard overhead. There was a shine to Gussie's forehead.

"It's so sweltering already, heh?"

"Hot as hades—*heit*," Gussie said. "My great-grandma Eunice Milligan, who they called Nicey, she spoke Jersey Dutch—fluent with it. I can still hear her saying that, *heit*. Raspy-voiced. She smoked a pipe."

He handled a tin bucket and spread fish heads into the garden. Exley pulled on a cigarette. Ora bounded out the side door and slung a purse over her shoulder. Her face was a terrain of coagulating eyeliner and acne scars. She wore an oversized shirt and worn bluejeans, and she was clearly nettled.

"Can you please get in by Emilia?" She was unlocking the car door, rushing to an appointment to donate her plasma.

"Yea-up, but I need to leave for work by noon."

"I'll be back," she said, reversing the car.

"You wanna come in and see Meal?" Gussie asked.

Exley babysat for Emilia when she was just a little one, when Gussie and Ora both worked nightshifts. He and plenty others in the tribe patchworked the childcare. Gussie was only a few years older than Ex, but it felt like more. It was probably all the fathering Ex had witnessed. He learned a lot.

"I would, but I don't want to hep her up," Exley said. "I gotta make this class."

"C'mon, Ex," Gussie insisted, moving inside. "Just for a minute."

Emilia ran to Exley as he entered the house. She clenched his calves and squeezed her face between his knees. Her fingernails were enameled with layers of magic marker. She wore a bracelet made of a cutup cardboard toilet paper tube, stamped with faded rainbows, ladybugs, and peace signs. It was adhered with scotch tape. The adornment was furry now, having been through several bathtub washes.

"Daddy washed-ed me with it still on," she explained. "I told him—I told him I wanted to take it off before he washed-ed me, but he didn't listen."

"Well I'm sure he didn't mean to."

Gussie made notations on a calendar. He was a man freighted with appointments and bill collectors and Ora, his wraithlike wife. She struggled to even be around the sick child. She struggled with the simplest of tasks.

Ex and Emilia puzzled on the braided area rug in the den. She didn't look ill, not now, with her swollen and squinting face in the mist and glint of the morning light. But cancer cells were clouding around her bones, casting a pall shadow. Emilia established the border of the puzzle all by herself, less aware of Exley than she had been.

"It's been a rough twenty-four hours with her," Gussie said, coming in from the kitchen.

"Her who? Ora?"

"Meal." Gussie began to comb back his daughter's hair with his hands. "She came in from playing in the yard yesterday with a chromium nosebleed—she didn't even know it. Thought it was snot. She wiped it all over her cheeks and ears, in her hair."

"Are you talking about me, Daddy?"

"Yes, babe. About your nosebleed yesterday."

"Last week, you mean?"

"No, yesterday, babe."

"*Nooo*," Emilia whined. "That was last week."

"Okay, baby," Gussie redirected her to the pile of unused puzzle pieces. "Last week." Exley strutted a puzzle piece across the floor, incarnating it to tickle and nibble Emilia's belly. "And then last night," Gussie continued, "she spiked a fever at like eleven. *High*—like 103. I spent the night sat up in her bed—no AC, hot as all hell. I ran ice cubes up and down her arm, even soaked the sheets with cold water. It was bad."

Gussie gathered Meal's hair into a ponytail.

Exley sympathized. He'd seen Gussie's tenderness on plenty of occasions. Gussie taught Ex how to care for Emilia—how to warm a bottle, how to swaddle her, rock her, how to diaper her while holding both teeny ankles with one hand. He could recall those initial training days, regarding Gussie's softness.

Meal still had the faintest blue vein running vertically—a half-inch, maybe—between the bridge of her nose and the corner of her eye: that remote inlet. Gussie would trace it with his ring finger during feedings, delicate-like, so as to not disrupt her suckling on the slow flow bottle of formula. Gussie would burp her after two ounces, demonstrating for Ex, and then pass the baby to him to finish the bottle. And Exley would burp her the same. Exley could still feel the intimacy of it—even now, three years on—the feel of Meal struggling to lift her head, to support it on her own, but the neck muscles not there yet. And her head—all its weight—falling onto his shoulder. How he feared the shift of her unfused skull, the soft, sunken fontanelle. The subtleties of her body. She'd burp, and the emission would put the quietus on the feeding. Exley would delicately pass Meal back to Gussie, and he would gently place Meal into the portacrib.

8

EXLEY DROVE, FOLLOWING THE STREAMS running off Erskine Lake, skirting the Wanaque Reservoir, and lumbering over the old Erie Railroad tracks that were nearly flush with the asphalt. The Escort needed struts. Ex recalled his da jerry-rigging car repairs on weekends. He remembered how sweaty he'd be, how hard he napped afterward, and he remembered climbing onto the couch and sprawling on his da's stomach. He remembered how the lifting of his da's chest would lift him— their breaths as matched as a man and a child's could be. Exley's memory dashed as he pulled into a parking spot at the high school.

He was late but took his time. Overturned desks and stacked chairs obstructed the halls. A janitor's long, shaggy dust mop leaned against a doorframe. The maintenance staff was already buffing out the blasphemies from the bathroom stalls.

The walls were still postered though, and a flyer for the E.R.A.C.E. Club (Everyone Respecting All Cultures Everywhere) was taped above the water fountain. This was *the* water fountain. His brother's. The stuff of legend. Exley thought it should be demarcated in some way, designated off-limits with velvet ropes and *No Flash Photography* signage. It should be autographed and galleried, given an audio tour option. It should be mounted in an emptied, whitewashed room of echoes. Exley turned the valve and watched the water run.

Mr. Chilowicz—who most students referred to as "Chill"—was already yammering on about covalent bonds. Exley failed chemistry, impressively—a forty-two on the final exam, with a curve. The mole was his mortal enemy. Mole calculations made him miserable. Having Chill for three weeks of summer school meant it wouldn't be as easy as showing up.

"Three tardies equals a failure for this abbreviated course," he informed the class in general and Exley in particular. The syllabus was projected onto the white board.

No more than ten students populated the class, ten failures. Green-tinged safety goggles hung by their elastics off a pegboard. The cabinets were packed with wash bottles, flasks, clamps, and test tube racks. There was even a mortar and pestle, not unlike the one his moeder used for grinding herbs. A senior who was denied walking at graduation held a compact mirror open, plucking her eyebrows with forceps.

There was a pay-for-pencils policy—to borrow one would cost the neglectful student a dollar. Exley saw the sharpened points fanning out of a soup can on Chilowicz's desk and had no intention of asking for one. He saw Sue a few chairs away in the window aisle. He whispered to her and pinched his fingers, making a squiggling motion in midair.

THE TOWN RECYCLING CENTER wasn't far from campus. Exley and Sue walked the tract of city land after class ended. They meandered the varying municipal buildings, storage sheds, and barns. They enjoyed the redolence of the geodesic dome containing alps of rocksalt. Sue described it as an enormous igloo. A de-icing dumptruck was reversed in its entryway.

One roll-off dumpster contained outdated electronics— big screen TVs, VCRs, and more microwaves than any hominid race actually needs. Another contained rubber tires—punctured, blown, or bald. Ex and Sue ended up at the shadowed entrance of a hangar storing amber glass. Barrels of beer bottles, mostly, and the shallow sea of shards littered underfoot—the bounty for some processing plant. Ex dopily sneaker-stomped the disorderly floor; he liked the crunching feeling. Sue, in her open-toed sandals, stayed back. She waited for Ex to fill her in on the Adams situation from the party.

"It was nothing," he explained. "Dude's a dick."

"And so you almost fought him?"

"It wasn't gonna be much of anything," Ex said sheepishly. He grabbed a bottle by the neck and flung it as far as he could into the hangar, the half torn Budweiser label flickering like a kite ribbon.

"Womack said it was about your brother."

Exley reached into another barrel, pulling his sleeve back from the grimy brim of it. He flung the next bottle even farther. The shattering glass charged him.

"Womack's another one," Exley said, stomping his heel and fragmenting shards smaller and smaller. "He needs to quit his talkin'. Everyone's got a comment, or a joke." Ex skidded a shard across the slab floor. "Or they want to tell fucking tall tales."

"Well what's the story then, Ex?"

"There is no *story*," he said, brandishing another bottle. "My brother was being fucked with and got sick of it. He punched a kid in the mouth and the kid lost a tooth." Ex turned over a bottle and the dregs dribbled out. "That's what happened. There's your story. Ancient fucking history, at that." He side-armed the bottle against the wall of the hangar.

They arrived back in the parking lot just as Mr. Chilowicz was leaving the school, smacking his thigh with his briefcase. "On time tomorrow, Mr. DeGroat," he shouted. Sue waved and Ex muttered, *Prick.*

"Do you wanna come by tonight?" Sue asked.

"Can't. I've got work."

Sue got into her car—a Volkswagen bug. She drove a manual. "You guys got that powwow coming up, right? I've seen posters." She put her foot on the clutch and started the car. "You going to that? I'll go with you, if you want."

"If I wanted to play tug o' war I'd enroll in summer camp."

"Alright, *jerk.* Don't get snippy with the ignorant whitegirl."

She poked her head out the window. "Call me when you get out of work."

9

VALERIE MANN WAS THE LAST breastfed baby on Stag Hill. She was forty-eight now and appeared unbenefitted from the milk. Considering all her moeder went through—not the least of which was applying warmed mullein leaves to her nipples before each feeding—it was a damn shame and shit luck. Val bled easily, clotted her wounds with cobwebs, and she steeped wild plumb bark in hot water for tea—said it helped with her breathing.

Val worked as a janitor at Mahwah High School but went on disability when the doctors told her she needed to have both breasts lopped off. Ever since then she kept to herself, or claimed to, but everyone knew she was shacked up with Rhetta Galindez. She kept quiet with closed shades and narrowed blinds and made calls to the ducks and particularly drakes in Rotten Pond and drank handfuls of river water. She boiled pine needles in a pot on the stove. She spread mustard seed around her home. And, if somebody ever did see her, she was in the same New Jersey Devils baggy shirt and cataract sunglasses.

Her alarm clock was set for 2AM, which explains why she turned in as early as six most evenings. She had to mouth down medicines at an ungodly hour, making her nearly nocturnal. The last ritual before sleep was to arrange the rust-orange pill bottles on her nightstand into something like a nativity. She slept on the pullout, mother-naked, and seldom slumbered under the sheets, preferring the wisps of fan air to blow through her bodyhair like a reminder of the cancer that coursed through her blood.

And when she woke at two, swallowed her pills—funneling them down her throat like firewood into a blast furnace—she'd sit on her stoop and wait and think and wait for something fresh to think about, waiting until the rest of the world woke up.

SHE FASHIONED HERSELF INTO AN ACTIVIST in her teens, starting an affinity group with fellow students at the segregated Brook School. She was the spoke, a screech woman when she needed to be. And her cause was the haulers—the contracted trash truckers, namely O'Connor Disposal, hired by Ford in the 70s to transport the poisonous sludge to their backyards. The haulers careened through Stag Hill in the wee hours— down Geiger Road, Split Rock Road, Echo Mountain Road— the leaky back valves of their trucks leaving glowing trails of slick sludge on their way to the mines. The ear-rending noise of the gear-grinding would scare babies, startle screech-owls, and the ruckus and racket would wake the elderly. The rigs swerved violently.

Meetings were organized at the Church of the Good Shepherd, a modest house of worship surrounded by acid-loving heath shrubs. No pointed arch windows, only a parish hall with pew seating along the walls. The friends and kin she gathered in the hall paged through Catholic missals, Assembly of God hymnals, and shared a small-bit of obeah—a hodgepodge of doctrine, really. It took some arm-twisting, some wheedling, for Val to convince all to come along, to commit to direct action—what she called "commotion time."

"They jeopardize our lives," she pleaded. She spoke with the cant of a coalheaver. "We'll be cadavers if we sit idle." She called for nothing short of a reckoning. She warned of a protracted death. "There'll be no more submitting, no bending knees—our elders have done enough of that, enough of the dirty work—in the mines, especially."

Her words invigorated them.

They came out of the woods like wildcats, coordinated though. Some threw rocks—pelting the hauler—aiming for the white space in the O, the C, the next O, the kloofs in the N's of the o'connor typeface. Others targeted the cab windows, shattering glass. They welded nails together for caltrops and peppered the road with them, puncturing tires. Val encouraged them to employ a sharps box of sabotage tactics.

Remission humbled her, though. Her activism stalled. She knew—*she just knew*—there were still some crafty cells swirling inside her, waiting for the right time to colonize again. Remission was only a lull, she believed. A lacuna in a life already prodded by a cursed finger.

SHE SAT ON HER STOOP, whey-faced, chewing the whitlows on her red, pulpy thumbtips. She was skint of spirit, reflecting on a time prior to poisons, pre-op. Her eyes followed a rustling sound in the viburnum bushes, some yards off in a spinney of sweetgum trees. She knew the movement to be human.

Val quietly lifted herself up, unfolded her hawkbill blade, and stealthily closed in on the spinney. She was surprised to find a French braided college student popping a squat.

"Oh," the girl yelped. "I'm sorry, I'm so sorry!"

Val concealed the blade.

"What are you doing here?"

"I'm here with my friends—our club." The girl buckled her belt and flattened her silkweight t-shirt. "We're an environmental club from Ramapo College. We're working on a project." Her breathing was labored. "Assessing the ecological damage on the mountain."

"Why are you out here?" Val asked.

"We're assessing the ecological—"

"Why *now?*"

The rest of the girl's group approached—three guys, laughing and carrying flashlights. One of them was holding a beer can. Another cast a beam of LED light on Val's face.

"Sorry, ma'am," a bushy-bearded one said, taking the girl by the arm.

Val watched them leaving. The girl turned once more.

"We're trying to mobilize a volunteer cleanup of the area."

Her group hurried her, redirecting her to the path.

She told Rhetta about it the next day.

They sat at the drop-leaf dinner table sharing a meal of mulligan stew that had been cooking for hours. Rhetta ducked beneath the rusted nail hanging from the pot-rack overhead. It had been pulled from Val's heel when she was a kid, covered in Crisco, and strung up to prevent the lockjaw from setting in.

"They go back to their gated communities, or their campus," Val ranted. "All the while we're locked down here on house arrest."

"Ease up, Val. They mean well."

"Drunk in the woods, more like it."

Val knew what was what. It was intruding, sightseeing—it was touristing their land: *gazing*. It was all they had read about in their textbooks, now fieldwork. It was a diorama of the dying, the soon-to-be-dead. And now they even had an interaction to gloat of.

"Exile for me," Val sighed, spooning stew into her mouth. "While they lie sprawling in the shade."

"Look at you with the poetry," Rhetta said. "You probably scairt the shit out of the poor girl, Val."

Rhetta was thickset—exultantly fat, she'd say—with bruised

thighs and kindhearted in the way she carried herself. Val, conversely, displayed an unwillingness to compromise on anything.

"Compromise was the comfrey the company boss gave my grandda for his knees," she'd say. "Knees like gravel after crawling in the mines his whole life. Compromise was the company house he raised his kids in, the company store his wife shopped at, the company groceries he bought at company prices with company money. All that deviling he did—they *all* did—for nothing. Fuck compromise."

10

THE BEDROOM WAS DARK: BLACK-PAINTED walls, towels and a tablecloth draped over the curtain rods. Exley blocked out as much light as he could. He doused the glim on the craggy salt lamp, erect on its neem wood base. The idea was to immure himself from the world, like one of those fairytale cottages situated in the deepest, skyless forest, only found—stumbled upon, really—for some fiendish reason. He took off his shirt and began to think again about napping on his da's chest, about being lifted. Instead though, he reached behind to the small of his back and felt the brass ring hanging there, tethered by a long fibrous string around his neck. His ma had given it to him, instructed him to wear it like that—long, down his back—to prevent nosebleeds. He'd been wearing it for years.

Exhaustion had set in, carrying with it a sort of soul ache. It was like the weariness of a warzone. His head hit the pillow and he dozed, only to awake again moments later at the revving of a car engine. He wanted to play watchman—felt obliged to even—but couldn't rouse himself. He put his hand down the front of his pants. Janet in pharmacy was twice his age, and he often watched her bend for a flavored water off the bottom refrigerator shelf before her break. He pulled off his ankle socks and turned one of them inside-out, making a scabbard of it. He stroked for a few minutes, finished, and fell asleep.

Unsettled sleep was the standard. Exley somnambulated like a sonofabitch. He'd move furniture, walk to his moeder's bedside and shush her, lift his pillow and sweep away phantom roly-polies. When he was younger, his parents would watch as he carried on entire conversations, eyes closed, in front of the mirror. They ignored his midnight arrivals in the kitchen, stifling their laughter as he flipped the light switch on and off, on and off—*on off on off on off*—until he tired of it and returned to his bed.

This wasn't that, though. He was awake, for certain. He'd heard his moeder coughing in her room down the hall, and he hated to hear the nebulizer whir to life. The clock read two—he had never sprung it forward, though—so it was actually 3AM. He dressed and furtively left the house.

He snuffled the awful sweetness of toadflax. He saw Val sitting on her stoop across the way. She immediately stood up and went back into her house, figuring the kid might be moonstricken, but she was definitely not in the mood to find out for sure.

Exley maundered the woods. He walked alone, in a solitary place in his da's forest, for contemplation. There was no lack of things to think on. The fuckedness of his being was deep and dense and nearly unnavigable. Sue came to mind first, how her low-cut top revealed the freckles on her chest. The time she got dressed in front of him—there was that. How she acted as if it were nothing and how he only averted his eyes to *seem* gallant. How she interrupted the dressing to straddle him, muss his hair, and her thighs—squeezing him—were cooler and smoother than anything his nature had ever known.

He considered how old and unattractive his moeder's face had become. Her nebulizer mask was as awful as the whiskers above her lips, her hair-bearing moles. He hated how the mask edges left indentations in her cheeks. He hated her clutter and her phone calls and her incessant death ledger jotting: she was a hoarder of grief and mourning. *For what?*

He thought about Zike. Zike was oozing. The EPA should dig a monitoring well in his gut. He was starting to resemble the mutant characters of his comic books, or at least their noxious origin stories. Ex couldn't tell him—not unless Zike did something unforgivable—just how bad he stunk. How his foulness followed him, glossing Ex's nosehairs for days. It was worse than the worst sweat-drenched big body Ex might've squared off against in the post. Worst than the slap of an opponent's back sweat on a boxout.

Risking a log cross, Exley lost his balance and rolled an ankle, and he could feel the pinch in his meniscus—a spreading heat in his knee as the pain settled. He should've tied his laces, but he enjoyed the lift and fall of his sneaker heels. He hiked uphill— calves burning—over felled trees and snags, bark-stripped, drilled with the belt-shaped excavations of pileated woodpeckers, beaking for carpenter ants.

Another tree, this one completely uprooted, was massive and folkloric. Its exposed, muddy root system was like the exploded end of a gag cigar. Green weed tufts and grasses interrupted the decomposing blanket of brown leaves. Exley stubbed his foot on a moss-covered, half-buried stone and cleared brush from around it. A forgiving breeze brushed up his shirtback. He left the stone looking unnatural, a terrestrial planet with a ring of space junk in its orbit—straw and needles and roly-polies stirred to a panic.

He followed relocated Erie Railroad tracks, slowly submerging into the subsoil. The rails were burnished, and he felt the rubber soles of his sneakers had something to do with that. He neared a clearing marked by a primeval tree with a hollow the shape of a flowing mantle. Human bodies could fit in there, and his parents' had done just that—he'd seen the picture every day of his life in the front hall. Each of them wearing flannel and his ma flinching in anticipation of the camera's self-timer. His da is behind his ma—his chin resting on her left shoulder—and a lens flare obscures their feet, giving them the appearance of floating.

Exley didn't learn to play basketball on blacktop, in a driveway, but on a concourse of trampled and rutted dirt at the joining of two glens. He covered a lot of ground on his night walks, and he often ended up there. A rusted rim was crudely attached to the trunk of a beech tree with four deck nails. There was no backboard, no net. *The sacred hoop*, that's what his da used to call it. He kept a pregnant ball hidden behind a gorse bush. The ball was so bald he didn't even worry about it being punctured by the brambles. A popping basketball: that was fantasy. The ball was so worn—its formerly dimpled rubber surface so smoothed—it was damn near indestructible.

The initials EX D were carved into the trunk with the same pocketknife Exley still carried on his walks. He did it years ago, and the letters enlarged, growing as he did, as the tree did. Hannah reprimanded him for scarring sacred nature, and now the initials were really grotesque, a deformed version of the original—clumsier and barkier. Someone once said if you could shoot in the dark, you could shoot when the lights were up. And so Exley was always the last one in at the close of day, ignoring the demands of his ma to be back on the porch before sunset.

He took some shots. The crickets alone drowned out the thud of the ball on the dusty forest floor. Though he was firmly sequestered, he could pretend airplanes flying overhead were aware of his shooting percentage. He could talk to himself, count down to the buzzer. He could retrieve his own rebound in dramatic fashion, saving it in the split second before it bounced into the brambles. The tree roots made it impossible to predict which way the ball would go.

But he didn't stay long. He nestled the ball back into place behind the gorse, surrounding it with stones and twigs so it wouldn't roll away with a wind gust. And he hustled, high-stepping through the underbrush, clearing brittle branches and ducking sturdy ones. He emerged at Cannon Mine Road and kept to the shoulder until he arrived at the Tribal Community Center. They held Lunaape language classes every third Saturday of the month, and they organized the food and craft vendors, the entertainment, and the games for the powwow there. The grounds included a full court with the keys painted blue. The hoops had chain nets that chinged like cash registers on swishes. Exley remembered how Freddie Conklin caught his finger in one of them trying to grab rim—the index flayed like a celery stalk, stringlike tendons dripping red. They called 9-1-1 on the office phone, but an ambulance never showed up.

Exley lined up in front of the hoop, pantomiming the one-handed shooting drills he'd done for years. He focused on bending his knees, keeping his elbow in, the follow-through, and the arc of the shot. He repeated the motion five times before taking a step back, and he repeated the ritual from all angles.

A car sped by—one he didn't recognize—and he wondered how long it would be before they were on Stag Hill, waking the tribe with horn honks and heckles. No, he thought. It was four in the morning. It wouldn't be that. He resented the bitterness in his heart, the suspicion and paranoia. He sure as hell hadn't put it there.

He tried to maintain focus on the shooting drill but couldn't. He rolled up his short sleeves behind his shoulder blades and headed home.

EXLEY ANGLED HIS BODY THROUGH PITCH PINE clinging to rock and arrived at the O'Connor Disposal landfill, which, for the past five years or so, had been doubling as a school bus depot. He immediately spotted the hunch of his uncle's back, but he briefly experienced the disorientation of seeing his uncle's face without glasses.

"Unky Orrin?"

"Thunder and lightning, youngblood. You must be trying to kill this man." Orrin had his hands on a hoop for a sugar barrel. Ratchet pawls and gears of every size were in a pile at his feet. He put his glasses on to see.

"Who else would be out here this time of night?"

"Metalers, scrappers," Orrin listed. "Competitors, killers, adders, coppers…"

Unky Orrin was Norval's brother, but he never came around much, wasn't welcome. Hannah accused him of being a phi-landerer, a bad influence, a bullshitter. And she kept him as far from their house as she could, often hexing him with the sign of the horns—in humor, but a hex is a hex.

Hale as a hellhound, Unky Orrin was a smoke-dried uncle with a wrinkled face like corrugated roofing and an elaborate zipper of hair—thick and twinelike—braided down his back. He often muttered to himself, dandering with his head down. He'd look good puffing a meerschaum pipe, but instead he had a metal tire pressure gauge between his wide, crackled lips. He dressed like a kook. He wore a Goodwill woman's fur with the seriousness of a skinwalker and an oversized Ramapo College hoodie closely resembling a cowl. The sleeve edges were deckled from his constant gnawing. His mind often skittered, speaking mostly nonsense but still with rare moments as eloquent as a scop.

"When's my next care package coming?"

"Soon," Ex said. "I'm gathering." He gestured to the pile of scrap at Orrin's feet. "You know what that's like."

Unky Orrin scavenged the landfills and the iron mines. *For materials, not money*, he reminded anyone who might bother to ask. He flexed his welding equipment and worked with the focus of a forager. Railroad wheels, brakeshoes, axles, switch stands, I-beams, rebar, electrical transformers: he scrapped for all of it. He hid materials from his hauls in an old hoist house and transported them back to his place in a wheelbarrow during daylight hours.

He used the scrap for junk art, primitive sculpturing—much of it was utilitarian, too. When Exley was still in elementary, Orrin designed and built a tire-park for the tribal kids. The sheer volume of Ford tires piled near the plant site was enough to inspire any old master. He chained up swings, sure, but the big draw was the dragon he designed. The treads were turned to dragon scales. One was sliced to a serpentine tongue. The township of Mahwah shut the park down within months of its completion. Some outsiders caught wind and notified Parks and Rec. It wasn't to code, they said. No permits had been acquired. Orrin had no grounds for building anything, they said, on city property. The municipal grunts with sledgehammers had a hell of a time demoing the dragon structure. The straight peen heads bounced off the rubber with each heave and each ho.

"You need to come see me about something."

"What?"

"How's your ma?" Orrin asked, changing subjects. He flipped over some timber with embedded bolts—hundreds of years old, likely.

"She's there," Ex answered. "In the kitchen. Doing what she do."

"Whoa-oh-oh!" Orrin shouted. He pulled a long, slinky line of copper wiring from under some pallets. Orrin regarded it as some archeological find, a hooked fish on his line.

"These used to fetch a pretty penny," he said. This was nothing Exley didn't already know. Copper wire was quick cash for his parents' generation, and he heard them fondly tell of it on many occasions. They'd descend into the deepest underground levels of the mines to dig it up. I-287 to 17 to 80, and you'd be in downtown Paterson at a junkyard with a man blacker than you measuring and weighing your haul. He might ask where you're from, squeezing a wad of cash from his jeans pocket. *You're an Indian?* he'd ask. *You look Black.* And you'd nod your head, anxiously, waiting for him to get back on task, back to counting your money so you could get back to Stag Hill and back to the mines for more digging. *My auntie always say we got some Indian in us*, he'd add. *Chickasaw.* You'd be hustling back to Mahwah—no goodbyes, no nothing—happy to be done with the conversation.

"Yea-up," Orrin yawned. "You need to come see me about something."

"What for? What are you talkin' about?"

"Not now."

Orrin tended to his scrap piles and ignored his nephew until he left.

11

THE PEDIATRICIAN TOLD GUSSIE that he could get a walk-in appointment at the radiology clinic if they made haste and arrived before lunch hour. They could be in-and-out. The doctor wanted to ensure Meal's lungs were still clear. She scrawled a prescription, handed it to Gussie, and wished Emilia good luck with a pat on the head. Gussie piggybacked Emilia to the car.

Rain was falling in sheets, the way it does in films. The wind, Gussie thought, probably had something to do with that. His wipers wouldn't wipe for shit, and whole sections of the windshield were distorted with wet streaks and fog. He twice had to pull the car over to the shoulder. He blasted the AC.

"It's cold, Daddy."

"I know, Meal. I'm trying. Daddy's trying."

He switched off the AC, shut the vents, and cracked his window. Rainwater sluiced into the car, splashing back at Emilia.

"Daddy! I'm getting wet," she shouted. "I'm getting wet!"

Gussie rolled up the window and banged the steering wheel. He smacked the console. He reached awkwardly and wiped the inside of his windshield with his hand. He cleared a small space—it looked like a nebula—but the sides immediately crept in, fogging it again. His hand stung from the smack. He felt like a fool for his rage. Felt like a failure for raging in front of his daughter. Felt remorseful for modeling that behavior. Felt sorry for opening the window in the first place. She had spiked a fever of 103 again—the night before—and here he was putting her at an even greater risk. She'd catch a chill, catch a cold, catch a pneumonia. Acid rain would eat away at her skin. They could skid off the road; they could both die in a wreck. Or, worse, she'd die; he'd survive. He'd be there holding his dead child at the roadside, getting rained on, waiting for an ambulance—*with his luck.* Or she'd be pinned under the overturned vehicle—unable to see her or to hear her or to know her ever again. His bald Goodyears. Her outgrown car seat. NJDOT's inadequate funding of road repairs. The booster they couldn't afford. Everything was in place for tragedy.

The rain let up, and he maneuvered back onto the road. He looked in the rearview—Meal's glassy eyes; the wet hairs running across her forehead; the yellow shadow from the hood of her poncho.

THE WAITING ROOM WAS PACKED—it seemed like everyone in Passaic County was waiting to get a look inside themselves that morning. The area smelled of nylon and too-strong courtesy coffee.

"Is it at all possible," Gussie asked the woman at the counter, "if my daughter could get in there and be seen before some of these people?"

"These people aren't all waiting for the same thing, sir." She propped the prescription behind the function keys on her keyboard.

"Oh, okay," Gussie said. "Because she's starting to spike a fever again, I think."

He cupped his hand around the front of Emilia's head.

"I need your insurance card," the woman said. "To copy."

Gussie slid the card to her. She stared down at it for too long a time—a fraud suspicion, a counterfeit stare.

"Who's the policyholder?"

"Ora Milligan," Gussie stated, slowly. "*Or*-uh. My wife."

The woman hobbled back to the copier—Gussie saw the loose sock at her ankle, a bad fit over a prosthetic leg. Gussie hugged Emilia to his thigh.

"Okay, sir," she said, returning his insurance card. "Shouldn't be too long."

Gussie and Emilia sat down on the only available seat in the waiting area. The heavyset man beside them rolled his oxygen tank back and forth on the ground between his legs and hogged the armrest. A teenager and his mother sat opposite them. The boy adjusted the crutches under his chair. The padding on the crutches was crudely cushioned with dishtowels and duct tape. The mother benignly simpered at Meal, but Meal gave nothing in return and curled herself onto Gussie's lap. He unhooded her head and brushed back her hair.

A flatscreen was mounted high on the wall. It showed a looping twenty-minute segment on "healthy living"—gluten alternatives, superfoods, outdoor exercise in spite of seasonal allergies. Gussie sent Ora a text on his prepaid, updating her. She didn't respond. A boy ignored his mother's pleas to stay in his seat, making repeated trips to the sanitizer dispenser instead. He put his little palm under the machine, the machine churned, and a dollop of foam squirted out. Soap dripped from between his lathering hands and fell to the floor.

Techs opened and held a wide door with their legs, their hips, their asses. They held clipboards and called names: Barbara, Wayne, Cathy, Richard.

Heat was radiating off Meal's body—Gussie could feel it. The moisture contained in the crumpled poncho wedged next to him on the seat made everything worse. Gussie lifted her off his lap.

"Can you tell me where we are in the line? *Milligan. Emilia.*"

"You're next, sir," the woman behind the counter said. She didn't consult any people or papers.

"Are you sure?" Gussie pointed to Meal sitting alone in the chair. "My daughter is burning up. I need to get her home and give her some Tylenol or something. This is taking too long."

The woman briefly looked over at Meal.

"You're next."

Ten minutes later, they were.

The tech, Ernie, led them into a dim, windowless room. "Like Ernie and Bert—*Sesame Street*," he said to Meal. He was tall and broad-shouldered and warm toward Emilia. She was receptive to him, but when she saw the hulking apparatus, she began to cry.

"We're not doing that one," Gussie said, crouching to Meal's level and shooing away the massive tunnel-like gantry.

"I don't want to lay on there, Daddy." Meal pointed to the long motorized table.

"You don't have to, babe."

Ernie was trying but only made things worse.

"You want stickers, Emilia?"

"*No!* No. No stickers. I don't want stickers. No stickers, Daddy." Meal stomped her feet. Her face was shining with tears. To think this was the same little girl with the blocked tear duct as a newborn. How they swabbed gunk from the corner of her eye and massaged along the bridge of her nose for weeks. All that for her to be capable of sobbing.

"Meal—," Gussie squared his shoulders with hers. "Meal, I want you to listen to Daddy." She trembled, but her eyes focused on his. "This is no big deal. This is going to be *soooo* easy. You just need to stand still, and Ernie is going to take a picture of your chest. That's all." Gussie looked over his shoulder at Ernie. "How many pictures?" Ernie held up two fingers—a peace sign—and swerved his head, approximating. "Just two pictures, Meal. C'mon, now. Stand with Daddy over here."

He signaled for Ernie to set up the shot. Meal began to cry again, but her body was moving. She never beamed voluntarily for pictures—never allowed someone to pose her. No amount of coaxing would change that. It needed to be candid, and this couldn't be that. That Gussie was even attempting that line of reasoning was laughable.

Meal, somehow though, agreed to stand on a chair against the wall. Without actually touching her, Ernie positioned Meal sideways. He held open a full lead apron so Gussie could put his arms through the sleeve holes and velcroed the back for him. Then Ernie handed Gussie a lead pad—no bigger than an oven mitt—and showed him where he was supposed to hold it on Meal's body: at her side, from the top of her belly button to just below her groin.

This request was complicated by the need to hold Meal's arms above her head, as if in a stress position, a strappado. As executed by the father. Ernie hustled—first pulling and adjusting the arm, then lining up the X-ray tube with Meal's little lungs, and then scurrying behind glass, behind his computer screen. Meal struggled—trying to loose her wrists from Gussie's grip; wiggling her torso away from any contact with the lead pad.

"It's okay, Meal. It's almost done. Almost done, babe. Just stay still for Daddy—stay still, Meal."

She cried and cried and cried as Gussie held his daughter's hands with his one hand and steadied the lead pad with the other, protecting her ovaries from exposure to the radiation. *I like to avoid imaging on girls*, the pediatrician had said. *They only have the eggs that they're born with, y'know.* That was almost a year ago. There had been so many X-rays since. The words repeated in Gussie's head as he held her in place—he might've even been mouthing them.

"Okay, we got it!" Ernie shouted from behind glass. "Okay, okay, okay!"

Gussie released his daughter's hands—her wrists were raw and red. He was holding her so tightly. He lifted her off the chair, frisbeed the pad onto the motorized table, and shunted the lead apron from his body. "You did great, babe," he told her.

"Who wants stickers?" Ernie ran at Meal with a spool of stickers, tearing them at the perforations. "Have as many you want, Emilia."

"I don't want stickers! No stickers!" she cried.

"I'm sorry, man. She's really not feeling well."

Gussie guided Meal's arms into the poncho.

"Take some anyway," Ernie said. They were cartoonish, smirking skeletons. They were dancing, clicking their heel bones together, with motion lines at their joints. The stickers depicted an anatomical jamboree in vibrant colors and zany designs—polka dots and zigzags. Bubble letter messages, like: *I'm in Pictures!* and *X-Rays are a Snap!* and *I Held Still!* There was even a skull with pulsating pink hearts for eyes. Gussie pocketed them, picked up Meal, and all but ran out of the building.

12

CARDBOARD DUTY REQUIRED GLOVES. You had to collapse boxes at breakneck speed because, for some reason, Aaron cared an awful lot about keeping the stockroom cleared. The corrugated cardboard could slice you up if you weren't careful. Exley volunteered for the task—it was better than fielding customer questions in the aisles. He delighted in compacting a cage full of cardboard detritus into a cube and corralling it with baling wire. It made him think of Unky Orrin, how—in only a couple of hours—he could gather a welter of metal and transform it into an art piece.

Exley was pallet jacking the bale when he heard Sue page him over the intercom. He finished moving the bale before heading to the front of the store.

Lib was in the checkout lane with shower-wet hair. She wore a military green t-shirt with *In Loving Memory* across the chest and *Leonard Van Dunk* below an airbrushed headshot of her brother. Park rangers killed Lenny over an ATV dispute. All the children Lib had hatched were hanging onto the shopping cart like hobos catching out on a freight car. She was in a clattery argument with Aaron. Sue stood near them, helplessly holding the scanner gun, looking cyborg with her forearm splint. Ex pulled off his gloves and smacked them together. He carried them by the fingers like a quarry as he walked.

"Exley!"

Aaron was eager to admit him into the conversation. "This woman says she knows you and thinks you'll be able to explain her grievance to us. Better than we understand it."

"I got these coupons, Ex." They were in an envelope, and she was waving them in Aaron's face. "And this man gonna tell me I can't use them. Like he don't see these three children I'm dragging along everywhere with me."

"They're expired, ma'am," Sue chimed. "If you'd just let me show you…"

"I'm not showing anyone shit," Lib said. "You all are gonna honor these coupons. I don't care how it's done. Get CVS corporate on the phone, for all I care!"

"Ma'am," Aaron pleaded. "If you'd just let us see the coupons again we could calmly explain to you why we can't accept them."

The twin toddlers knocked a box of Heath bars off the shelf.

"Can I see the coupons, Lib?"

Lib passed the envelope to Ex.

"You better make this right, Exley. Your ma raised you to know wrong and right." She cricked her neck and rolled her shoulders, breathing loud, contemptuous breaths. She set a pair of deadeyes on Aaron.

The fine print on the tatty and crinkled coupons was difficult to read but easy to comprehend. Exley flipped through them— one for a six-pack of pre-mixed infant formula; one for a diaper rash cream; another for buy-one/get-one jugs of hypoallergenic laundry detergent.

"These expired last month, Lib."

Aaron grinned.

"Really, Exley?" He handed the envelope—now with the coupons outside the flap—back to Lib. "This is some bullshit. You all know that, right? Do you see these kids?" She bent to the Heath bars and began piling them back in their box.

"Exley," Aaron said. "Would you mind…?" He pursed his lips at the exit.

Ex took the box of candy from Lib's hands and put it on the counter. Sue reached down to replace it on the shelf. Ex picked up Lib's twins—first one, then the other—and plunked them down in the shopping cart. He began to escort the family out of the store. Lib left in a huff. She shoved the front of the cart into the too-slow sensor doors. Her twin toddlers lunged forward. The baby wailed.

"What the fuck, Exley?"

There was heavy foot traffic on the walkway. A girl in soccer cleats and shin guards held a can with a slotted lid, tagging for her traveling team.

"Don't *what the fuck* me, Lib. The coupons are expired—what do you expect me to do? Why'd you even have me paged? I look like a damn fool being called up for that." He lowered his voice and moved further from the sensor doors, which had continued to slide open and closed. "Don't you understand what I'm doing here?"

"Your manager is a needle-dicked jerk." She bent and shoved the coupons into her purse. The baby's bare feet got caught as she lifted him from the cart. "And you're no help, Ex. No help at all."

"I'm no help?" Exley bounded in front of her as she walked toward her car. "I've given you shit tons of formula, Lib. What the fuck you coming at me for? How is this my fault? Why are you even in the store? You act like this town doesn't have drug stores on every corner."

"Get it straight, Ex," she spit. "Remember who your people are."

Exley watched her leave, marking the *R.I.P.* on the back of her homemade t-shirt. The twins trailed behind, gamboling in rain puddles and soaking their sneakers. Ex leaned against the wall and lit a cigarette, listening to rainwater gurgle down the drainpipes.

13

THE MOST HISTORICAL BODY BURIED at Ringwood Manor is Robert Erskine's—ironmaster and part-time mapmaker. He took over the ironworks in the late eighteenth century, and that means *all of it*: the forges and the fullers therein; the hearths, the anvils, and the slack tubs; right on down to the cross-peen hammers, the chisels, the tongs, and the hot cut hardies. At night, Erskine would sit at his fireside with his folding pillar compass, straightedge, and fagot of cedar pencils, and he'd sketch maps while the workers made shot and munitions to fight American wars.

Not far from the dirt and ding and worms that decayed Erskine's body, excreting it to dust, was the apparition of the Ramapough longhouse. Logs defined the structure-to-be like a blueprint—a T-squared tech sketch on vellum—but on soil with tree trunks. The site was the subject of a zoning dispute. The tribal council could not secure the permits needed to begin assembly on the longhouse. So they settled for logs—logs with faces carved into them, an open-air venue for council meetings and reflection. A spiritual space. Holy outline. Like a rustic lot with logs instead of concrete parking curbs. The longhouse represented the universe, albeit a woody one. Gussie Milligan went inside the universe, fell to his knees, and became part of it.

He was riven, a man with his skull split by a squiggle down his cranial vault. *A sick child.* Ora accused him of being all doom-and-gloom, but how couldn't he be? Who could just read a gardening rag in a rocker or remove the lattice, crawl under the porch, and drag the jack stands out for an oil change? Gussie was despaired. World altered. Earth shaken. The holler was out of joint, catastrophic and joyless. Meal was ill, and so they all were, and their lives were stalled.

Broadleaf weeds carpeted the longhouse. Knawel clumb and curled over the timber. Gussie pulled what he could from the plot, weeding furiously. He yanked hairy bittercress in bunches only to have seeds explode from their capsules and land elsewhere, perpetuating more growth. Milky sap greased his knuckles while pulling prostrate spurge. He eyed the reddened spots along the midveins, kneed forward, and scraped as much as he could to clear the surface. He was weeding. He'd weed the world if it would clear his mind, if it would make things right.

Gussie's mind inevitably went back to Meal, though—the contortions of her crying face; the febrile heat she emanated; the feel of her perfectly oval wrists in the brutal grip of his large hand. Who was Ora to criticize his pessimism? Where was she—as a parent, as a wife? She was as scared as he was, but she shut down, retreated. He at least fulfilled his roles.

He stood up, wiping his jeans. There was an opening in the canopy directly above the location of the longhouse. The highest tree branches formed an irregular opening, and an unseen flue connected Gussie's skyward gaze and the cloud clearing. He gathered the pulled weeds and lofted them elsewhere, well outside the perimeter of the longhouse. He walked back to the trail, got into his car, and drove to work.

14

THEY WERE IN THE LAB experimenting with a top-loading balance, pipets, and burettes, figuring the density of an unknown solution. Sue partnered with Ex for lab and was okay with doing the bulk of the work. Ex woke with a pimple on his ass and had trouble stool-sitting comfortably, without torment. He pitched Sue's lab binder so as to blind Mr. Chilowicz to his presence there and fiddled with a Bunsen burner.

Chilowicz was summer school casual: an unbuttoned poplin shirt revealing a tuft of hair like grayed nonesuch; Delft blue shorts with maritime flags on the cuffs; a white belt; tasseled loafers. His feet were anchored on the rungs of his stool as he respooled the spinning reel on a fishing rod. His tacklebox was gaping open on the black tabletop. Not in teaching mode, but prepping for the weekend.

Sue's hair was pulled back in a bun. Seeing her neck was seeing a spook, the nape whiter than her tanned arms and face. Ex connected the rubber hose to the gas line, forcing it onto the serrated nozzle that he always saw as a croc snout. He loosened the gas tap.

imagine Zike though, accelerating down a marbley trail. This
rider had knee braces and a kidney belt. Zike never bothered with
those precautions. He was deft but madcap. His ankles would
get tender and sore, so he'd soak bandanas in egg whites and tie
one around each. The rider swerved around a mudhole and hung
a left over Mahwah's oldest, moss-covered, stone bridge, while a
flock of starlings appeared above the forest, swirling in the shape
of a vortex.

15

THE GUTTERS ON THE DEGROAT HOUSE were off-pitch, sagging with stagnant water and leaf mold and when the muck overflowed and thudded onto the roof below, the clumps were indistinguishable from drowned birds. By Exley's estimate, the porch roof was blotched with an entire deluged flock.

No one was home, which was odd. Usually his moeder would be napping through a soap or in the alcove on the phone with a university grad student—a member of a research team, discussing how many health surveys she could conceivably get completed by the tribe. He checked the bathroom floor, the yard, and feared what he'd find in her unmade bed. There was a grocery list on the kitchen table on top of newspaper pages spread about as if she were housebreaking a pup. Hannah's A&P lists were diaristic— not lists but long scrawls of description and superfluous detail.

I do believe Exley would enjoy a London broil tonight.

Nectarines are nearly in-season, worth a try.

EggsEggsEggs XL eggs.

Milk, two-percented.

Yogurt raisins? Yes, please!

Only do deli counter if line is less than five—FIVE!

Navel oranges for the navelgazers.

Exley heard a friendly farewell honk, looked out the window, and saw Elsie's car pulling away. Hannah hobbled up the porch steps, clopping a bronze cane with a foam grip. She waved to Elsie without turning around, a sort of dismissive thing. Stapled paperwork was rolled under her armpit, and she coughed at the top step. Ex met her out there.

"Where were you?"

"On the town, on the town with Elsie." She plopped into the wicker chair and fanned herself with the paperwork.

"What's that?" Exley loomed like a father.

"I had to see the doctor."

"Doctor?"

"Yeap."

"What about?"

"Oh. Tests," Hannah answered. "Tests, tests, tests."

"Why?"

"Because that's what they do—they run tests. They hook you up to this machine, plug you into that one. Take your blood," Hannah patted her arms at the elbows. "Take your urine, take your shit by means of the teeniest wee little dipstick. We donate our bodies to science well before we ever croak, y'know."

Exley fumbled his words as he leaned against the porch railing.

"Son," Hannah said, decisively. "Let's not worry. Okay?"

Looking off past the gourd birdhouse—moldy in a piebald pattern—to the woodlot, Exley didn't say anything. His moeder was his moeder, stubborner than she even bragged to be.

"What happened with Libby the other day?"

"*Libby?*" Exley repeated, still looking off.

"Smarten up, boy."

"What's there to say? She came into CVS, acting insane. She wanted them to honor some bogus coupons. And then she called me—*me*—to back up her claim. I don't know if she thought I would pull some strings, convince my manager, I don't know, Ma. I don't know."

"You couldn't help her?"

"Ma, think about that for a second." Exley was animated now; his hands sliced the air between them. "I'm the *last* person who should help her. I'm already delivering baby formula to her doorstep on a weekly basis. Why would we even want my manager to know I'm connected to her? What's she even doing there—of all places?"

"Okay, Exley," she said. "I get it. The woman is struggling. Don't be so harsh."

Moeder and son fell silent.

A rough-winged swallow chirped over its clutch of eggs. Exley's eyes followed the sound but continued higher to the clouds. The trees in the holler hid so much: the warbling vireo placidly singing until it pinned a moth underfoot; a stinkpot wading in a shallow stream, snapping at some mustard greens. Follow the horseshoe bend downhill, where—Ex's ma would say—the devil broke his apron strings and fractured rock filled a natural embankment. One of those hairpin turns was parallel to the trail where Zike once went headfirst over his handlebars and shattered his sternum. The dirt and basalt bits of gravel wouldn't wash from his wounds for weeks.

"How's that sweet thing Meal been? I heard she's not doing so well."

Exley didn't know what to say. He didn't want to answer. His muscles seemed to stiffen then slacken with weakness at the very thought. Meal's bitty body bent over a floor puzzle. Meal sweltering in her still bedroom with Gussie running a damp cloth over her face. The way her body sprawled in exhaustion across the sofa. But then he thought of better, brighter moments—that distinct, rank smell of the last formula drops as he unscrewed the nipple off the just-finished baby bottle. And the performance he'd put on for infant Meal—the *pew* he'd draw out while pinching his nose—and the wet laughter she'd respond with. It was the joyful thoughts that pained him most.

"That's what I'm hearing too, Ma. Not doing so well."

Hannah hoisted her body off the wicker chair, and she squeezed her son's upper arm.

"We'll find our way to health, habnab."

"Yea-up," Exley said, avoiding her efforts to meet his eyes. Hannah was halfway through the door when she turned back to her son.

"I need your help for the powwow, Exley. I need you to get folding tables from Zike and bring them to the fairgrounds. Elsie told me they have three or four. I don't want you to wait until the last minute either. I told the tribal leaders they could count on us."

"For real, Ma?" Exley huffed. "I'm not going to the powwow. It's the last place I want to be."

"You think I don't know that? I'm your moeder. You're so frosty, so offish, Exley. And, to be honest with you, the powwow is the number one place you *should* be. Think of Meal. She'd feel your presence there, for sure."

Exley walked off the porch.

"We'll find our way, Exley," his ma said again. "We will."

16

August 1982.

The Ford assembly plant had shuttered operation two years prior. For the unemployed, it meant closed doors there and anywhere else they went looking. No balm of Gilead could sooth their spirits. No nibble of tansy could ease their stomach pains. They were defeated men.

For the Ramapoughs, it meant the cessation of haulers making midnight runs to the mines, hauling paint sludge. It meant the opportunity to go berrying in the meadows beside the plant like they used to. Other than that, it didn't mean much. The plant never hired Ramapoughs, anyway.

Overgrowth cloaked the area. Moss and hardy ivies climbed the outer walls of the plant. Alehoof crept along the empty parking lots. It would be some time before the purchase of the land and the demolition of the structure, before the construction of the Sheraton.

Unky Orrin was one of a passel of scrappers then, scavenging the scene for valuable residue and oddments, both inside and out. They were the unbidden masses. They borrowed boltcutters, scaled barbed wire fences marked by the empty threat of KEEP AWAY and PRIVATE PROPERTY signs. They broke up machinery like Luddites, loading up crates and sacks. They hotwired forklifts and sneaked pickups onto the property, parking in the shadow of the water tower—a globose egg on rusted white stilts, canting east.

One afternoon, Orrin shouldered an office door and spent an hour at a supervisor's desk, his bootheels smudging a desk pad calendar. He smoked half a pack of cigarettes and ransacked file cabinet drawers. He found a penciled rota, a payroll, timesheets, and an advertising brochure that offered walking tours to the public. *Hop in your car and have a look at the biggest show of all—U.S. industry at work.* A CAR A MINUTE! a miniature man in overalls shouted on the back fold of the brochure. "And a thousand gallons of sludge a day," Orrin muttered to himself. He thought about the 200 million-year-old faultline beneath his feet and wondered if not iron mining, if not the auto industry, if not his fanatical scrapping, would a seismic shift be the force needed to alter this reality?

HANNAH COULD TAKE THE FIRE OUT OF A BURN. She'd inherited the skill in adolescence. Her ancestors tended to miners, the most remarkable feat having been done by her great-great-grandma Jorie. An Irish immigrant—a Fenian named Dermot—worked the insert molder. He was pouring hand ladles one morning and scalded his inner thighs on a spill. It gave him a never-ending headache. Jorie applied her palms to his thighs and felt the intensity of the heat. She closed her eyes and extracted the fire from the welts. No amount of Hannah's inherited hoodoo—not even of Jorie's caliber—could counter what was coming that August afternoon, though.

They wouldn't know of the intensity of the fire until nightfall. The day went about as normal on Stag Hill. Norval and Hannah were no longer newlyweds, but they hadn't lost their flirtations. Zike had free rein of the front yard. Norval tiptoed behind his wife and shot a stream of water into her ear from pointblank range.

"Oh, for heaven's...Norv!" she shouted.

She tilted her head, tugged on her earlobe, and, from that angle, caught sight of Zike funneling a handful of dirt into his mouth.

"Norv, oh—," she tried to find the words. "Would you get out there and tell your son to stop eating dirt?"

Norval held the pellucid plastic water pistol under the kitchen faucet. His thumb pinned the flimsy plug to the side as it refilled.

"Let him be, Hanny. It's harmless."

He plugged the pistol and tucked the weapon in his waistline. Hannah was tapping on the window glass and calling to her son. "Zike! Don't eat the dirt, hon. You're gonna come in here with collywobbles later, begging for medicines."

Norval came up behind Hannah, headlocking her with a hug. He sniffed her hair and kissed her ear. They appeared well. There was no knowing what contaminants swirled within them on a cellular level, so, for the time being, their dark skins were silklike, untainted.

"Let the boy be, Hanny."

Orrin came trudging up the road, sweaty and smeared with grunge. He set down a galvanized minnow bucket and creel, both full of metallic pickings and fragments. He knelt before Zike and smoothed the dusty dirt at their feet. He took up a twig and slowly spelt something in the ground. Zike smiled at his uncle.

"Here comes your brother, the cheat."

"Give it a rest, Hanny. Will ya?"

"Minnie said she saw him with some whore on his lap just weekend last."

"Where?"

"Mothers."

"In Wayne? Minnie's full of it. How you expect Orrin to get out there?"

"Mothers in Greenwood Lake."

"Maybe."

Norval walked out onto the porch and clodhopped down the steps, the water pistol still tucked in his waistline. He put his hands on his hips.

"You can leave that creel here. You borrowed it from me months ago."

"This?" Orrin asked.

"Mine."

Orrin noogied Zike's head and stood up to meet Norval. Hannah joined them outside. Orrin flicked his brother in the chest. There was a bib of sweat on his.

"How's Minnie?" Hannah asked.

"Leave it alone, won't ya?" Norval said.

"I been good, Hanny. I have."

"Pish. Save it, Orrin. You backslidden more times than I can tolerate to tell."

Orrin heaved the minnow bucket onto an old trestle bed set on sawhorses in the side yard. He emptied the contents of the creel into the bucket and closed the lid.

"Where's this all from?" Norval asked, closing an eye and peering through the aerator holes.

"The Ford plant. Looks like I won't be scrapping in the mine for awhile."

"Why's that? Park rangers been coming around?"

"Nah, not that," Orrin said. "It's ablaze. Been burning since noon." He pointed to the sky. Smoke tendrils were braiding up and up.

"Which one?" Norval asked. "I thought that was them kids messing out there."

"Peters."

"Hell outta here."

"I'm serious. Cotton told me about it. I'm heading there now. See what's what."

"I'm coming."

Norval tossed his repossessed creel to Hannah and the water pistol to Zike who failed to catch it. But he picked it up and sprayed the dirt where Orrin had written with the twig and it splattered in streaks and made mud droplets.

"You better bring back dinner if you're heading out there."

"Alright. What you want?" Norval asked his wife.

"Roy Rogers."

"Bet."

THE BROTHERS DEGROAT CROSSED A GREENSWARD before reentering the woods. Orrin's minnow bucket rattled with his stride. Their boots crunched the understory, the leaves being so brown and brittle that a wildfire wouldn't be all too unlikely.

"Don't mind her," Norval said.

"I won't."

"She's pissy because she got spit on at the grocery store."

Orrin paused and turned to Norval with a seriousness he seldom expressed.

"Well not spit *on*, spit *at*," Norval clarified. "At her feet."

"Somebody do that to Minnie I'll put a reaphook to his gut."

"Yeap, you say that. Do the protector bit. But where are you on doing right by her?"

"Don't talk to me about that smallbore gossip," Orrin snapped. "You know that's bullshit, through and through bullshit!"

"This is plaintalk, brother. Plaintalk."

They had nearly trekked a morgen, it seemed. Orrin kept

switching the minnow bucket right hand to left and back again, and Norval never bothered to take a turn, so he had no way of knowing how heavy and burdensome it was.

"I do right by Minnie," Orrin said several minutes later.

"Alright then. It's settled then." Norval took a couple steps, springing up over an old stone structure. "But if you're associating with slatterns and stragglers, then I got a right to know. 'Cause you know I'm hearing it from Hanny nonstop, three sixty-five."

They came to a stream, still a mile from Peters Mine, and kneeled on the shallow slope of the bank. Orrin pointed to a frenzy of lacewing naiads—which they had been seeing less and less of—swimming between stones. He fell back on his bum and rested.

"How long you thinking you can keep this up?"

"Keep what up?" Orrin asked.

"This scrapping." Norval tapped the lid of the minnow bucket with his fingernails.

"Long as I can," Orrin said. "Good money in it, y'know."

"I know, but it don't seem like a long-term plan is all."

"The Ford plant ain't going nowhere. Nobody buying up that land for a while, that's for sure. And the mine—the mine ain't going nowhere."

"The mine's burning up right now."

"One of 'em is."

"Fire is fire, though."

"Yea-up," Orrin drawled. "They go out."

Norval raised up, swept off his clothes, and continued walking. Orrin was slow to stand and rejoin his side.

"Scrapping is solid work," he shouted ahead to Norval, feeling assured of himself now. "Where else am I gonna find work, work without a boss breathing down my back, spitting at my feet?"

"You're right," Norval conceded. Orrin caught up.

"I mean, you know it better than me. You got a wife and the kid."

Neither of them spoke for some time after that, not until they were nearer the mine.

THEY CAME UPON AN ENORMOUS BOULDER—an erratic—displaced a million, a billion years before. Its look, its feel—Norval gawked as if it had appeared there overnight—invisible dust concretized into rock. He swore to Orrin he'd never seen it, never crossed it. It was foliated with white layers like rivers running. Its broad side—flat as a baby that rests on its back—was white speckled with quartz. Orrin watched noiselessly as Norval held his wrist to the rock. The plaited lanyard compass needle spun silly, havocked by the presence of iron ore. It was Norval's grandda who learned him how to do it. Learned him about sediment deposits. Ancient basins. Learned him mudstone and shale. Intense heat. Pressure. Norval would be teaching Zike soon enough.

The smell of the fire was strong now. And the smell wasn't just woods, it was tinged with the smell of linseed oil or polyurethane. They were just a few rods off. The heat was more than Jersey humidity. Crackling and groaning could be clearly heard now. And, between the trunks of white oaks, they could see the sheets of flames flooding from the maw of the mine.

It could've been vandalism—intentional, or criminal even. Teen kids using rootstalks for punks and setting sizable fires, for kicks. Small fire after small fire until their ardors got them going. It could've been an inability to contain what they'd created: an inferno. Or maybe it could've been a comet, as some speculated. Few accepted such bad science, though. It could've been the cherry on a Pall Mall blown into a mound of brown leaves. That could've spunked it. Either this way, that way, or some other, fires were familiar. Whatever it was, it stirred up history, riling revenants.

Peters Mine was crammed full of hoisting shafts and headframes, stockpiles and ingots, and all of it stoked the pyre. It was a hellish sight to see on a sabbath day. Scrub oaks and shrubs, debris and ruderals, were adusted at the entranceway to the mine. Peters Mine had acted as a receptacle for mining equipment for hundreds of years, a pit for people's trash nearly as long, and the primary disposal site for Ford's paint sludge dumps for decades. And so the aged coatings of dyes and varnishes and anthracite fuel only stimulated the blaze. There wasn't much of anything in there that wasn't combustible.

Woodchoppers once felled trees there, sawed them, and piled them in cones. They looked like tipis but were covered crosswise in withes and enclosed with moss clumps. The woodchoppers would set them afire, sit, and rue for a fortnight. They'd cough and wonder at the particulate in the air, surrounding them. They would pillow on rucksacks, and the lot of them would be wreathed in char by the end of the burn. The cones would eventually collapse and smolder for days in addition.

The Ramapough men who moiled in the mines would come up and out with something like soot wart. Raise drillers, drifters, and muscular men who ran muck machines. Oilers and molders and chippers. Pattern makers and cranemen. Grinders. Frog builders. Mule drivers and test-hole drillers working for company dollars. Making those wagonwheels turn. The foundries, the furnaces, the forges—it was all the Ramapoughs and their labor. Cutting and heading nails. Stocking ore. Green clouds of smoke would settle overhead only to turn blood red by the twilight of shift's end. It was like glacier lights. Limekiln workers would cut hoop-poles and wood for charcoal. Ramapoughs running the hoist. Ramapoughs working overtime at the slitting mill. All of them suckers for superstition. An iron melter chasing off his haranguing wife from coming too close to the mine. A watchman taking aim at mine rats with a spade. The thirteenth level of the mine unworked, untouched—holding a darkness never dreamed of. An ankle sprain on the angles of tailings. The heels of the coremaker's hands scalded to slickens. And not a one of them ever discounted the bodies buried in the shafts and the pits, loamed over and one with the lodes and the veins. It was a fiery catacomb.

Norval and Orrin beheld the conflagration. It wasn't only them bearing witness, though. Others from the tribe were there: Norval's sister-in-law, Black Mag; Hew Milligan who was chugging a beer and holding the remaining six-pack by its yoke; a bunch of Van Dunk kids, dripping wet, much too close to the flames; and Cotton. Cotton shouted *Lo!* when he noticed the DeGroats' arrival, excitedly pointing and flailing his arms at the mine. The Van Dunk clan, led by headman Hadley, tried to dash the flames with shovelfuls of soil and aggregate. It did nothing. The dense air was relentless, a hot wall like walking in the line of steam from a teakettle.

Orrin approached Cotton but Norval stayed put, his eyes fixed on the flames. He shifted his weight and spoke aloud to himself.

"That mine just eats men alive, don't it?"

THE FIRE INTENSIFIED, REACHED HIGHER. The onlookers backed off, skittered downhill. Night officially fell, and when it did, the scene was without detail. The flames were a wash of sopping-wet watercolors on an absorbent surface. It burned for days on end. No fire engines bothered to respond. The Ramapoughs just continued to live, existing through a film of smoke.

The sky was full of light the first few nights like an unrelenting fire-flaught. The tribe brought out their aluminum beach chairs at eventide and watched as they would fireworks. Kids lit sparklers and saluted the auroras above the tree canopy. The sky shifted colors depending on what was burning. The local paper said the fiery sky could be seen from Manhattan.

It simmered for weeks.

Nobody knew what was spreading, or nobody thought much about it. But chemicals were dispersed, carried by gales and gusts and settled on rooftops. Ash flurried down and dioxin specks breezed into open attic windows. You'd have to click on your wipers to clear your windshield in the morning. It was a rime on railings and awnings. If it hadn't been so hot, August would've been mistaken for a first frost in October. What was already in the ground and in the rivers and in the taps was in the houses now, squatting. No amount of dusting could change that cataclysm.

LORE

The kids used to purposely slip and spill downhill, down Sludge Hill, their feet-bottoms slicked. They'd spill like hoop snakes, topsy-turvied and putting undue pressure on the neck and spine, on the nervous system. They'd splash in the rainbow muck and murk of mud puddles. They rolled Ford tires, building momentum by running alongside them for several strides with a skinny stick, more often a branch with a prominent burl. Once they came upon the enormous rear tire of a scoop loader with the most menacing ruts and ridges in its tread pattern. They took turns tucking their bodies within it and went headlong. Like a hoop snake. The hoop snake swallows its own tail, see. It is a living wheel with high levels of toxicity. Don't look into the elliptical pupils of its eyes. Don't provoke its venomous braided tail. It hunts accordingly, a biological wheel on the attack—rolling, rotating, and then arching back into arrow straightness for the sting. If the stinger misses, it will suck into a tree trunk or even a gneiss boulder and swell. The folk taxonomy for the wily and feared critter is *debated, often a mouthful. And, some have said, it gags on its own nomenclature. What isn't up for debate, though, is the fact of the hoop snake's errant sting swelling a gneiss rock into Houvenkopf Mountain.*

17

THE CHILDREN OF STAG HILL would escape daily into the fastnesses and gorges of the mountains. They were overridden by schoolmarms and hectoring classmates and left no option but to run, rip-roaring and roisterous through woods. They wouldn't ignore but rather avoided the white blazes on the trees marking trails—they wanted none of that. A footpath, to them, was a betrayal. They preferred to forge through firs and birches, shucking the bark as they pleased, as they went. Go, go, *go*. So much, for them, was predetermined. They needed, at the very least, autonomy of geography.

They slid down what they dubbed "Sludge Hill" on car hoods and hubcaps—an orange stream at the foot of it. They shinnied oaks, splashed in umber puddles, and plashed twig effigies to burn in the clearings. A pinwheel with ladybug-patterned vanes would scud across an open lot, and the more impish among them would give chase. They'd trek to the Foxcroft mansion ruins— hide-and-seek, manhunt, kick the can—and *olly olly oxen free* until their lungs ached. Sometimes they'd climb the ancient stone cistern and check its water level. If adequately filled, they'd treat it as a swimming hole, yattering as youngbloods do.

Other times they'd play with mammets and nodding dolls, make brush-brooms of boughs and withes, peel lichens and prepare stew potions. They yo-yoed phlegm wads on tenuous strings of spit. Rotted, discarded lumber would make for a dandleboard; a carburetor for the fulcrum. Girls and boys with sticks poked the webby nests of tent caterpillars between branches. Foam rockets were launched with air pressured foot pedals. Dirt bombs were indiscriminately lobbed. Girls buried action figures and army men so that boys could resurrect them, but burial plots and tomb locations were lost to distraction and disorder.

They played store with pebble currency. They bartered and exchanged with one another until a solitary ruiner executed a stickup and finessed the profits. Someone would be pegged with a grayed tin dipper. One would make a tragic-figure of herself. They whittled with switchblades, calculating bloody vendettas. They dwarfed themselves with hunched shoulders and walked drowsily across the glade. They pretended to be some soft-brained peer they all knew from recess. An old calico dress would be strung up with clothespins to create a fort. The afternoon would almost always end in a mock strangling of two or more miscreants.

Sometimes they'd stay close though, in the yards, especially the younger ones. They'd drive Tonka trucks on their knees, often making head-on collisions of scoop loaders, cranes, and bulldozers. This is what Emilia did with her cousins—Madge, Agnes, and Jerome with the cleft lip. They crashed the construction vehicles together until Jerome—who cried with regularity, usually as if on cue—pinched the skin between his fingers. The triumvirate of Meal, Madge, and Agnes called him a *crybaby*. Jerome uttered a curse.

They all began to chase each other around the yard, ducking behind grills and curling up next to the crumbling transom of an old johnboat. Oars, lawn chairs, propane tanks, and more provided a gauntlet for them to navigate as they tagged each other. The blade markers on a yellow snowplow distracted Jerome. He boinged the reflective antennae and giggled with amusement. Gussie ran into the backyard and interrupted the chaos to remove an exhaust fan and a push mower from the field of play.

"What're you all doing?" he shouted.

"We're gonna push each other and die each other," Emilia said with a grin.

"Nuh-uh. No way. Don't talk like that, Meal." Gussie turned to all the cousins. "And watch where you're running—the lot of you. This yard isn't suited for play. It's full of landmines." He gestured across the road to an opener space.

Gussie watched Meal pick up a matted tennis ball turned olive drab from dog slobber. She charged her prey and pitched the ball at Jerome's back. It bounced off his shoulder blade. "I died you!" she shouted.

"Meal!"

"Sorry, Daddy."

"Why don't you all play mudpies?" Gussie suggested. He shoveled the safe soil from their raised garden beds into buckets and dumped into a burlap-lined cratch. He dragged the black garden hose off its reel and saturated the soil, leaving it there with a slow trickle. He gave the kids sieves, pails, and sandcastle molds and told them to go at it. "This is what me and my cousins used to do."

Gussie lifted off Meal's shirt and her cousins requested the same. They stood shirtless around the cratch—perfectly waist-high—and patted down mudpies as if it were the most fulfilling pleasure they'd ever known.

THERE WAS A DEEP MINE COLLAPSE months prior. Nobody knew it. Thinking back, there were intimations: the give of a patch of soft grass underfoot; a distant creak in the still of the morning; an alteration to the path the water washed away from the foundation of the house.

Gussie was balling the used foil from baking sheets and cleaning the countertops. He placed a slice of white bread into a Tupperware so the snickerdoodles he'd just cooled would stay chewy for longer. He periodically checked on the cousins in the yard through the window. Jerome had become preoccupied with a bundle of bamboo garden stakes. And he was concerned that Madge and Agnes had forsaken their mudpies for cat's cradle by the raised beds. They used his green garden twine to create their matrix, exchanging it back and forth between their attenuated fingers. Meal was left alone.

He sponged the kitchen table, adjusted chairs, and looked out the window again. He watched Meal place a mudpie on a ledge and put her fingers in her mouth. He was inclined to yell to her but didn't.

Granular sediments spalled into the steep-walled mineshaft below the surface of the earth. The overburden suddenly buckled inward like Exley's dented chest, creating a cavity. *Suddenly*, but not so much. There was nothing sudden about the over three-hundred years of iron mining in New Jersey. Nothing sudden or secret about an over five-hundred page geological survey sitting in the archives of a government building, methodically outlining the pits, shafts, and underground pathways. It should've been no secret that the land they lived on was vulnerable. Gussie didn't react as swiftly as he would've liked to, as he believed a father should.

Meal was shrewd enough to step back from the ground sinking before her. The cratch fell into the sinkhole as Gussie grabbed his daughter under her armpits and carried her away from the void. "Stay there!" he shouted to his nieces and nephew, each in other areas of the yard. "Back up!" he revised. The dirt and rocks and dandelions that passed for a lawn descended into the widening hole like an escalator. The sound of it, Gussie supposed, was like that of an earthquake but quieter. It was like a floor giving out and dropping to the level below. Jerome hugged the corner of the tool shed and started to cry. Madge and Agnes climbed into a raised bed, flattening a section of plants. Agnes stood on tippy-toes to try to see into the sinkhole. It stopped swallowing in under a minute—maybe even less than that. Gussie carried Meal toward the house and gave the sinkhole a wide berth. He coaxed the other children to follow the same route. Gussie kissed Meal's face and fell to his knees so he could sufficiently clutch her. He sent the children into the den with the Tupperware full of snickerdoodles.

Gussie leaned over the sink and assessed the yard through the window. The sill made an indentation across his chest. The diameter of the hole, he estimated, was ten feet, and he was immediately concerned with how close it came to his house. As for the depth, he had no concept. It was deeper than he was tall, of that he was sure. The black garden hose had fallen over the edge and snaked into darkness.

18

THE CORRUGATED SCRAP PATIO SLABS leading to Unky Orrin's tumbledown digs were shoddily placed, so each of Exley's steps was hobbled. It was a ramshackle cabin, a stick-built work-in-progress. Its original intent was a hunting shack. Orrin and Norval constructed it in a remote location, but not so remote Orrin wouldn't be able to easily ask for favors. The walls were cobbled together with a patchwork of materials and cohered with roughcast or loam or joint compound. In truth, it wasn't much more than a frame and bark structure, but it kept out wind and rain. If you were to steady yourself on its walls you'd no doubt get a fistful of flinders.

Exley found his uncle behind the home, crouched in front of a small black alienship grill, cooking bluegill over briquettes. Exley suffered the sound of the scraping tongs against the grates. He watched from a safe distance as Unky Orrin searched the premises for a wire brush, tipping cans and flipping crates. He stopped, as if to think, and wiped a wart on the palm of his hand with a red mechanic rag. Then he sneakily discarded the rag at the edge of his property and plonked a rock on top of it.

The area resembled the O'Connor Disposal landfill and the grounds of the abandoned Ford plant and the entranceway to any of the mines. Junk and refuse were scattered everywhere. This wasn't a trash heap, though. First and foremost, it was Orrin's artist studio. But it was also a spot for hunting prep, a welding shop, and catchall for his many hobbies and gambles. Pelts were stretched over poles. He had both carcasses and clothes on a line. His Ford hubcap collection extended from the outer wall of the house to the rafters of the lean-to that was held in place by a windowsill planter, trough, and slates. Stolen EPA signs were stacked like a deck of cards in a far corner, waiting to be melted down. And his art pieces were in varying stages of creation and completion.

One half-completed piece was propped onto a mangle press that Orrin used as a worktable. The worktable was clothed in newspapers and fabric scraps. A quern was at the piece's center with a railroad tie running vertically on top of it. Brass hinges and doorknobs were hammered into the sides to resemble limbs. Screw clamps were welded to a deep pan to create a sort of featureless face. Hex nuts, couplings, and bolts were patterned up and down the railroad tie, and acorn caps and pinecones formed a mane around the pan. Cans of aerosol paint—capless and with modified nozzles—were both stood up and toppled under the worktable. The sculpture had recently been sprayed with black and titanium silver streaks, and the excess paint dripped down the pan face as if weeping.

Orrin crouched beside the grill again, and Exley made his presence known. He let down a plastic CVS bag that had been slung over his shoulder.

"Unky," Exley said. "I've got your things."

"Youngblood," he stood and clapped his hands several times. "The care package, yea-up. The care package. It's appreciated."

The bag included hygienics—toothpaste, bar soap, roll-on deodorant, and dental floss—but also packs of Pall Mall cigarettes. Exley stacked them onto the mangle press.

"Will you stay? Have you got a minute?"

"Sure," Exley said. "I'm around."

"I've got the makings of a meal here," Orrin pointed to the grill. His arms were covered in seta-like hair, and it altogether made for scabrous skin. "Let's go inside, though. Let's go inside."

Exley ducked his head under the doorway and followed Orrin's path. An inverter welder was just inside the cabin. His toe stubbed a tin can spittoon full of dip globs. Orrin sat down in a folding chair and kicked off his boots. He wasn't wearing any socks, and Exley could make the mosaic warts and the seeds at their centers. Orrin reached behind and shook a bottle of salicylic acid extracted from the bark of a white willow.

"The *salix*," he said, applying it to his feet with a C-fold paper towel. His thick-lensed glasses shifted down his nose.

Orrin was wearing a knit cap over his hair; his long braid was swirled into a topknot. Perspiration was running down his face. He wiped it away with the same sheet he washed over his feet with, and it still reeked of chemical.

"It's like a sweat lodge in here."

"Funny." Orrin flipped off his nephew. Self-made sterling silver rings were like gnarled twigs pried over his knuckles. They were the same as the ones he'd gifted to Zike, only skull-less. Unky Orrin was a wodewose, thoroughly so.

"Drink?"

"I'm good."

Orrin sugared his beverage, sipped, and licked at the starchy orchid root contained therein. His lips were almost powdered, so he wiped across his mouth with the back of his hand.

"Y'know, I would love it if you outfitted me with some tube socks before the arrival of fall."

"Harder to smuggle," Exley said. "I can only shove so much down the front of my pants." Ex was still looking for a safe place to sit. The floral-printed couch was moth-eaten and timeworn. His legs were tired from walking though, so he decided to hell with it.

Orrin had whiskey glasses all over his place. They were half-filled with tap water and skimmed with foamy saliva and floating, tailed loogies. Eddies of black bile. He hocked up the gruesomest grit and sputum every few minutes. Even still, he sat in that folding chair like the sagamore of his domicile, just waiting for the opportunity to get all lectury with his brother's son.

"You're right, youngblood. You are *right*. You've provided me with surfeitings for seasons. You know I thank you for that."

Exley rolled his eyes at the vocabulary.

Orrin didn't have a proper fridge, but a larder full of desiccated meals and a cooler brimming with convenience store icebags, most melted to bulging water balloons. He slogged to the larder, hid behind a cabinet door, and returned to Exley, lofting a gross amount of weed in his lap for his recompense. Unky Orrin didn't package his homegrown marijuana in a shrunken ziploc but as a smudge stick, bundled with red yarn.

"I can't take all this, Unky. It's too much."

"Hell, I know you can't, youngblood. I'm not letting you." Orrin put a Luden's lozenge into his gulf-like gob. His tongue grotesquely sloshed it around. He started to speak again, but it was all dental clicks and inadvertent glicking, saliva spraying onto the linoleum floor between where he and Exley sat. He belched and gathered himself.

"Break off some and put the rest over there." Orrin pointed to a kerosene heater, the kind that catch fire and burn down homes.

There was an altar built around the heater that climbed the wall like black mold. Oval portraitures of family members and past relatives were backlit by caged hand lamps hanging from hooks. Wires and extension cords made for a sort of drapery. Prayer cards weathered to a woodcut resemblance were Blu-Tacked to the frames. Slow burn emergency candles were repurposed as votives. Rosary beads vined and intertwined with fresh, handpicked pale corydalis. Statuettes of Saint Joseph and Rip Van Winkle and shepherd boys stolen from the manger scene vied for position. Raffle tickets and scratchoffs were collected in ashtrays. And combination locks, diner matchbooks, whittled wood curios, and bottle caps were arranged as a boy would his toy soldiers on a rainy afternoon. Power strips lined the path to this altar like some ornate and regal runner.

Welding equipment and jugband instruments shared the floor space. Orrin picked up a banjo and jammed his fingers into thimbles. He began to pluck an uncomplicated pattern. There were a few washboards leaned against the couch, hollowed log drums at the front door, and a sweet potato whistle and ocarina in a basket at Orrin's feet.

"Getting ready for the powwow?"

"Heck no, youngblood. You know only rawhide drums are allowed at the powwow." Orrin chuckled to himself and plucked a riff. "Me and your da used to play on the weekends at the Cliff. People'd be slapping hands and buck dancing, drunk as hell." He shook his head. "Your ma *hated* it."

"She hates you for more than your music."

"Yeap," Orrin conceded. "More than you know. Your ma's hard, Exley."

Orrin rested the banjo against the wall and took off the thimbles, one by one, and dropped them in a cigar box. He sat stilly.

"You need to stay soft, youngbood," he finally said. "You're still in the gristle—you're not hardened bone like your ma."

"Give it time," Ex said. "I'll get there."

"No, stay soft."

Black-knot fungus grew on a branch of the chokecherry tree outside the window. Exley heard a mallard quack, probably wandered over from Rotten Pond. Orrin had a habit of feeding them bread crusts when they showed.

"Ma's on me about going."

"And what—you don't want to?"

"No," Exley said, looking directly at his uncle. "What do I wanna be there for?"

"I know I joke, but you should go—it's important."

Orrin reached for a pad of corn cushions from a drawer. He crossed one leg over the other and stuck them onto his feet.

"What's so important about tug o'war?"

"You know it's more than that, youngblood."

"It's drinking, too."

Exley lit one of Orrin's cigarettes and whished his hand back and forth through the lighter flame. Then he pinched the flame between his fingers like he was feeling something tacky.

"You know what they used to call the tennis courts in Rio Vista?"

Exley stared at his uncle through the lighter flame and shrugged.

"The colored folk burial plot." Orrin paused. "They called it *the colored folk burial plot*. That was actually on a sign at one time, too."

"Okay."

"You know why they don't call it that anymore?"

Exley shrugged again. Orrin leaned forward and smacked Ex's knee so hard it hit into the other, injured one.

"Because they built a fucking tennis court on it!"

The mallard sounded closer now. The quacking was right outside the door, soliciting. Exley rubbed his knee. Orrin pointed out the window.

"See these plants out here?" He poked the air, again and again. "We know what to call all these plants but not ourselves. Nobody never has. Hell, we can name every weed from here to the Hudson Valley, but we can't name ourselves."

"Speak for yourself. I know what I am."

"You know what you are," Orrin repeated back. "Good. I'm glad for you. But let me ask you this: Who else knows what you are? Who else calls you what you want to be called?"

Exley looked away from Orrin. He looked at the clock, at the hands of the clock, at the missing numbers.

"Listen, youngblood," Orrin stood up. He was on his heels, not wanting to apply pressure to his toes. "Who else you know—outside of *us*—that got poison control on speed dial?" He knocked an empty Old Milwaukee can onto the floor. "I keep hauling these cans down to the recycling center, but what's Ford doing right now? What's the EPA doing?" He sat back down. His body slumped on the folding chair. "What about this don't you get, nephew? We're raised from a common earth—

that's how my grandda told it to me. And, as Ramapoughs, we've shared a common toil. And we ain't gotten jack shit out of it. Outsiders come in here to laugh or to gawk or to taunt. Businesses show up to cut and slash, to level our hills, to deface our monuments. They fill our valleys with trash. The park rangers—what do they do?—they shoot you clear off your ATV, clear off your land."

His brow was seeping sweat and tracking dirt with it. Exley flicked the sparkwheel on the lighter.

"You done gabbling at me?"

"Yea-up," Orrin said. He hacked. He made a fist at his mouth and his body bent. His hand searched for a whiskey glass, found one, and he hocked a glob of mucous into it. "I'm done now."

"You alright?"

"I'll survive." He wiped his mouth with his sleeve. "Y'know. Your da never got it either. Not fully."

"Maybe that was smart of him, wise. Knowing all you know sure sounds like a headache."

Exley got up and waded through clutter to the door. He felt full of heat and glutted. His uncle didn't move from his chair. He hocked and spit again, as if in farewell.

"We still got more talking to do, youngblood."

"What about?"

"Not now. You ain't ready for what I need to tell you. And, honestly, I ain't ready to tell it." Orrin switched from the folding chair to the couch, rearranged a pillow, collapsed, and closed his eyes. He'd forgotten all about the bluegill burning up on the grill out back. "We'll talk soon, nephew. Maybe after I see you show up at the powwow."

"Wouldn't miss it for the world, Unky."

Walking the patio slabs away from Orrin's property, Exley noticed another junk sculpture set between the hornbeams against the cabin. It was plinthed on an upside-down metal washtub, as a mesa, which was surrounded by so many fallen catkins that it gave the appearance of shag carpeting. The sculpture was a body form—ferrous legs and arms figured from wrought iron Gothic sconces and strap hinges. It had the copper-aluminum coils from an AC for a solar plexus, and nickel-plated safety pins were crooked open like porcupine spines and welded to the torso—the ganglia of a nervous system. What would be the upper chest was sequined with IC chips and inductors. Drill bits for nipples. A dishwasher solenoid for genitalia. A copper yoke for a face. Dirt bike chain as a chinstrap beard. Beady red eyes like a loon. Most off-putting were the twin longneck oil funnels sprouting like yellow antennae from the headpiece. The entirety of the sculpture had been spraypainted black, but Orrin had begun blanching it in stripes.

Exley accidentally kicked a blue propane torch while his eyes remained fixed on the sculpture as he left. Its red beryl eyes were watching him, and it creeped him out something serious.

PART 2

VERSIONS & VARIANTS (CONT'D)

We are the Ramapough Lunaape Nation. We are Ramapough Mountain Indians. We are the Ramapough Lenape Nation. We are Tappan-Hackensack Indians. We are Munsee. We are the Ramapough Lunaape Munsee Delaware Nation. We are heteroglots. We are heteroclites. We are Jonkanoo. We are John Canoe. We are in whiteface. We are in blackface. We are illiterate mountaineers. We are hillbillies. We are Jersey Dutch. We are isolates. We are pioneers. We are tenants. We exist in negative terms. We are other. We are white-Indian-Negro. We are quasi-Indians. We are pseudo-Indians. We are racial. We are biracial. We are triracial. We are not scientifically determined. We are mixed. We are mixedblood. We are mixed up like a dog's breakfast. We are a breeding population. We are forked tongue. We are black. We are red. We are high-yellow. We are ashen. We are dun. We are palefaces. We are redskins. We are Charlie's man. We are rock jumpers. We are a separate caste. We are mine people. We are a reservation. We are a ghetto. We are a trailer park. We have no tribal *affiliations. We are unclean. We are disposable. We are the whole indefinite disintegrated mass thrown hither and thither. We are white trash. We are black trash. We are black black. We are trash trash.*

19

MAY 1996.

Zike woke up to the howling of the Van Dunks' half-beagle, half-basset hound, Buster. His head throbbed at the temples, and he was self-conscious about the smell of his morning breath. The mattress he shared with Lib was rock hard, more fit for a corpse than a cooling board would be. The bedsheets were sutured together from several sets, and Zike was coiled within them like a mort cloth. Even drunk, he slept lightly so as to make sure he didn't cozy up to Lib. Pillows and stuffed animals were riprapped between them to make doubly sure he didn't touch. Lenny had passed out on the floor next to them, and there's no telling what sort of crude violence he would be provoked to if he woke to see Zike DeGroat spooning his kid sister.

The Van Dunks resided in a log chapel that had long been de-christened. There was nothing sacred about their shouting matches, their cusses, their spray bottle training of their cur. Lenny had a few years on Zike, but he knew him from the dirt bike trails. Zike's relationship with Lib was nebulous, at best.

They had a similar class schedule at school, if they so happened to attend. Kids often referred to them as The Twins—their outward appearances warranted it. You wouldn't know Lib hid a female body under her Cannibal Corpse t-shirt. And it wasn't uncommon for Zike to ask her to put black eyeliner on him before first period. They were two of only four or five metalheads in Mahwah. Their JNCOs and wallet chains were dead giveaways. And they were each growing out their uncombed hair at comparable speeds. Sometimes it would tangle if they got too handsy, kissing—the tips of their tongues stabbing—with fingers climbing from the napes of their necks to the crowns of their heads in the way young people choreograph passion. Other times, though, they appeared as strangers with a likeminded wardrobe.

Zike staggered into the bathroom for an in-and-out shower with no soap. He only rinsed because the water was so cold and frigid—the generator hadn't kicked on yet. The husk of smoke from the prior night's bonfire peeled off his skin and emanated the kindling anew. It was enough to gag.

He stared at himself in the vanity mirror and was pleased. His rounded shoulders were like upturned beggar bowls. Bis and tris were defined as if inked. The lines and curvatures of his anatomy were on par with a comic book drawing. Chunks of muscle piled in a pattern of crags and plates, like Thing, only with darker skin. His complexion was the imprecise halftone printing on a splash page of an old Marvel issue, black dots bleeding into the gutters.

Lifting the toilet seat, he was overwhelmed by the waft of still urine. The Van Dunks never flushed—septic issues. He sighted Lib's razor on the edge of the sink. He pressed his thumb against the blades while thinking about the privacies of her body, the hideaways with which he had only trifled. Zike squeezed a blob of Aquafresh onto his finger and brushed it over his teeth. Smiling in the mirror, he saw an American flag of paste and froth melting out of his mouth.

Iris Van Dunk grabbed Zike's arm as he left the bathroom.

"Your ma's been calling, Zike."

"Oh, yeah?" Zike said. "What she say?"

"She wants you to call her. She sounded kind of…" Iris circled her hands like she was conjuring long spurned powers. "…kind of, worried."

"She's always worried, Mrs. V."

Zike followed Iris into the kitchen. She sat cross-legged at the table and started doodling spirals and crosshatch shading in the margins of a Kmart circular. A slipper teetered on her toes.

"You all left beer cans on the patio last night." Zike turned to look out the window onto the yard.

"Just looks like a couple," he said. "We'll get it later."

"*A couple?* It's a whole case worth."

There was an open pack of hamburger patties on the dish rack. A pool of red surrounded it and channeled into the sink. There was also a torn package of hotdogs dribbling its opaque water, forming a conflux with the burger blood.

"Yea-up. There's that, too."

"I'm gonna grill 'em up."

"For breakfast, Zike?"

"It's good for ya."

The phone rang. Iris turned it over and checked the caller ID.

"Your ma again."

"Don't pick up."

Zike carried the warm, wet hamburgers and hotdogs out to the grill.

Hadley Van Dunk yelled from the next room: "Answer the damn phone!" He lumbered into the kitchen, scratching his ass and yawning. "Why's the phone keep ringing so early?" Hadley worked the container terminal in Port Newark but had been laid off. Route 17 and 21 were the worst for traffic in the mornings, and the lates he accumulated hadn't helped his job security.

"Hannah keeps calling for Zike. Apparently he doesn't want to talk to her."

"Clearly." Hadley pinched yesterday's sagging coffee filter from the brewer and dropped it in a garbage bag attached to a cabinet doorknob. "Hell would he want to talk to his moeder for? He's here all the damn time."

"They've got their troubles, Had."

"Well we should start charging rent."

"Is all you got is criticisms for our kids' friends this morning?"

Hadley cupped his hand under the faucet and slurped the tap

water. He swished it around and spat it into the sink. "What else you fishing for?" He picked at his teeth with a long pinky nail.

"How about a *Happy Mother's Day?*"

"Hell, you ain't my moeder."

"I would've raised a better son if I was."

"Lenny proves otherwise."

Iris snatched a steak knife off the table and pointed it at her husband.

"Keep it up and I'll cut you up like a joint snake. Say I won't."

"And I'll re-form like one, too."

"Forget you."

The grill lid filled with propane gas and balled into flames when Zike dropped a match in between the grates. Instantaneous heat made his eyes tear and the fire singed the hairs on his knuckles. The smell was vile, but he sniffed it anyway.

Zike thought about whether he'd be able to get away from Lib. He wanted to see Elsie. Elsie with the choker and the pixie cut and the barrettes on both sides of her head that were so useless but so come-hither. Her family had just moved from Hillburn where there was another, even smaller, community of Ramapoughs. It was right over the New Jersey-New York border. It had been communicated to Zike on more than two occasions through Elsie's envoy, Bede, that Elsie was interested in *maybe* dating and certainly meeting up.

Lib came out onto the patio in a long shirt that extended below the boxers she was wearing. She stretched her arms up and rocked back on her heels. Zike immediately began slapping the patties and hotdogs onto the grill. He rolled the dogs with the spatula and pressed the hamburgers, too.

"Is that breakfast?"

"What?" Zike said. "No appetite?"

"I don't care. I'll eat that for breakfast."

She sat down on a warped patio bench and began cleaning wax from her ears with a fingernail. Brash yelling came from the kitchen.

"Is that Lenny?" Zike asked.

Lenny barreled onto the patio, shirtless and with his Nine Inch Nails medallion necklace swinging. He rocked a lazy mohawk which he sometimes sectioned into spikes with cornstarch and beeswax. More often than not, though, it looked as it did now: a flap of crinkled hair falling over the remainder of his shaved head and shading his face.

"What the fuck is wrong with her?"

"What?" Lib asked.

"I just woke up and she's on me about job applications." Lenny cupped his hands around his mouth and yelled at the kitchen window: "The stores aren't even open yet!"

"Dude, ease up," Zike said.

"For real, Lenny. It's fucking Mother's Day."

"Oh, shit!" Lenny turned to the kitchen window again. "I'm sorry, Ma! Happy Mother's Day!" He kissed the windowpane. Zike and Lib went into an uproar. "What?" Lenny asked, laughing with them.

Fat dripped onto the heat shields, sizzled and smoked.

"Hell yes!" Lenny said.

"One of each?"

"Nah, DeGroat. Gimme two burgers and two dogs. Pinkish on the burgers, but make sure them dogs are barking!"

"You're disgusting," Lib said.

She emptied sugar packets onto the glass patio table, leaned in, and started sorting the sugar into the letters of her name. She was surprised to see the tiniest reflection of an airplane in the glass. It moved rapidly—past the umbrella hole, to the edge, and then vanished. She looked up to follow the flight path unfiltered by reflection, but that version vanished too, into clouds.

Lenny unwrapped a string of firecrackers from red tissue paper. The burgers were bubbling fat on the tops, so Zike flipped them. Lenny snuck up behind and dropped the firecrackers over Zike's shoulder. They fell through the grates and exploded in Zike's face.

"Yo!" Zike shouted. "Are you fucking serious right now?"

"Not cool," Lib added.

Zike threw down the spatula and grabbed some firecrackers of his own. He lit the fuse with a match and tossed them at Lenny's chest. Duds.

"Luck of the draw, bro."

"I'll get you later, motherfucker."

There weren't any buns left, so Lib got white bread instead. Zike and Lenny made meat sandwiches—two hotdogs side-by-side between two hamburger patties.

"You guys are disgusting," Lib said.

"Yea-up. Say it one more time, won't ya?" Lenny had a mouthful of undercooked meat. Bits of ground beef shot off his tongue. "*Disgusting.*"

Lib directed her attention to the blue five-gallon water bottle between her knees. She sliced and sawed the bottom off with a retractable utility knife. Zike and Lenny cracked open Budweiser cans from Mr. Van Dunk's steel cooler. They decided to play Metal War until Lib finished crafting a gravity bong. Metal War was War but with the faces of metal musicians instead of pips and court cards. Lenny had made almost fifty of them by cutting faces out of magazines and gluing them onto index cards.

Lenny shuffled the cards while Zike plugged in a JVC ghettoblaster. It blared the demo tape of a local grindcore band, originally known as Blood Girdling Scream but going by Nosebleed Nancy Boys now. The lead singer—who Lenny claimed to have chilled with once—snarled the lyrics. The message was paranoid and political, and it definitely dabbled in occultism, but nobody could make out much. The thrashing, down-tuned guitars drowned the vocals in the mix. The overdriven bass signal sounded like a jammed-up jigsaw blade. And the drums were low-pitched and mic'd all wrong.

"This is muddy as fuck," Zike commented.

"The singer is dope, though. Admit that. His range is incredible."

"His voice is buried," Zike said. "I can't even judge."

"Put on the new Sepultura," Lib said. She'd begun to stab the bottle cap with a pen, working to puncture it.

"Fuck outta here with that!" her brother said.

"Sorry, Lib," Zike added. "Not a chance."

"Focus on your project there, sissy."

It was true that Lib was an experienced maker of the gravity bong. Even if they only had a nickel bag to split amongst the group, she could create these giant water cooler bongs that made the bud hit four times as strong.

She smoothed a square of aluminum foil on the patio table, firmly rubbing out the wrinkles. Then she wrapped the foil around the spout and sealed it shut with the rubber band from Lenny's Metal War deck. She dented the center with her thumb, pricked holes in the foil with an earring post, and packed the weed into the foil bowl.

"Fill that bucket with water, please."

Zike did as Lib requested, holding the bucket by its wire handle under the spigot. Lenny fanned the Metal War cards in his hand like some two-bit magician.

"How much longer, Libby?"

"Don't rush her, Lenny."

"Easy for you to say, Zike. Not all of us are copping feels."

"Uncalled for," Lib deadpanned.

She turned the holes in the bottle cap into slits, and then carved the slits into a hole. Zike lugged the bucket of water and lifted it onto the patio table. Lib submerged the water bottle and then screwed the cap back on, grinding the foil bowl. She pinched some of the bud and pulled it up a little ways through the cap hole.

"Okay," she said. "We're all set."

"'Bout time," Lenny groaned. "Most elaborate bong ever. I don't know why you're even bothering with that cap."

"You make it next time then, Lenny!" she shouted.

"Will do. Now back off. I'm taking first hit." He strong-armed his way to the gravity bong and struck three matches before he managed to keep a flame. A drawn-out and strained lyric arrived clearly over a drum break—*My des-o-la-tion.* Lenny held the match to the bud and a tumbling cloud of white smoke billowed in the water bottle. It built and built on the surface of the water, filling the contained space like a dust storm rolls over an arid prairie. *No destination*—came across clear, too, but then the voice garbled as the guitars returned. Lenny untwisted the cap and put his mouth over the spout. He pushed the water bottle deeper into the bucket, forcing the white smoke into his lungs.

"Holy, holy!" Zike said.

"He's a fucking ham," Lib added.

Lenny removed his mouth from the spout in such a vulgar way that the contortions on his face seemed all the more warranted. Lips pursed into a trampled prune and his cheeks folded like accordion bellows. His brow immediately glossed with sweat, and he coughed in what sounded like a foreign language, the sincerest parody of what they were hearing from the ghetto-blaster. He growled.

Zike took a hit next and reacted similarly. Lib passed on it. After belting Zike on the back like a choking infant, Lenny began to deal the cards.

Mrs. Van Dunk opened the door to the patio to let out Buster. His short wrinkly legs barely moved, but he succeeded in reaching the patch of dirt he preferred to piss on. He had a yam-sized tumor on his hind leg, and it dragged against the ground, chafing and stippling blood.

Between coughs, Lenny managed: "Happy Mother's Day, Ma...again."

"Shut it up, Leonard," his moeder snapped. She slammed the door and left the hound outside.

Lenny finished dealing half the deck to Zike. "You get next, Lib," he told his sister. Zike evened his cards while Lenny, opposite Zike at the patio table, began to relish the cards he'd dealt himself. "Ready?" Lenny swigged a beer.

"Stop arranging your fucking cards, Lenny." Zike hammered the table with his fist.

"Can this *not* end with you both in a headlock this time?"

"Shut up, Lib," her brother said.

They put their first cards down.

"Oh shit!—grudge match!" Lenny yelled, pointing to Zike's Oderus Urungus card. He had turned over Dimebag Darrell.

"That's mine."

"No fucking way," Lenny said. "Evenly matched, sure. But you lose because *you are* Oderus Urungus, you fucking space ogre."

"You're an asshole, Lenny."

"Thanks, sissy," Lenny said, sliding the two cards into a pile under his elbow.

Metal War always played out the same way: Lenny had final say. He was the sole judge of the matchups. And he'd alter his argument depending on who held the cards. Holding the Dio card would give him the win. *Dio sings about wolves, man.* But if you pulled the same card, he'd have a substitute explanation that meant a loss for you. *Dio slays a stage dragon, man. Lame.*

Zike threw down Buckethead. Lenny flipped Iggy Pop.

"Mine," Zike said, collecting both cards. Lenny grabbed his wrist. "Iggy Pop isn't even metal, Lenny."

"Doesn't matter. Iggy's got an enormo-dick."

"Buckethead thrashes, dude."

"No, no, no," Lenny explained. "Buckethead wears a KFC bucket…on his head."

"I think he's got you there, Zike."

"Thanks, Lib." Zike evened his cards again. "This is a fucking hustle."

At turns, though—and if the opportunity for a good joke presented itself—Lenny could be fair. Zike's Henry Rollins beat his Lemmy card, for instance. "He'll punch you in the face and write a poem about it. Lemmy is old as fuck…and those fucking moles."

Otherwise, Metal War was mostly an occasion for Lenny to hear himself talk and to philosophize about the metal icons that regularly populated his consciousness. Rob Halford's studded leather jacket was hardcore, but it wasn't as badass as Freddie Mercury's glittered leotard. Ozzy bit animal heads, so Phil Anselmo and his mic-grip muscles were no contest. Slash was never a winning card for Zike because their afros were too similar, cancelling them both out of the competition. Rob Zombie won because he was horror as fuck. Vince Neil lost because he took Jack Daniel's through an IV and drove drunk and left dudes brain-damaged. Lars Ulrich: automatic loss. James Hetfield: automatic loss. Danzig was a wildcard, but—as determined by Lenny—won every time. Satan—a cackling and caped Mephisto from an issue of *Silver Surfer*, red as the hell he inhabits—was the other wildcard. Most Metal War games ended with Danzig versus Satan in a no-holds-barred death match. Winner: Danzig.

"Stop dragging," Zike ordered. "Put your card down the same time as mine."

"I am, man. I am."

Zike slapped down Sammy Hagar. Lenny pulled David Lee Roth.

"There it is!" Lenny shouted. "Hagar's a bitch with a perm."

"David Lee Roth isn't even in the band anymore," Zike reasoned.

"Nope. Doesn't matter. Dude could wear a wrestling singlet and still get laid any night of the week."

"Are you guys almost finished, or what?" Lib was pinning a Megadeth patch onto her denim jacket. "Oh fuck me!"

Buster had flopped on his side—his legs trembling, his tumor jiggling—in the piss puddle that had only just absorbed into the soil. The hound's eyes were vacant, and his tongue spilled from his mouth. Whines and snorts issued from his snout as he liquid shit in his place.

"Yo, that dog is alien!" Zike blurted. "That's a fucking alien exorcism. It's turning itself inside-out. What the *fuuuuuck*?"

"He gets these seizures," Lenny said nonchalantly, shuffling his cards. "Gets them all the time now."

"I feel so bad for him." Lib crouched close to the hound and patted his belly.

"Better it happen out here than inside," Lenny said.

"Not like you clean it up anyway."

Lib hosed off Buster and dragged her Doc Marten through the dirt to cover the muck. Lenny slipped a Pantera t-shirt over his torso, and the three of them squeezed into Iris's '84 Ford Fiesta without her knowing. Lenny had his permit but had been joyriding since thirteen. He jammed *Vulgar Display of Power* into the tape deck and turned the volume knob to the right.

Zike and Lib sat in the backseat together. The roof fabric was drooping down and the carpeting had a foul smell. The floors took on water whenever it rained. Lenny would bail out the backseat with a mug or say *fuck it*, drive off, and watch the tide roll in at his feet whenever he came to a traffic light.

"Hold up," Zike said. "I need a cigarette."

"What am I, a chauffer?" Lenny asked. "You two just gonna sit back there and pretend I'm driving you to prom?"

"Can you run in and steal one of your ma's packs?" Zike asked Lib.

"Ma quit again—broke them and flushed them just a couple days ago. There were shreds of tobacco all over the toilet seat."

"Your da?"

"Are you out of your mind?" Lenny said. "He'd literally castrate us." He pulled out of the driveway and started headbanging.

"Go to the Dollar Tree," Zike directed. "I need to get my ma something."

Lenny turned the volume down. "Are you for real?"

"It's Mother's Day, man."

"Haven't you been ignoring her calls all morning? How many days has it even been since you've been home?"

"Just drive to the Dollar Tree, will ya?"

Lib stretched out in the backseat. She rested her head on Zike's shoulder, and he shrugged. Lenny drove through Fardale— he didn't signal even once. They passed a Catholic church. Parishioners were parading to their cars after shaking hands with the priest and the deacon. They had bulletins in their hands and key fobs under their chins. Lenny pointed out a middle-aged man in a raffia hat. Zike pushed the passenger seat forward and craned his head out the window.

"Nice hat, asshole!"

The man shook his head and pushed a small child ahead.

They drove on, and Zike grew quiet, musing out the window.

"What are you thinking about?" Lib asked.

"Nothing."

But Lib immediately thought it was Elsie. Zike knew it was Elsie, and he knew what Lib suspected. He didn't know how he'd survive the ordeal unscathed. He wanted Elsie—he was sure of it now. But he didn't want to risk his friendship with Lib. He didn't want to risk his health by inciting Lenny's wrath either. He put his arm around Lib and smelled her hair with his eyes closed. He opened them, still being that close to her, and admired the mousse dandruff on her scalp. It edged her part like plowed snow.

ZIKE SHOPPED AT THE DOLLAR TREE with the gusto of a pre-K kid pocketing a birthday fiver from grandma. He browsed the aisles for the best items, defining "best" as absurd or ironic and, necessarily, cheap. It didn't take long for him to fill his arms: a waterproof bouffant cap; a Mardi Gras feather mask; a FAITH ceramic refrigerator magnet with a cross for the T; a single, microwavable Velveeta mac and cheese; two-pack of super glue; a bag of crinkle-cut paper shreds; and an air horn. His moeder would be thrilled. The total came to just under ten dollars. Lib and Lenny threw thumbtacks at the ceiling corral of foil balloons near the exit. None of them popped, but the manager was ready to pounce.

They took turns using the air horn in the car. Lenny ended up hogging it, honking at anyone within sight. Zike yelled at a group of middle-schoolers on BMXs: "Nice pegs, tweeners!" He threw up the Danzig fist. One of them in a backwards hat answered with dual middle fingers.

Zike pressured Lenny into detouring somewhere he could browse comics. Nightbat and Joker's Child were too far away, so they settled on the flea market in Ringwood. A burly vendor with arched eyebrows and a felt cowboy vest had milk crates. He unloaded them endlessly from a wood-paneled station wagon.

"You go in," Lenny said. "I'll wait." He sat down on a bench outside the Rec Center.

"You coming, Lib?"

"I'm gonna wait out here, too," she said.

"Don't take for-fucking-ever." Zike waved off Lenny's command.

The tables were arranged around the perimeter of a multipurpose room. Zike tripped on the buckled parquet flooring. Light shone through the skylights and refracted off the bags of the display comics on easels. He inhaled the smell of cardstock and ink and the accumulated dust of the vendor's personal collection—it was heavenly. His comic browsing was sacrosanct. He didn't tolerate being rushed or interrupted or haggled with. He had no cash on him after the Dollar Tree spree, but the exposure to the merchandise was enough.

Only last week he'd traded for a copy of *Fantastic Four* #45. It was in poor condition with a center crease down the cover, a popped staple, and foxing at the corners. But it included the first appearance of Black Bolt, the black and blue-outfitted leader of the Inhumans who could strip mine the summit of a mountain with the smallest utterance. His voice was a savage weapon. His exposure to the Terrigen Mist, a mutagen, was what gave him his powers. He was Zike's favorite character. It was well worth the Suzuki frame chassis and a set of Bridgestone soft-terrain tires with tall knobs he traded for it. He'd stolen the chassis over a year ago, so he didn't think twice about making the deal.

Now he was after *Fantastic Four #46*. It featured Black Bolt on the cover, his arms and legs spread into an X formation. It wasn't unlike a metalhead pose. The words THOSE WHO WOULD DESTROY US! appeared between his legs in a green typeface. Zike rifled through milk crates looking for the top edge of the issue—an earth-core red cloud that he'd studied in a tiny picture of an outdated *Wizard*. From the price guide in that same magazine, he knew a mint or near-mint copy of the issue was too expensive for him to even dream of. But, unlike most collectors, he really wasn't averse to poor conditions. Rodent chew, dust shadows, oily fingerprint smudges, full-page folds, spine breaks—he wasn't prejudiced against any of it.

"Got a specific need today?" the vendor asked. Just a table width apart, Zike could see the man's felt vest was severely pilled from years of washing. His eyebrows arched even higher with his question, and there were a trio of bristly hairs sprouting from the tip of his nose.

"Nah," Zike said. "You don't have any Lee-Kirby *Fantastic Fours*, do you?"

"No, no, none of those," the vendor said. He scratched behind his ears with both hands. "There's a guy who does the convention in Hasbrouck Heights at the Holiday Inn. You might go see him next time."

"That right?"

"Got a lot of value in his collection, though." The vendor removed the backing board from a Todd McFarlane *Spider-Man*. "Bring your wallet."

LENNY, LIB, AND ZIKE WENT RIGHT BACK to drinking at the Van Dunk home and continued through the afternoon. Lenny shoveled a Tombstone frozen pizza into the oven and fetched an old Sprite can bowl from his bedroom closet. Lib ground the last of their weed onto the indentation in the middle of the soda can. They cyphered in a triangle pattern and took turns exhaling into the exhaust fan above the stove.

The oven timer went off, and Lenny licked his fingers before pulling the pizza out.

"You fucking dingbat!" Lib shouted. "You forgot the cardboard again."

The pizza had melded with the cardboard tray.

"Fuck me."

Zike grabbed forks from a drawer and passed them out. They each began scraping and peeling the pizza from the cardboard. Viscous mozzarella cheese webbed between their forks.

"Let it cool," Lib said. "Like last time."

"I'm not waiting for shit," Lenny said. "I'm starving over here."

The phone rang.

"If that's you-know-who, I'm still not available."

"Zike, for real?" Lib said. "How many times am I gonna have to lie to your ma?"

"Until I say. Pick it up."

Of course, it was Hannah again. And she pressed Lib—calling her "Libby"—telling her it was *really* important she pass the phone to Zike. "She says it's important, Zike."

"Bullshit."

"Just talk to her."

He huffed and flung the mass of tomato sauce, cheese, and rubbery bread off his fork. "Thanks," he said to Lib, taking the phone.

"What's up, Ma?"

"Where've you been the past two days, three days?—I don't even know what it is."

"I've been here."

"Then why haven't you taken my calls? I've been dialing this number nonstop."

"Busy, Ma."

"We can't find your da, Zike."

Lenny was pantomiming across the kitchen. He held his hands over his heart and thumped them out and in against his chest, out and in. Smooched his lips together. Mouthed a sentiment to Zike to pass on to his ma. He ran out of the kitchen, made some noise in the hall, and returned holding the Dollar Tree bag. Pointed to it, with jabs.

"I almost forgot, Ma," Zike started slowly, sounding dopey. "Happy Mother's Day."

"Did you hear what I said?"

"Ma, ma. I got you gifts. I'm gonna bring them over later. I just gotta help Lenny with something."

Hannah must've moved the receiver, repositioned it closer to her mouth or something, because her words came through clearer.

"We cannot find your da. He's been gone two days now. I need you to look for him."

"Call Unky Orrin about it."

"I did, Zike. He hasn't seen him."

"Maybe he got a job."

"Since when have you known your da to get a job? And—even if he did—you telling me he wouldn't stagger home drunk with the pay in his belly?"

"Shit, Ma," Zike waved his hand at Lenny who was eating his portion of the pizza. "I don't know what you want from me."

"Zike. Listen. Your da is missing. I need you to go look for him. I can't do it myself. I'm stuck here with Exley. He's full of anxiety, your brother."

"Let me talk to him."

"He's in the other room."

"Let me talk to him, Ma."

Hannah called Exley's name. Her voice sounded distant, an echo deep in a mine.

"Yea-up?" Exley's voice was soft.

"Ex, what's going on?"

"I don't know. Da's not home."

"Don't worry about Da. Alright?"

"Alright."

"You good, li'l bro?"

"I think."

"He's all out of sorts." Hannah was back on the line. The mine echo, again: "Exley, hon, lay on the couch."

"Alright. I'll go look for him, Ma."

"And then come home, Zike. I don't need you *and* your da out there with me not knowing your whereabouts."

Zike hung up the phone.

"What did she say?" Lib asked.

"Nothing."

Zike left the kitchen and went into Lib's bedroom. He sat on the edge of her bed and gazed into the mirror on her dresser. He surveyed the room in the reflection: her Slayer poster; her CD tower; her clothes on hangers but not hanging, only folded over the chairback; her unzipped makeup bag—a mouth with too many minuscule teeth. There was a bump to the mirror, a warp, and it disfigured everything it reflected with a funhouse effect. The room—all of it—was widened and narrowed like a cinched waistline. Zike put his head between his knees and zeroed in on the braids of the carpet and was desperate to find and reestablish his axis.

"You alright?"

The bedroom skewed and Zike's nausea swelled. He shuffled past Lib and out the door. He leaned against the bathroom sink. He heaved, heaved again. And he puked. Lenny joined Lib at the door.

"What the fuck, bro? The toilet's right there!"

Zike dropped to the floor. He hugged his knees and slapped his shins. The curdy puke clogged the drain and the sink held a shallow pool.

"Dude, what the hell is that? What am I looking at right now?"

Lenny and Lib inched forward, studying the sink. The ragged casing of a hotdog floated at the surface of the fallow brown beer and bile.

"How did you manage to eat the hotdog but not the skin?" Lenny asked. "That shit is intact!"

Zike reached up and behind his head, pulling a towel off the rack. He wound it around his whole head like a turban, held it in place, then unwound it and mopped his face.

"Let's go ride," he said, standing.

"You sure?" Lenny asked.

"Zike, you look like shit. How many rips did you take?" Lib put her hands on his waist.

"I'm good," he said. "I'm good. Let's go."

CANNON MINE TRAIL WAS HARDPACKED but could be marbley after heavy rain. Zike's Honda could handle it, but Lenny rode a contrived and clapped-out Kawasaki KX500 from the early eighties that overheated and rattled like a pressure cooker bomb. Zike was, by far, the better rider. Lenny was a muscly spode who often bobbled on the studders they'd made his freshman year. He'd lift off his t-shirt as though he were getting ready to fight someone and flex his arms behind his head. The bellicose pose drew attention to the helmeted and bat-winged skull tatted on his shoulder blades. BUILT TO RIDE was on a banner beneath it. He did this posturing for an audience of two: Zike and his kid sister. Zike laughed. And Lib couldn't care less about her brother's physique.

Lib plugged in the earbuds of her Discman. She sat on a stack of tires in a culvert next to a collection of discarded Blendzall empties. Zike three-fingered the chain, checking its slack. His chain broke loose the month before and whipped his back like a medieval flail. He hadn't taken any chances with specs since then.

"You ready?" Lenny asked. He was already wearing his knockoff Oakley sunglasses, desperate to look the part. He looked bionic behind the polarized lenses.

"Give me a sec."

Zike adjusted the bark busters on his handlebars and slapped the Blessed Virgin graphic on his seat fairing as some sort of superstition. But he thought it bad luck to look at the Misfits logo Lenny had stuck to her groin, so he blinked long behind his hologram goggles. Neither of them wore any more than the eye protection—no helmets, no gloves, no pads. Zike had an unused kidney belt in his bedroom—a birthday gift from his parents—but he felt his movements would be limited if he wore it. The feel would be too unnatural.

"Alright," Zike announced. "Let's do it."

Lib barely acknowledged them as they began riding. Zike's massive body on a dirt bike resembled the Hulk on a trike, a circus bear on a bicycle—it was comical. Lenny followed a good distance behind, wobbling and clipping the trail edges and beaver dams. Zike pushed it, accelerating through the river valley, buzzing past the downed trees at the ridgetop of Houvenkopf Mountain. Zipping downhill, he blipped the throttle at turns, bounding through mud bogs and splattering Lenny with his roost. Lenny got a soil sample to the face, and Zike didn't feel bad about it. Even if the mud did include a smear of meadowlark yellow and candyapple red, he didn't feel bad.

Rotten Pond was off to the right. Zike was cloaked in a blur of trees—a blizzard, a May squall. He could make Unky Orrin's forlorn cabin through the stunted chestnut oaks and the thick colony of purple-flowered loosestrife. He lost Lenny to the skunk cabbage and reed grasses and milkweed. Zike's shirt was mildewed with mud, but he felt empowered and adequate and skilled on his dirt bike. There was no audience—no Lib looking on, no phone calls from his ma, no school scuffles with other students. He approached a hillock, squeezing his waffle grips tightly, and whipped his bike. He nailed a nac-nac off the small jump. No one was there to see it, but he didn't even care.

His stomach began to cramp. His nausea returned. A grouse flew out of a field of goldenrod as he rounded a bend. Following its flight was like watching a success story, what with the banks covered in trashed radiators, rims, and barrels dented to hourglasses. Zike's face sweat chilled at his top speed, and the slicing glare of the setting sun blinded him moment to moment. He made it back to the start, his stomach still twisting. Lenny was there, spread-eagle on a boulder of gneiss next to Lib. Zike accelerated coming in, skidding at the curve, acting the part of a cocky rider.

Suddenly though, Zike's forearms locked up like cinderblocks, and he couldn't pull the brake lever. Blood collected underneath his skin and his nerves dulled. His fingers wouldn't bend. He went into the next turn too fast and did an endo into a berm. His face smashed against the crossbar, and the bike ricocheted out from underneath him. Lenny and Lib ran to the embankment and huddled over Zike's tossed body. He was scummed with mud and paint sludge. Flares of indian turquoise, colonial white, and brittany blue smeared his shirtfront, elbows, and knees. All those Ford colors. They were everywhere in the woods. He rolled over on a lava-like jut in the ground. The hardened sludge was porous and could be chiseled away like clay. The metal angles of his bike cleaved the mound and revealed the rainbow of colors beneath.

"Zike, are you alright? You hurt?" Lib asked. She pushed the hair from his face and held it back.

"You greased it, dude!"

"I'm fun," he said, his eyes downcast. "*Fine*, I mean. I'm fine." There was a ragged hole ripped at the center of his shirt—a bizarro superhero symbol. "My chest is killing me." Lib grazed her fingers at the cotton fabric and saw the bloody scrape.

"It looks awful," she said.

"The pain inside is worse." Zike started to get up. "Broken ribs or chest plate or something." He winced and began to limp in the direction of his bike.

"What happened?" Lenny asked. "I never seen you lose control like that."

"Arm pump, bro. Worst case I've ever had. I couldn't move my fingers, my hands."

Zike massaged his forearms as he found his dirt bike in a ditch full of bracken ferns. He inspected the damage, shaking his head the entire time.

"Blew out a fork seal."

"Dented the subframe, too," Lenny said. "Cracked the belly pan, and your steering stem is fucked."

They heard a whistle and looked over to the glade. A form— not unlike a buck deer in flannel—high-stepped through the smooth alders. The man wore a coonskin cap like something out of a Davy Crockett TV special. His gingham shirt flapped free at his front but was tucked in the back. He waved and whistled again.

"Is that your uncle?" Lib asked.

"Yea-up," Zike confirmed. He leaned the disfigured dirt bike against a treetrunk and picked at his scratched up decals on the seat fairing. Unky Orrin's wheeze could be heard twenty yards out.

"Kids," Unky Orrin said, nodding to Lib and Lenny. "Zike, I been looking for you."

"I already talked to Ma on the phone—no worries."

"What about?"

"What you mean?"

Orrin stared at Zike, trying to figure him.

"I need you to come see about something," Orrin said. "Your ma don't know about it. It's for you to know."

"I'm busy, Unky. I don't got time."

"Like hell you is," Orrin said, getting firm. "I see the busy you been up to." He gestured to Zike's exposed, bloody chest. He walked off a ways, out of earshot from Lib and Lenny. Reluctantly, Zike followed.

"Well what is it you need?" Zike asked. "Come by your place?"

"Nah, not there."

"Where then? I got plans with my friends. And then I got to bring Ma her gifts. It's all back at Lib and Lenny's."

"I need you now," Orrin insisted. "No telling how long it's gonna take."

"We can't do it tomorrow?"

"Now."

Zike walked back to his bike. Lenny was crouched, measuring up the damage to the engine.

"Can you walk it back?" Zike asked.

"Do I look like triple-A?"

"C'mon, Lenny. My uncle needs me for something."

"For what?" Lib asked.

"I don't know. He's being a fucking weirdo."

Lib hesitated, then asked: "You're not going to see that Elsie, are you?"

"Didn't you hear what I just said?"

"I'll take the bike," Lenny interjected.

"Thanks, man. I'll hit you up later."

"Your uncle," Lenny said, "thinks he's a fucking medicine man."

Zike followed Unky Orrin to the edge of the glade. They stepped over a patch of mugwort, of which Orrin snapped a sprig, sniffed, and folded it into the rolls of his sock. Entering the woods dimmed the scene. The sun had sunk below the horizon, and—with his wounds and aches—Zike saw himself as something feral, a figment. Unky Orrin braced Zike's wrist.

"The fuck?"

"Nobody's told you about those Van Dunk kids? Warned ya?"

"What the fuck you talking about?" Orrin's grip pained Zike. He still had the numbing feeling from the arm pump.

"Hadley was always in trouble."

"And?"

"And I suspect he's passed it on to his children."

"I hang out with who I want," Zike asserted. "Tell me what this is about now. Why you need me out here with you in the woods?"

"It's about your da," Orrin said, his eyes on the footpath before him. He picked up a bottle cap and it plinked into his sagging breast pocket, joining acorn nuts and rivets and what-all.

"You find him?" Zike asked. "Ma was freaking. He been on a bender, or what?"

"How old are you now?" Orrin sized up his nephew. "Sixteen."

"Fifteen," Zike corrected.

"That's enough."

"Enough for what?"

Orrin ignored Zike's question. He stopped walking, unbuckled his pants, and dropped them halfway down his thighs. "We're going to Peters Mine," he said. "You go on ahead. I'll follow." He pulled his shirt around his waist and yanked his pants back up, tucking the shirt completely.

"We walking all the way to Peters Mine?" Zike complained.

"Walk."

ZIKE TRUDGED IN THE DIRECTION OF THE MINE. Unky Orrin followed behind several paces, like a scout leader gauging a boy's foraging skills. The speaking between them stopped. Zike thought about trivialities. He struggled with the where and the when of breaking it off with Lib. He picked at the gravel embedded in his chest. The blood was coagulating in the same dunnish color as the basalt bits. The costs of his dirt bike repairs would take months to hustle. The subframe alone would cost two bills. Maybe he could hammer it out himself. He'd need Lenny's hands and vises to steady the part, though. And Lenny wouldn't be around if he and Lib weren't together. At least not at first. Zike could imagine Lenny letting it go after a couple weeks, maybe. It really all depended on Lib's reaction. If she was okay with it, then Lenny would have no reason to beef with him. He thought of his Grandma Edie's arthritic hands as he tried to straighten his own. The stiffness remained. Tired out, his feet stumbled over a fallen branch. His heels crunched the understory, and he noticed Unky Orrin's steps were sounding farther away. He turned around.

"I'm still with ya," Orrin assured.

The scrap and trash broke up the sylvan beauty of the hike as they neared their destination. Barrels and buckets and garbage bags fringed the trail leading to the adit of the mine. Zike knew the location as a place for kids to set off firecrackers and smoke cigarettes—he'd done much of the same. Scenic views of the ribbed mountains and the valley-cleft could be had, too. You just had to climb above the mine entrance and scale a boulder wall. It could be accomplished with bare hands and moxie. Unky Orrin frequently scavenged the mine. Zike had heard plenty of tales concerning his big hauls. He climbed a few more steps and saw the gaping adit staring back at him. And all he could make was more trash at its core. His uncle had stopped following.

"You go on ahead now," Unky Orrin shouted, a good distance off. "You need to see it, nephew. You need to know what it is we all dealing with here, what it can do to a man. It's no joke. Make sure your ma gets the note, ya hear?"

Zike was confused at the statement, and he felt off—disoriented too, in a literal sense—as Orrin receded into the woods.

Alone there. He heard wingbeats and the pecking of a common flicker in the oaks. He crept closer to the adit of the mine. A ragged son—weary but sobered—with blood and sinews and muscles. There were pallets strewn across the clearing, but one— almost centered—was concealed by a crumpled blue tarp. Zike saw a callused foot-bottom—a hard, rust-orange heel—showing through the folds of the tarp. He moved in closer. He saw other skin: a hairy, left shin; knobbed knuckles no better than a dog chew; a black neck. Zike curled his finger through a grommet and threw back the tarp.

His throat went dry, and he gagged. He looked away from what he saw, looked skyward, saw—instead—a gibbous moon. A gray pall gradually passed. He looked down again and saw his da's nakedness.

Naked, but faceless. He beheld the bloomed skull, like the frayed fag-end of a rope. The splayed fibers of a cablewire. A bloody clump of fungus. Magma flow. He looked from the feet to the head, alternating: *This is my da. This isn't my da.* The face skin flapped like the unbuttoned epaulettes of a flak jacket. His scalp was doffed, his dome butchered—a heap of bison meat. The hair had been blown back into a bloodied helmet plume. There were no eyes.

Zike stepped back, unsteady. He'd once watched his da piss behind the skinning shed. And what he saw then looked the same as what he saw now, only slightly smaller. The beer paunch made everything appear less. And the carbuncles in the crevices of his groin were revolting. The position of the legs and arms were such that he wouldn't be able to recognize the body if it were alive. His da wasn't limber. His body was stiff, rigid. *This isn't my da.* Zike mopped his face with the hem of his shirt and was startled at the hole ripped at the chest, the absence of it. The fall from his dirt bike seemed forever ago.

His da's uncovered corpse—he left it there, and it was enormous, seeming to overspread the width of the mine. He found the pile of neatly folded clothes. The plaid shirt, the cargo pants, the tortured boots and tube socks with threadbare, diaphanous heels. *This is my da.* Of course his da would do the chore of folding the clothes, displaying them. But Zike wouldn't recognize the absurdity of it for years.

Zike found the note between the leg folds of his da's cargos. The paper was crisp with sharp creases. The penmanship was sloppy but steady. There weren't any cross-outs, no erasures. No rubber eraser fibers fell out as Zike unfolded it. It wasn't a note his da had labored to write. It all came easy. Its content was boilerplate, as though he'd found a manual for it—a how-to for suicide notes. That was something Zike knew for sure—his da was a man who knew how to follow instructions.

He stood there—his legs like lumber—reading the note countless times. It felt like a covenant between him and his da. Zike read it until it was too dark to read. Until its meaninglessness became meaningless. Until it was just an ink blotch on a yellow page.

20

EXLEY DREAMT OF HIS SEVEN-YEAR-OLD BODY sprawled on his da's stomach. It was midafternoon. His da was napping. He closed his eyes and opened them and was his seventeen-year-old self on his da's stomach. He felt the lift of his da's chest lifting him. He felt safe. But then anxiety overtook him as he spotted a camping lantern on the coffee table beside the couch. The lantern's mantle emanated a blinding white light. He was worried his da would wake up. Ex squinted and reached to close the valve. He stretched his arm, but he couldn't reach it—his fingertips grazed the glass. The smell of naphtha sickened him. His vision blurred looking into the lantern, like staring into the sun. He gingerly shifted his body, worried about disturbing his da's sleep. He lifted his body slightly, reached once more, and successfully shut the valve. But now the light source wasn't a camping lantern—it was a Bunsen burner.

Mr. Chilowicz was sitting across the living room on a recliner. He was dressed in his casual summer clothes with his tasseled loafers propped on the ottoman. *I told you not to fuck with that Bunsen burner, DeGroat.* Exley panicked. He quickly turned the needle valve and the flame grew. Like a film transitioning to its next scene, his view of Chilowicz was burned up in a flare of excess light. He curled into a fetal position on his da's body. The heat of his da's chest became stifling, and then hot to the touch. Hairs spiraled out from his shirt collar, sizzling like live wires.

And then Norval gurgled—the clearing of a throat. Exley looked up and into his da's waking face but it wasn't his da. Zike's face, full of scarring and fissures, stared back at him. Exley rapidly averted his eyes and nuzzled into the comfort of his da's plaid shirt, but it wasn't that. It was Zike's cratered chest with all its raw, grafted tissue and wrinkled mud-brown skin. Exley's legs jerked and kicked over the Bunsen burner. The carpet caught fire as though it were soaked in paint thinners. Flames climbed the curtains and the walls, and the flames sucked at the ceiling like a starving babe. Exley ran from the room, looking back only to see his brother still stretched out on the couch—faceless now, but in repose—and melting into a heap of molten metal.

EXLEY AWOKE WITH HIS BEDSHEETS shackled around his ankles. He heard his moeder coughing in the kitchen and anticipated the clicking on of the nebulizer. She'd been coughing more, so he'd been wandering more. He'd spent most of the month of July roaming the woods. He'd watched fireworks on the Fourth from the summit of Houvenkopf Mountain. He climbed the ruins of

Foxcroft mansion and sat atop the stone cistern and could see the display across the New York border in Sloatsburg. The colors glowed like a corona above the uneven canopy of the trees, a fuzz.

It was deep summer now. Spring jackets and the waxy fragrance of magnolia blossoms were faint recollections. He hadn't spoken to Sue for weeks, nothing more than the meaningless small talk they shared at CVS. He spent his time alone, withdrawn. He didn't even jerk off all that much. He was bored with most everything.

He often thought of Emilia, though—little Meal—her body temperature rising on such sultry days. Exley looked to the sky, searching out the dog star, thinking about Meal's diminutive body lazing in that large and leather chemo chair. Gussie had grown more nervous, fidgety during interactions. It seemed he, Ora, and their daughter were in a dead heat for unhealth, each their own sort. Gussie described in awesome detail how the tumor snuggled Meal's pelvic bone and would not let go. The chemo was intended to shrink the tumor, Lord willing, prior to scheduling surgery.

Exley was sick, too. Sick of his surroundings—those woods, those archways of leaves, those darkling hills that turned him swarthy. So instead of wandering the woods he snatched his ma's car keys off the hook, tightly closed his fist to mute their jangling, and ducked his head into her Ford Escort. He shifted into neutral, thinking he'd roll the car down Stag Hill, turn the key in the ignition when he hit Cannon Mine Road, and not have to worry about his ma making a fuss. But then he remembered the whirr of the nebulizer, how—after a few minutes—it droned and deafened. And he was relieved. He started the car and drove out of those destitute mountains and into the affluence of Cragmere.

He didn't park far from where he'd parked for the start-of-summer party on Masonicus Road. He stepped out onto the cobblestone curb, not bothering to lock the doors. He wandered a different Mahwah now—not the wilderness he knew so well, but the freshly paved, well-lit, avenues of the moneyed.

So he made it a point to ignore the sidewalks. He rambled over manicured lawns and in the middle of streets. And the signs appealing to courtesy and obedience to local laws and statutes— he ignored those, too. Forget vehicles. The DEAD END and NO U-TURN signs seemed personally addressed to him approaching on foot. He meandered the cul-de-sacs, the winding roads. This was smalltime civil disobedience. *A home invasion*, he thought. *These people. They can be so sensitive about what they think is theirs.*

He began to walk the front yards, angling his body through middling elder-hedges arranged checker-ways—landscaping designed to keep people out. His knee was feeling strong, so he didn't hesitate to hop a worm fence constructed from rust-resistant cedar. These residents would unspool razor wire if it weren't so unattractive. He scaled their ha-has, leapt over their sewer ditches. They just had the loveliest storm drains imaginable!

Exley trampled their pavers and pea gravel. When he crossed a lawn, he'd pause after several steps in an effort to imprint and flatten the luxuriant grass. He passed both seasonal and patriotic flags bracketed beside front doors. The star-sewn pleats of porch buntings were ridiculously nationalistic. He noted the guardian lion statues on either side of a circular driveway. Noted the gnomes and nature boys with bug jars and St. Francis of Assisi cupping a bird in his hands while another has alighted on his shoulder. Noted the jockey with gloss black skin in bright red racing silks bearing a lantern. Exley smacked a DOG CONTAINED BY ELECTRIC FENCE sign. He thumped granite birdbaths with sunflower basins. He spun the three-hundred-sixty degree rotating heads of owl decoys. And he even thought about pissing in a tiered and illuminated fountain topped with a pouring rustic pot. A pump and a weatherproof cord powered the continuous flow of water. All was artificialized. Their beds of nonnative flowers rankled him.

A brick-front colonial with a stationary wheelbarrow stuffed full of flowerpots got Exley's attention next. There was a glow in a second-story window. It had to be a kid's bedroom. There was a mason jar on the sill glimmering with fireflies. Exley's ilk never nabbed fireflies for bedside lighting. They would capture them and rip off their luminescent butts, smearing the neon glow across each others' faces. They'd chase and cast spells until their faces dimmed, and then they'd do it all again.

The babbling of water over rocks could be heard from behind a privacy gate. Ex hoisted himself over and landed in the backyard. The inground pool had a slate step structure at the far end, and the water filtered through and cascaded down. Ex removed his shoes and socks, rolled his shorts high up on his thighs, sat at the edge, and submerged his sore feet in the water.

In the summer of '94, Exley's parents got him and his brother an inflatable cauldron pool for forty bucks at Big Lots. The ground behind their house was so gravelly and jagged that they had to throw down weeks' worth of newspapers to soften the surface. Their ma was fanatical about the liner. *If that thing tears there's no getting another one!* Norval would usually yell for her to relax. "Let them have their fun, Hanny," he'd say.

Their fun was wrestling. Zike had learned all the moves from *Monday Night Raw*—suplexes and stunners and sleeper holds. The inflated brim of the pool was perfect for chokeslams into the turnbuckle. Exley could recall his brother's body on his—his oily muscles, the slickness of his skin. Ex was helpless—a ragdoll for his brother's amusement. "Go easy on him, Zike," their ma would yell from the back door. "He's a baby still."

That pool was still in the backyard, but it was deflated, coated with algae and slime. Its walls had buckled long ago, and the crevices became breeding grounds for bucktoothed mosquitoes. Larvae skittered over the sunken tarp eager for flight.

The reflection in the inground pool distorted Exley's face. It sent his crimped hair sliding off his head. The ripples swirled the rest of him. He lifted himself out of the pool and dried his feet beside a row of bamboo citronella torches. There were— from what Ex could tell—no mosquitoes in Cragmere. No varmint, either. The same could be said for Fardale, for Rio

Vista. These sections of town were enclosures, pest-controlled idylls. Ex slinked through the balks between this yard and the next and made his way back to the street. There were two Mahwah PD cruisers out front. He veered left as two cops stepped out.

"Stop," one shouted.

Exley did. The two cops adjusted their utility belts, doing that thing cops do with their fingers and hands—replicating the shape of the actual weapon while gripping the holster.

"You live there?" the lead one asked.

"No," Ex answered. His voice was subdued. "I was just passing through."

"Then why are you on the property?"

The other cop stood with his arms akimbo, his thumbs tucked in his belt. His head turned on a pivot, looking up and down the street. He appeared to be expecting an ambush.

"I was passing through."

"If you don't live there, it's not your property."

A plane flew overhead. Its lights flashed, and Ex thought—as he always did—about destinations. He pulled a Virginia Slim from his pocket.

"Don't light that," the cop said. "You from the mountain?"

"What's it matter?"

"Well if you're not a Mahwah resident we're gonna have problems."

"Keep your hands out of your pockets," the other cop said.

Exley had simply replaced the cigarette into his pocket and left his hand there.

"I'm a resident," Exley said.

"You live on Stag Hill?"

Exley didn't respond. He saw another plane in the sky, too high to even consider its destination. Too high to be heard or even to be regarded.

"Listen," the cop said. "You can't just cut through people's yards. How'd you get here?"

"Walked."

"You walked that whole way?"

"Yea-up."

"Smells like bullshit to me, Ken," the other cop said.

"You need to leave this neighborhood. Get back to your home." The cop pointed at the mountain, the woods. "We catch you here again and you're cited for trespassing. We can't be getting calls like this."

Exley didn't say anything.

"You get this?" the cop asked. "We're letting you go with a warning."

It didn't mean anything to Exley. He turned and slowly walked to the end of the block. He didn't retrieve his ma's car. He didn't let on that he had a vehicle.

He left residential Cragmere and walked along the business route parallel to Route 17, feeling like vapors. It wasn't hard to reenter the zone of invisibility. He only had to hug the medians, stay close to the Jersey barriers and guardrails, hunker against an abutment. His people had been disappearing for decades, and it was always only a long walk or a short drive into industrial wasteland.

The parking lots of strip malls were fun to walk. If an overnight security pickup was making the rounds and dared question your being there, you could talk back and take comfort in knowing the patrolman was as powerless as you. Exley pushed a wayward shopping cart even further toward the perimeter. He flirted with the idea of pushing it all the way across the intersection, letting it clatter into the jughandle island full of lilac bushes and bulrushes. The jughandle island with the THIS AREA IS MAINTAINED BY DYER LANDSCAPING & LAWN CARE sign. He longed to disrupt the banality of it all.

Some storefronts had lights that shone all night; others were dim or shuttered with rolldown gates. The Sunoco station was radiant. Ex considered the artistry of the motor oil canisters stacked in the window of the attendant's booth. He wondered if they'd ever been bought or rearranged or inventoried.

He walked through the CVS parking lot, following a path he wouldn't during work hours. The store was dark, but the block-lettered sign on the exterior was a bright, blinding red. The birdnest in the bottom swoop of the S was still there.

He was haunted by his dream, his being on his da's chest only to have it turn to his brother's. The thought, the vision, left him forlorn. His da was dead. Zike was all but done. And the Mahwah cops seemed intent on being dicks. They were so bloated, he thought, those cops. Both of them—even the younger of the two. He shouldn't have even allowed them to speak to him. He should've booked it, hopped a fence, and watched as they struggled to lift a leg over it. Bellies gutted on the barbed ends of the chain-links. Intestines opening up and hanging like drapery. Or maybe they would've just put a bullet in his back.

HE PACED HIMSELF RETURNING to his ma's Escort. He half-expected it to have been towed. He had no permits, no parking privilege on those streets. All it would take was a resident with an incontinence issue to look out a window and recognize that Ex's junker didn't belong on that block. But it was there, and he drove the speed limit until he was clear of the neighborhood. The lawn sprinklers went off in synchronization as he drove—one after another after another. The fountains of water and the oscillating sprays and the glistening greens gave the impression it was all in his honor, which, of course, it wasn't.

21

EXLEY LEFT HIS CVS SHIFT with diabetic tube socks shoved down his khakis. Unky Orrin could shut up about it now. Home held his interest less and less as the summer wore on, so Ex drove to the Mattress Factory instead of climbing up Stag Hill. Gussie worked the shipping gate at the back of the building, sitting in a folding chair with ratchet tie-down straps in his lap. The job was mostly waiting—waiting for some customer to make a selection and splurge on a new mattress. He and a few other guys edged close to the open warehouse door. The facility had no temperature control and the upright mattresses in heavy-duty plastic sucked up all the air. Exley pulled his car up to the loading dock.

"Gussie. What's up?"

Gussie seemed startled at the sound of his own name. He hadn't even looked up when Ex pulled in, assuming it was a customer and that he'd be required to lift a mattress.

"Ex. How's it going, youngblood?" Saying hi seemed to be an exertion. He went immediately back to his lap, daisy chaining the excess strap. Exley nodded to the other guys on the loading dock—Tone, a white dude, and Theo and Dew, who were Ramapoughs. Theo and Dew could've been twins but weren't. Each was bald in the same pattern and wore t-shirts inside-out with the seams showing as if they were starting a trend. Lifting belts hung loosely around their lumbars. Tone shuffled invoices, thumbing the white, yellow, and pink pages of each.

"You coming off work, Ex?"

"Yeap. I fucking hate that place."

"So leave. Quit."

"I would, but Ma needs me to help with the bills."

"Work here," Theo interjected.

"Yeah?"

"Yeah," he said. "I don't think they hiring, though."

"But we've been trying to suffocate Tone there between the mattresses for months now," Dew joked. "When we succeed, we'll let you know there's an opening."

Gussie barely laughed.

"How's Meal doing?" Exley asked.

Gussie shook his head once, like a twitch. He melted the frayed end of the tie-down strap with a grill lighter.

"Poor, poor," he muttered. It sounded like labored breaths. "Poor girl, Ex. She…I don't know."

"I know," Ex said.

Gussie slid a roll of packing tape down off his forearm. Ex hadn't noticed it there, not until Gussie took it off. But, fitting it on his forearm like that, it was like a sleeve wrap—something symbolizing a period of mourning. It wasn't that, though—it was clear tape. The kind that's a hell of a time to get started because you can't very well see the location of the last tear. And such was the case for Gussie, who caressed his pinky finger around the roll, feeling for the slightest ridge. Nothing was coming easy to him.

"I'm bringing her to chemo every day," Gussie said, proudly.

"Ora ain't doing shit. Ora's in the wind. She can't take it, she says—can't square it or see it. The garden's gone to shit—it's a jungle."

"I know, Gussie. She should do more—for you *and* for Meal."

Exley could feel his maturity in his mouth.

"Fuck her, though, right? It's all me. I'm the one going on all these appointments. The X-rays, the scans, the blood work. I'm the one talking to these doctors, oncologists…all the time, Ex!" Gussie squeezed the roll of packing tape between his hands, shaping it into an oval. "You should hear how these people speak. Like—I don't know—*marveling* or some shit. They keep talking about its aggressiveness." Gussie looked up from his lap and made direct eye contact with Exley. "I mean, am I supposed to be proud of that? What the fuck do they expect me to say to that?" Tone, Theo, and Dew receded into the warehouse. "It's like it's not a sick person to them, Ex. It's like my daughter's just a disease they want to study."

"I hear you," Ex tiptoed. "But maybe they're just trying to figure it out proper-like."

"Meal wakes up moaning in the night, though, Ex. She moans

about pain in her legs. Says they feel stiff, like she can't move them off the bed. So I go in there, and what do I do? What can I do? I console her. I hold her to my chest. I massage her thighs and her calves. Then she yells at me not to touch her, that it makes it worse. 'Stop hurting me, Daddy,' she says. Which leaves me feeling shitty as death."

"I'm sorry, Gussie. That's awful. Can I do anything?"

"Nah, youngblood. What can you, right?" He wiped at the corners of his mouth like he'd wipe tears from his cheeks. "We got this house bullshit to deal with, too, now."

"House bullshit?"

"I didn't tell you this? The sinkhole?"

"You told me about the sinkhole. The city's gonna fix it, right?"

"They say so, but they've also got inspectors and engineers and whatever else coming in my yard all the time, and now they tell us the house is *uninhabitable*—their word. They say it's not safe for occupancy, that the foundation is fucked." Gussie held his hand in front of his body—a kung fu pose—his hand flat and at a slant. "Like this," he says. "On an angle. And it's only slipping worse."

"Fuck. What're you guys gonna do?"

"I don't know, Ex. I don't know at all." He hung his head between his legs for a moment, and then popped up. "I tell you one thing, though. I'm not putting my sick child up in no hotel room while the city of Mahwah fills a hole in my backyard. Not happening."

"Can't they just stabilize the house for the time being?"

"Ex. I don't want to talk about it anymore."

Exley hoisted himself onto the loading dock. His legs dangled. His heels tapped the vinyl under-siding in an alternating pattern.

"You been playing any ball?" Gussie asked, calmer now, cooled.

"Little bit."

"The knee doing any better?"

"I think so. I haven't pushed it too much, but it feels strong."

"We're in a men's league," Gussie said, circling the warehouse with his finger behind his head. Tone, Theo, and Dew reemerged from the maze of mattresses as if under Gussie's command.

"For real? When'd you start that?"

"Just a couple weeks. We've only had two games."

"In Mahwah?"

"Nah," Tone said. "In Ramsey. At the high school."

"I need to do something to keep my mind right," Gussie said. "I can't just be living that sickness."

"Ora let you play?"

"I *told* her I was. She's got nothing to say about it."

"You should join up," Dew said.

"I'm seventeen, dude."

"Ain't like nobody's checking IDs, man."

"He's right," Gussie said. "You should play. If your knee is strong enough, I mean."

"It's good," Exley assured them. "It's good."

"So, you down?"

"Bet," Exley said. He hopped down from the loading dock

and leaned over the open door of the Escort. "You all know I'm a ball hog, right?"

"That's good," Theo said. "We're washed-up and overweight anyway."

22

IF YOU ASKED AROUND AMONGST THE ELDERS, Cannon Mine Road should've never been there. Stag Hill used to be inaccessible by car. Only hikers gone astray ever staggered into the area, usually dizzy with dehydration. The thoroughfare that the County constructed in concert with the Mahwah township council cut clear through the woods, forging a path for eviction, for a mass exodus. They left piles of cleaved branches and twigs along the shoulder of the road for over a year. The idea was to allow for a resort—something to rival the Poconos of Pennsylvania. A woodsy getaway within driving distance of Manhattan.

The Ramapoughs resisted, though. They rose before dawn and ran transport chains with clevis grab hooks across the path forged by the construction crew. When the men showed up and laughed, bulldozing through the barrier, the Ramapoughs got up earlier the next morning and pushed junkers onto the path. Excavators flipped the cars upright between treetrunks, but the move slowed work enough for the Passaic County Sheriff's Office to send in a group of uniformed grunts. Most of the Ramapoughs had records, and so they backed off. A small cadre of youngbloods continued to delay the project through vandalism—bashing in windows and engines on the motor graders and asphalt pavers, on the compactors and rollers. The crew started towing the vehicles out on flatbeds at the conclusion of each workday. Tribe members that lacked the physical prowess to bust up and barricade campaigned for their cause instead. They printed up pamphlets on a ditto machine and passed them throughout Mahwah, sliding them under wipers on car windshields in the A&P parking lot. They tried to reason with Mahwah residents at large, that the destruction of the forest wasn't in their interest either.

In the end, it wasn't the tactics the Ramapoughs used or regard for a native tribe or fundamental human decency that kept the resort investors out. It was the road itself. Too many curves. Grades too severe. Unsafe for leisurely travel. The local politicians were pressured into abandoning the project when the investors decided the job wasn't adequately done. Other Mahwah community members—folks from Fardale and Cragmere and Rio Vista—complained about an influx of traffic to the area. All that remained was an access road. It was just what O'Connor Disposal needed to efficiently haul sludge deep into the forest. Now there was accessibility: for intruders, for harassers, for spectacle-seekers, for teenage tourists looking for a thrill—looking to terrorize or to be terrorized. The Ramapoughs, with the construction of the road, were exposed.

A HUMMER H3 CRAMMED FULL of private school kids—from Oradell, from Ho-Ho-Kus, from Franklin Lakes—barreled up Cannon Mine Road in the sweltering August night. The driver swerved recklessly, snapping branches and twigs on the climb, with zero regard for the solar flare metallic finish on his truck. A case of Natty Ice was on the floor of the backseat, its thin, cardboard flap torn completely off. The occupants—four boys, and one girl sitting on laps—spoke over one another, their volume increasing.

Shh, the driver said. *We're getting close.* They were nearing Stag Hill, expecting to find mythical men or beasts or some glimpse of storied violence. They were enlivened after a night of drinking and pushing and goading. They could live off of Stag Hill for the following week with gossip and embellishments. Each individual occupant could tell the tale in locker rooms and hallways and classroom corners badly managed by substitute teachers. And they could encourage others to go deeper, to put the car in park, to get out, to knock on doors. *Let's see what* you *can do*, they could say.

The driver of the Hummer had cauliflower ears and flashed his highbeams on and off at every turn. The woods swallowed the light, and the darkness heightened the trepidation of the group. When they finally arrived at Stag Hill, they didn't note the kiddie pools, the neon-colored shovels and pails, or the gardens. They saw decrepit homes and trash and dirt. They didn't think of teakettles on stovetops or dog-eared magazines on coffee tables or people asleep in their beds. They drove slowly through the dirt lot, idling and inching along.

Do it, one of the backseat passengers whispered. *You do it*, the driver answered. And an arm reached from the backseat over the driver's shoulder and pressed the center of the steering wheel. The horn blared and waned and intensified again. The other passengers stuck their heads out the windows and war whooped.

Go go go. The driver did doughnuts and kicked up a dust storm. The engine rasped and the kids all screamed. As the truck came to a stop, they saw a figure standing stone-still at the edge of the road with shoulders hunched. From just under thirty feet off, she looked like a gargoyle. The driver turned his wheel and directed the headlights. He clicked on his highbeams and they spotlighted a woman in a baggy shirt and dark sunglasses with wide, rectangular lenses. The dust was still wafting as the woman lifted her shirt over her head and tossed it to the ground. Nobody in the truck said anything. It took some time for them to process what they saw.

A middle-aged woman. A belly clawed with stretchmarks that overhung denim shorts. Bad posture. Face pockmarked. Hair in a bun. Skin the texture and color of ground cinnamon. And two ragged curves where breasts should be, scars—lighter, like taupe—sloping down and away toward the ribcage. *Go, man, go!*

The driver clicked off the highbeams, peeled out, and accelerated down Cannon Mine Road. Valerie Mann watched them go, squinting through the dust, and committing the plate number to memory. She picked up her t-shirt, slung it around her neck, and sauntered into her house. She worked the wrinkles from a white pharmacy bag on the edge of her nightstand and pulled open the drawer for a pen. Her rummaging woke Rhetta on the pullout.

"What is it?" she moaned.

"Kids," Val muttered, moving items around in the drawer. "Cowards. Come by in daylight—they won't."

She found a pen, jotted the plate number down, and folded the pharmacy bag three times like a letter. She put a couple of rust-orange pill bottles on it and went back out to the porch.

23

ORA PLOPPED INTO THE PASSENGER SEAT of the car smelling of deet, her skin always slicked with insect repellent when she'd been working in the garden. Too many times she'd been bitten to near death by mosquitoes and chiggers, her ankles polka-dotted with red wheals.

"Why don't you use the lemongrass oil?" Gussie asked her before pulling away. "Witch hazel, even. Something that's not gonna kill us all when you enter a room." Emilia was strapped in her car seat, and Gussie adjusted the dash vents, wondering how long until the AC started blowing cold.

"You're a hot mess," he told Ora. His wife waved him off. Her hands were grimed—soil under her nails and the calluses at the base of the fingers with brown crud patterned in the hardness. She never used gloves; she was a natural woman. Just clawed her hands into the dirt as an excavator would and pried the earth loose. Streaks of green, too, down the palms and up her wrists— all that from pulling weeds, stubborn ones she needed to wrap around her fisted knuckles and yank and wrest from the raised beds. The brief cut-off of circulation, the blood backing up—she was a martyr. She mortified her flesh.

Gussie appraised her acne scars, her mussed hair: a madwoman in overalls.

"You didn't have time for a change of clothes?"

"Would you shut the fuck up, Gus?" she snapped. "I didn't know the blood lab was a fucking banquet hall."

The trunk was packed with crates and pallets, full of eggplant, chard, bulging snow peas, and cabbages with earwigs, aphids, loopers and their frass no doubt still between the layers of leaves. This was to be one of the final hauls for the Milligans to the Fardale farmers' market. One of the final hauls of the season. The garden had been overgrown and under-watered, neglected. Ora would pull weeds but didn't prune. She'd corral the top-heavy cherry tomatoes with bamboo sticks and twine but ignored the gourd vines choking out the broccoli and chili pepper. Did nothing about the squash leaves shadowing the low-lying endive and asparagus. She used to sprinkle ground cayenne from a gallon jug around the borders of the beds to keep critters away, but not anymore. It became as though she were intentionally feeding the entire ecosystem. And, oh, how they would feast.

Meal mouthed the words to a pop song on the radio. Gussie watched her in his rearview. The mirror was never on the cars behind him now; it was always on his daughter. This was a serious joy: to see her singing, in a placid mood, in an imaginative world.

She's not sick, he thought. *This isn't happening*. And thinking that way made him woeful.

THEY ARRIVED AT THE BLOOD LAB close to one in the afternoon. Gussie carried Meal in, and Ora walked a few feet ahead of them. The hallways of the building were dim and outdated. Ora pulled on the door to the lab, which wouldn't give.

"Lunch?" she said. "These people have some nerve."

Gussie slouched against the wall and sat Meal between his knees. The carpet was firm as though someone had spilled massive quantities of glue on it. Ora paced, complaining about the wait.

"You act like people aren't supposed to eat lunch."

"Some jobs require employees to go above and beyond," Ora said. "Like in the medical field. What if we needed blood work done urgently?"

"Then we'd be in the ER."

Meal got up and walked along the wall, her hand dragging against the ridges of the wainscoting.

"C'mere, babe." Gussie extended his arms to Meal, inviting her back to his place on the floor. "Don't touch the walls."

"Why can't she touch the walls?"

"I don't want her getting a cold on top of everything else."

"You're ridiculous. You know that?"

"Her immune system is compromised." Gussie lowered his voice as a man walked out of an adjacent CPA office.

"I don't know where this is coming from," Ora said. She

was standing over Gussie now, bellicose. "You had no problem letting her make mudpies with contaminated soil in our yard, but you care that she touches a fucking wall?"

"It wasn't contaminated, Ora. I took it straight out of the beds."

"Still."

"*Still* nothing."

"It probably mixed," she said.

He loathed her. This wasn't his wife, his lover. This wasn't an ally. She was someone else—a crueler, compassionless version of herself. She'd been that way for so long it seemed. And he had so much ammunition to draw on.

"What about when she was a newborn, Ora?" He stood up now. "What about how you couldn't be bothered to sterilize her bottles in the microwave? Knowing damn well the water we rinsed the bottles with was full of poison." He raised his eyebrows at her. "Or what about all the other times you half-assed it? What about diluting her bottles with water because you wanted to scrimp?"

"I *never* did that."

"No, not *you*," Gussie said. "It was me that did that."

"It probably was you!"

"Uh-huh. Me, Ora. *All* me."

"All you."

"When's the last time you were in here, Ora?" Gussie gestured at the locked blood lab door. "When's the last time you brought her for an X-ray? When's the last time you took her to chemo?

Spoke to her doctors?" He edged his face toward her, mouth agape. "Huh? *Huh?* Exactly, Ora. That's what I thought."

Meal was sitting between them—her legs out in front of her, her face staring up at them, lonesome and forsaken.

The deadbolt on the blood lab door thudded. Lights went on inside. The blinds on the window opened to reveal an employee—a short Pakistani woman with a mouthful of food.

"C'mon, babe." Gussie lifted Meal off the floor. "Let's get this over with."

The space was lobby and reception and lab all in one, partitioned with cubicle walls. The panels were sparsely decorated with a calendar, insurance coverage sheets, and bulletins. One printout read NO CELL PHONE USAGE ALLOWED and included an image of Daffy Duck speaking into a candlestick telephone. Potted cactus plants lined the baseboards, and wildly propagating spider plants were hanging from brass ceiling hooks. The room stunk of reheated eggs.

Meal sat on Gussie's lap as the Pakistani woman—*Amy*, her nametag showed—processed the paperwork. Ora stood behind them with her arms crossed, looking on like an overalled auditor. Looking out of place and unrelated. Amy led them behind another partition.

The blood-drawing chair had wedgewood blue cushions. Amy told Gussie to sit down.

"Me?" he asked.

"Hold her on your lap," Amy said. "This isn't a pediatric chair."

He worked his hands into Meal's armpits and lifted her up, worried she would squirm and fight it. This wasn't how they usually did it. Not to say it usually went smoothly—it was harrowing each time. And so Gussie made appointments at different labs, embarrassed of how Meal typically behaved. He didn't blame his daughter, though. He was just acutely aware of anyone's judgment of her. Each lab employee would have words of comfort and consolation as they left, but those same employees would be less tolerant if there was a repeat performance. Tears, yowls, thrashing. That was expected the first time but frowned upon every time after. *It'll be easier next time*, staff always said. And they acted inconvenienced if their prophecy proved false.

Amy, it turned out, wasn't simply office staff. She was the clinician. She pumped the foot pedal to accommodate Gussie's height. She brought down the padded flip arm. It was the same nervous anticipation as an amusement park ride.

"This arm across her body," Amy instructed Gussie. "And your right hand bracing her arm in place. You'll need to be firm." She looked Gussie in the eye for the first time. Inches away, he could see the mascara webbed between her lashes. "*Don't* let her budge."

"Like this?"

"Like that. You want to straightjacket her with your body." She turned to Meal. "When I say to, sweetie, hold this tight as you can." Meal was handed a glass vial with a rubber stopper. "When I say to."

The partitioned space for the drawing of blood was only a few feet from an actual wall. These narrow confines were strangely comforting for Gussie. What should've been suffocating was reassuring. He felt cloistered. Time slowed—stopped even. *Nobody was sick.* Just a woman prepping, following procedure. Routine. He was mesmerized by it.

He fixated on a framed painting, too. One executed in the typical mass market Impressionism common to office walls. It depicted a Dutch landscape—windmills, cows grazing, a mauve sun and sky. The entirety of the painting was done in the same, short, upward brushstrokes used to create the pasture of timothy-grass. He wasn't restraining his daughter then. He was hugging her.

The snap of elastic ripped Gussie from his reverie. Amy twisted a teal tourniquet above Meal's elbow. Gussie worried about pinching the skin—anything to set her off. Meal was fine with it, and Amy mechanically unraveled the skinny tubing of a butterfly syringe. All her equipment rolled or clinked on the metal tray of a cart. Ora eyed the vial rack.

"How many of those do you need to fill?"

"It's fine," Amy said, casual. "It always looks like more than it is."

Gussie glowered at Ora. Amy saw it.

"Okay," she said, raising the butterfly syringe, slacking the tube like a sewing needle and thread. She pressed Meal's forearm from the wrist to the elbow crease. Rubbed the skin. Gently smacked it. The skin pinked. Amy examined the arm over the lenses of her glasses.

"Deep veins. Let's try the other."

They switched everything to the opposite arm. Amy pressed, rubbed, and smacked. Her lips puckered in concentration.

"Hector," she called over the partition wall. "Do we have any warm packs? Hector?"

A voice came over the wall. *Let me look. Hold up.*

Hector hurried onto the scene in his scrubs and white-on-white Air Force 1's.

"Last one," he said, tossing the bag to Amy. She started by squeezing at the center of the pack and then squeezed it all over. It reminded Gussie of the mylar bomb bags they used to play with as kids. Small silver packets with Vietnam scenes on the label—fighter jets, Patton tanks, and helmeted soldiers. They'd squeeze the bags and wait for them to inflate, and then pop. Gussie was as volatile as the bomb bag—his ass was going numb, his thigh cramping under Meal's weight. Amy patty-caked the warm pack back and forth in her palms.

"I think we're good," she finally said, setting the pack on Meal's forearm. Rubbing it in a circle. Rubbing. "Her veins are so deep. I'm only trying to find a decent vein." She raised the warm pack. "I think we're good. I think we're..." she trailed off.

While tightening his grip on her arm, Gussie barred Meal against him and managed to also avert her eyes from the needle puncture. If his daughter had to be drained, he wasn't going to allow her to witness it.

Meal's body jerked at the poke of the syringe. Gussie struggled to restrain her. She'd never reacted so strongly to it.

"I think it's hurting her," he said.

Amy ignored him.

"It keeps rolling," she said. Meal whimpered. "Hector. On here." Amy nodded for him to hold down Meal's arm. Gussie, apparently, wasn't doing it well enough. He was more focused on averting her eyes, pinning her face to his chest. He thought she would strain a neck muscle trying to watch what they were doing.

"See how it rolls," Amy said. She made room for Hector to have a go at it. "Rolling, right?"

"I don't…"

Hector turned to allow Amy to take the syringe back.

"We have to try the other arm again," she said.

"Are you serious?" Ora asked.

"Has she had anything to drink recently?"

Gussie and Ora looked at each other.

The same process was carried out on the original arm. Pressing. Warm pack. Puncture. Meal was uncontrollable now, convulsing and crying loudly. Ora began to restrain her, too. She cupped her knees and tried to keep her legs from kicking. Meal slumped down Gussie's lap. He saw the scene for what it was: *trauma*. He saw his small daughter being forcibly held in place. Four grown human bodies on her. Her helplessness.

"Look at the painting, Meal," he said. "Look at the painting on the wall. See it?" He didn't know if she did or not. She kept struggling. "You see those cows? I bet they're mooing, babe. They look hungry. Look at all that grass. That's so much grass, Meal. Do you see it? And what about that sun, huh? Purple. It's a purple sun. I don't think I've ever seen a purple sun before. Close your eyes, Meal. Close your eyes and dream you're there—running through that grass, playing by that windmill. It reminds me of our yard, babe. Think about our butterfly bush and all the butterflies we get fluttering around it in the afternoon. Think about picking cherry tomatoes from Mommy's garden, Meal. Think about how those seeds explode in your mouth. You see the painting, Meal?"

He kept talking, but it wasn't working.

"Emilia," Ora said, bending to whisper into her daughter's ear. Gussie couldn't make what she was saying, but Meal was solaced. She surrendered as her moeder spoke softly. The three of them there—contorted bodies and tangled limbs. Their heads so close: a hydra or something. For Gussie and Ora, their faces hadn't been that close in months, close enough to kiss. Gussie got caught up in it. The smell of talc on her. The unblended powder on her cheeks.

"There we go!" Amy became a different person as the tube ran red. "That was a toughie," she said. She seemed triumphant. Ora touched heads with Meal and then backed off. The vials filled rapidly and Hector racked them. Amy untied Meal's tourniquet on the last one.

"All done," Gussie said, combing back Meal's hair. "All done, all done, all done," he repeated until they actually were.

While pressing a fold of gauze on the puncture wound, Amy tore open a princess Band-Aid and reached to stick it onto Meal's arm.

"No," she cried. "I don't want it."

"Pick your own then, sweetie. You can pick it."

"No. I don't want *any*."

"I'll hold the gauze on there," Gussie told the clinician. "Are we done here?"

"Does she want a lollipop?"

"Do you want a lollipop, Meal?"

"I don't like lollipops," she said. "I don't like that painting, Daddy. I don't like *her*."

"Okay, okay. That's enough. Let's go. We're going." He lifted the flip arm and passed Meal to Ora. "I'm sorry," he said to Amy as Ora walked Meal out of the lab.

"Make sure she drinks a lot before she comes next. Okay, Dad? Will make it easier to get that vein."

"She will."

Darkness clouded Gussie's vision as he walked outside. A cicada went off like a phaser effect in the leaves of a street-side tree. *Was that the sound of mating or dying?* Gussie couldn't be sure. His eyes adjusted, and he hustled to the car.

"Drive fast," Ora told him.

"What do you mean *drive fast?*"

"The farmers' market."

"I know where I'm taking you. I'm not an idiot."

"I'm late already. Half the day's gone. I'm not gonna sell a thing."

"It's just like you—"

"How's it just like me, Gussie? What's just like me?"

Gussie looked into the rearview. Meal was nodding off. Her hair flopped forward over her face.

"Our daughter just went through all that, she hasn't eaten or drank anything, I don't know if she's falling asleep back there or fainting from low blood sugar, and all you care about is getting to Fardale as quick as possible."

"Oh, you know what?" Ora said. But she never said what. She didn't say anything. Gussie dropped her in the plaza parking lot where the farmers' market tents were pitched. He helped her unload the crates and pallets of vegetables from the trunk, dropping them onto the curb, leaving the rest for her to do.

He kept his eyes in the rearview the whole way home. He wanted Meal to wake up. He wanted to know she was okay—not lightheaded or woozy. He wanted her to snack, sip a juicebox. No. He wanted her to keep sleeping—to get her rest, to slip into a serene state of consciousness. He wanted her to see spinning windmills. Slow cows stepping with halting hooves. A mauve sun. Timothy-grass tickling her ankles. No. *No no no.* He wanted her to wake up and never sleep again.

24

EXLEY AND GUSSIE ARRIVED TOGETHER at Ramsey High School a week later. They got there early, before anybody else. They banged on the door to the main entrance. A grizzled custodian opened it for them and set a woodblock in the doorjamb to keep it that way.

They walked the darkened corridor to the gym. As they opened the double-doors, stale and stifling heat wafted over them.

"What's the story with the AC?" Gussie shouted down the long corridor to the custodian. The man took his time, walking bowlegged, repeatedly removing his cap to wipe the crown of his bald head.

He walked right between Gussie and Exley and made for the other end of the gym.

"Craft fair this weekend. Somebody must've shut it off."

"How long until it cools?" Gussie asked.

The custodian stopped, turned back, and said: "You're gonna be hot, boys."

THERE WAS A RAM'S HEAD LOGO at center court with beady eyes and yellow horns. A banner was hanging on the wall behind the bleachers that read: WE BLEED BLUE. Gussie tied his sneakers with double knots while Exley sat on the hardwood and stretched. Neither of them remembered to bring a ball. They heard the AC fan kick on.

"There we go," Gussie said.

"Anything new with Meal?" Exley ducked his head to his knees.

"Let's just focus on ballin'. Deal?"

"No doubt."

Ex high-stepped behind the basket. He put his hands on the wall as though a cop had ordered him to. He stretched his calf muscles and his Achilles on his right leg, his left. His palms peeled off the clammy protective pads on the wall.

Two other players entered the gym looking serious. One had black knee socks, and the other had pixelated camo compression sleeves. They weren't as old as Exley expected the competition to be.

"They ours?" Ex asked.

"Nope."

"How many do we have?"

"Counting you? Seven. But Dew's old roommate, Willy, won't be here. He's a Jehovah's Witness and goes to church like four times a week."

"That's a short bench, man."

"You're telling me. Good thing we recruited your youthful ass."

"Shit. You better lower your expectations. I've barely been playing."

"Still better than us old-timers."

Exley watched the two opposing players shoot around. They both took turns draining consecutive jumpers. And one of them—the guy in the black socks—was wet from behind the arc.

"Those guys don't seem so old."

"They're not," Gussie said. "Your boy with the socks played D-2. Caldwell, I think. And the other dude redshirted at Seton Hall before catching a drug charge at a house party in South Orange."

"Using or slanging?"

"Slanging."

"Fuck me," Exley said. "I need a cigarette."

"Don't scare, man. You've got the edge," Gussie rallied. "You're in your prime. The prime mover."

THE PARKING LOT WAS IN BAD SHAPE. Weeds sprouted from blacktop fractures in long, sawtooth rows. The neglect left a tract of crude tectonics with the weed rows interrupting the white lines of parking spaces. Exley leaned against the exterior of the gymnasium and pulled on his cigarette. He twisted the toe of his sneaker on a leafy weed and closely monitored the arriving players.

Sizing up the competition—doing *that* again. He couldn't help himself. He examined bodies—builds and heights—

comparing himself, considering who had the advantage. He'd been doing this since biddy ball. The players rolled up in quick succession now. Players who kept their gear and sneakers in their trunks; players accessorized with headbands and hefting duffles; players with sweat towels around their necks. He thought of Womack, how he wore his towel the same, but twisted, snapping it at unsuspecting teammates. Womack got Exley good plenty of times—the sudden crack of the sonic boom; the sting of the tip; the keloid-like welts it left. It wasn't mean-spirited or anything, but it was still humiliating to have your legs give out with the snap of a towel, to hobble onto the court with a handicap. The pain faded only after the game began, when Exley would be able to gain redemption through a crossover or reverse layup on the baseline.

Tone, Theo, and Dew arrived in an old Scirocco hatchback with a laughable spoiler. Dew was sitting in the back, and he pushed Theo's seat forward, crushing him against the dash. "Hold up, bro!" Theo yelled.

"I need some air, man. I'm dying back here."

"Well hold the fuck up. I'm still buckled in."

Dew angled his body out of the coupe, planting his feet on the blacktop. He looked mythically tall once he extricated himself from the car and stood upright. Exley resisted the urge to immediately comment on the ruinous state of his sneakers: a hole in the toe box was patched with cardboard and duct tape. "You need a new whip, Tone. For real," Dew said.

"My car is bomb."

"That air conditioner is busted, though," Theo said.

"It's no better in there," Ex said as they came closer. He flicked his cigarette.

"Is Gussie in there?" Theo asked.

"Yeap. But he's just sitting there. We don't have a ball." Tone unzipped his duffle bag and scooped out a well-worn and fleecy ball. He bounced it to Exley. Ex dribbled low, circling his legs, and then tested the grip of the ball.

"How is he?" Dew asked.

"He don't want to talk about it."

"Fair enough," Tone said. "Here, Ex." He pulled a rust-orange t-shirt from his duffle and tossed it at Exley. "Number six good with you?"

"I'm not picky." Ex held it up. The front said CALIFORNIA. The reverse said KINGS. "Clever."

"I thought you'd appreciate that one."

"I'll be right in," Ex said as the others hastened into the gym. He gave himself a pep talk. Bent his knee back a few times. It felt good, dependable, but he wouldn't know for sure until he ran up and down the court a few times. The sun was setting and storm clouds were covering overhead. Thin, black wisps extended from their bottoms like tentacles, like twigs. Eastward, there were no clouds. But there was a sulfurous sky. So yellow. It was as though the sun had exploded without making a sound and its sallow insides were embers falling to Earth.

THE PREGAME WARM-UP WAS CHAOS with balls bouncing every which way. The paths the balls took off the rim were unpredictable because the bricks they were throwing up were so god-awful bad. Ex watched Theo hit the side of the backboard on three straight attempts before punching the ball on the final miss into the bleachers. Ex stayed to the side, sawing the sleeves off his team t-shirt with a car key. He suggested layup lines to Gussie, and the rest of the team agreed.

Their final player, Deep Desai, walked into the gym with his bulldozer chest and a tight fade. He held a black basketball with white ribs under his arm, and his jaw seemed to dislocate with every chew of his bubblegum. Dew elbowed Ex from behind. "Secret weapon," he said as he rejoined the rebound side of the layup line. "He bought a mattress for his condo about a month ago and we all got to talking. Found out he balled, and we recruited him on the spot, Calipari style. Fucking blue-chip, this kid."

Deep greeted everyone, even giving Exley daps as though he'd known him for years. That sort of swagger seemed comical here—a men's league. But Ex wasn't about to mock it. He was more concerned about Deep being their go-to, the franchise. It fucked with Ex's fantasy. Clutch free-throws. A buzzer beater. Dropping forty. An emphatic block into the stands. He had all the scenarios worked out in his head, and those all became a lot less likely with Deep on the floor.

The refs blew their whistles and both sides convened at center court. They circled the ram's head, and Exley staked out position at a horn tip. He flexed his knees and amped himself up, taking comfort in being the youngest player on the court. Gussie volunteered to start the game on the bench, and he crouched at the makeshift scorer's table—a folding chair and a student desk—penciling in everyone's names and numbers into the stat book. The lead ref spoke through his whistle prior to tossing the jump: "Hot enough for ya, fellas?"

White Flight—their opponent—maintained the tip and pushed the ball. Their shirts were gray and had a sponsor name across the back, UPDIKE's. As Ex backpedaled down-court onto defense, his heels slipped from under him and he nearly ate it. The farcical temperature in the gym combined with the sudden burst of air conditioning had created a layer of condensation on the hardwood. Everyone—even Deep and the collegiate rejects on the other team—were losing their footing. Theo and Dew collided in the paint, unable to keep pace with their men. Tone tippy-toed at the perimeter. And Deep stole the ball, slipped at midcourt, and managed to bullet the ball up ahead to Ex on the breakaway. Only problem was his aim. He thrust the ball so hard that it actually knocked the fire extinguisher off the wall. It clanged loudly against the floor and the custodian poked his head into the gym to assess.

"Let's go zone," Gussie shouted as he checked in at the midway point of the half. "Two-three."

The game was getting away from them. White Flight established a ten-point advantage, mostly by exploiting the lumbering bodies in the paint—Theo and Dew were loggers in Timberland boots compared to the quick steps of White Flight's slashers. The guards pulled up for short eight-footers before the defense had a chance to collapse the lane. Exley tried to help out, but he didn't want to fall too far back from the three-point specialist with ghostwhite skin he was guarding. The guy probably had seven or eight years of experience on Exley. He lazily hovered around the three-point line waiting on a kick-out, but he also had no handle whatsoever. So every time the pass did come, Ex got up on his body and pestered him with pokes and swipes at the ball.

As for an audience, the bleachers were mostly filled with the players from the two teams scheduled to play next. They dribbled in sitting positions, jawed at one another, and tore into Tone, who they called Rik Smits every time he touched the ball. Exley saw an older man, too. Not a player, but a relative maybe. There was something familiar about him. He was on the top bleacher and had a camcorder on a tripod. Ex didn't know what to make of it—a local pervert? A scout? Whoever it was, he kept the camera on the Great White Hope that Ex was responsible for containing. So, in effect, the camera was on Ex, too.

Gussie called a timeout right before the half. The California Kings not so much huddled as moseyed in the general direction of the sideline and milled about—gulping water, wiping sweat.

The temperature had barely dropped. Too many bustling bodies. It was brutal.

"Who needs a blow?" Gussie asked.

"Me," Dew said. "But not the kind you're talking about."

Exley's attention was on the cameraman.

"Ex, you good?"

"Yea-up. I'm fine."

"You're carrying us, man." Deep patted Ex on the back. "I can't buy one. That ball is slippery as shit."

"It's the sweat," Theo said.

"Keep cranking 'em up, Deep," Gussie encouraged. "Shoot through it. We're still in this." Everybody glanced over at the flip scoreboard. "Ex. Look for your shot, youngblood."

"Who's the creeper with the camera?"

"Who?"

Ex nodded at the bleachers and wiped his face with the collar of his shirt.

"That's your boy's father," Tone said. He indicated the shooter Ex had been guarding. "Harry Adams."

"*Harry Adams?* That's Harry Adams? I didn't even recognize him." Harry Adams was the older brother of Nelson Adams, Exley's pink-lidded arch nemesis. Harry had gone to school with Zike. "What's he filming for?"

"Highlight footage," Dew joshed.

"Apparently he does it every game," Tone said. "I agree it's fucking weird."

Ex knew Harry from years back, but with Harry's hair loss and Amish beard, he might as well have been a stranger. Ex was pretty certain Harry had no idea who he was either. Still, it provided even more motivation for Ex. A one-off, inconsequential men's league game was suddenly magnified. Wiping the bottom of his sneakers, Ex sprinted back onto the court. He stole the inbound pass and hit Deep on the wing for a three. Deep poked an A-ok sign against his temple three times to celebrate.

HARRY AND EXLEY CROSSED PATHS walking onto the court for the second half. Harry muttered something, but Ex didn't catch it. No matter—he felt better than he had in months. He stroked jumpers from the baseline on two consecutive trips down the floor. Tone passed him the ball in the same spot for the third time, so he pump-faked, drove the middle, and made a circus shot off the glass.

Sweat was beading into rivulets down his forehead and burning his eyelids, but adrenaline or focus or his ailing moeder's mumbo-jumbo prevented him from even noticing. He was unconscious now. Experience and physical know-how came together. His knee might as well have been made of metallic implants, indestructible cyborg sinews and muscles. He felt nothing. He felt healthy.

Each dribble-drive, every bounce pass, individual steps: all aspects were carried out without thinking. Exley was in a natural state of being. Trillions of pores on his body breathed like microscopic Buddhas. It was a feeling that only a Latin phrase could convey. White Flight's guards tried to trap him at the top of the key, but he split the defense with a behind the back dribble and hit a scoop shot over their tallest defender at the basket. On the other end, he got up in Harry's gut when he caught the ball beyond the three-point line. *Shoot it*, Ex taunted. Harry tried to throw a cross-court chest pass, but Ex deflected it, jamming his finger in the process.

Next time down, Ex hit another baseline J. That spot had been money for him for as long as he could remember. His da always called it his "sweet spot" after rec league games. Dew batted away a loose ball, and Deep pitched it to center court for Ex to finish on a fastbreak. He smacked the backboard on the lay-in, leading him to believe he still had some post-injury hops. Harry was slow getting back on D but bumped Ex as he landed. *Fucking cherry-picker*, he said. The comment surprised Ex, and for the first time in a while he noticed the camcorder on the top bleacher.

Harry Adams waved off their point guard and brought the ball up himself. He did a goofy stutter-step at center court and passed the ball to the wing. He cut through the lane and looped back up on the other side of the frontcourt. The power forward grinding in the post and getting nowhere kicked it back out. Harry caught the ball and popped a set shot from NBA range. Drained it. Ex had failed to get a hand in his face. Harry trotted down the sideline blowing phantom smoke from his fingers like a

Wild West gunslinger. It was all for the camcorder, for showtime, for posterity, for nothing.

Keeping pace, Ex said to him: "Lucky shot. Hope your daddy's camera was in focus." He curled through the lane, losing Harry with a pick from Dew on the block. Tone fed Ex the ball at the foul line, and Ex swished it. *All day.* Exley pointed at the ball as it fell through the net. *Sign that!* he said to Harry.

Harry couldn't hang—not with his shooting and certainly not with his quips. He held the ball overhead with two hands, pivoting in a full circle, looking for an open man. Ex was all over him with a stifling, harassing defense. Worried about a five-second call, Harry swung his elbow and caught the bridge of Ex's nose. Ex staggered back but kept his footing. There was a bit of blood, and Exley dabbed it away with his t-shirt. The referees convened and called it a basic foul.

"How is that not a flagrant?" Gussie yelled from the sideline. He played the role of coach well. Fatherly, but also prone to violent expressions of emotion.

Harry approached Gussie.

"Stop complaining. Everything's been going your way." He turned to Exley. "This is a *man's* game."

Deep walked the ball up the court. White Flight had fallen back—with a comfy lead, they figured there was no need to press. But Harry Adams didn't abide by the same logic. He pushed chest to chest against Exley, and when Ex put his hands on Harry to create some space, Harry swatted Ex's hands away. Ex hated the feel of his sweaty skin on someone else's. And here was Harry facing-up, his hot breath blowing over Ex's entire being.

"You're beasting," Ex said.

Harry whispered back: "Man's game."

Tone fed Deep at the wing. Deep backed in, dipped his head and shoulders into his defender, stepped back, and shot a short-range fadeaway. Deep yelled *Off!* on the release. Players crashed the rim, vying for the rebound. In the throng of bodies, Exley and Harry didn't even bother with conventional boxouts. Their arms locked up. Like a helix. Like a braid. The more each of them struggled to pull apart, the closer they got until they were nose to nose. The rebound went long, but the refs blew their whistles in bursts and ran in to break up the tussle. Harry freed his arms, backhanding Ex with a slap on the jaw while doing so. Ex pushed Harry with both hands. Refs and players tried to break them up.

"Fuck you, scrub-ass," Exley yelled. He pushed his sweat-wet red hair out of his face.

"You're soft, fucking miney."

Gussie restrained Ex, and the refs separated Harry.

"*Miney*, huh?"

"How's your brother?"

"How's about you shut the fuck up?"

"Heard his dick don't work no more."

Exley busted free of Gussie's arms, charged Harry, and managed to reach his hands around his neck. Harry's face contorted in a way that showed terror—eyes widened and teeth clenched. The bay lights in the gym rafters went dark as the players freed Harry from Exley's grip. The custodian was standing at the entryway to the gym, his hand on the master light switches.

"I'm about to call the cops, fellas."

The referees ejected Exley and Harry, but Gussie quickly made the call that they were all done, a forfeit. Exley headed out before anyone. He passed Harry's father near the scorer's table—he hadn't even noticed that he'd come down to court level. They briefly made eye contact, but Ex kept walking. He turned back only to look into the bleachers. The camcorder was still perched on the tripod—its robotic, stilty body. Its glass, convex eye. Ex was too far to see his own warped reflection in the lens. He was too far to see an illuminated red dash. Too far to know if he was still being recorded.

25

IN THE CVS LOCKER ROOM, Exley used a narrow putty knife to pick at an RFID label on a package of Gillette razors. It was a precaution he had to take if he didn't want to trip the electronic surveillance system. The doorknob jiggled, so Ex quickly hid everything away in his locker. Julie, who worked in cosmetics, came in smiling. She sat down at the break table, crossed her legs, and flipped through a bridal magazine. Ex re-tucked his polo and left.

Sue was bored at the cash register, doodling a parade of obscene cartoon characters on receipt paper. Leaning in on the customer side of the counter, Exley admired the work.

"Not my best," Sue said.

"Looks professional to me."

"This thing," she said, holding up her forearm in the splint. "It turns me into an amateur."

Exley tapped the velcro tags on the splint. "When do you get to ditch that?"

"I don't know. Now. Never? I haven't gone back to the doctor for a follow-up. So I just keep wearing it, in case."

"Isn't it uncomfortable?"

"No—it's not, actually. I like the snugness. It's like a part of me is being hugged 'round the clock."

"Hugged, huh?"

"Yeah. Like those two bruises under your eyes are hugging your nose."

Exley grew taciturn and aligned candy boxes on the shelf at his waist. The sensor doors opened and closed, opened and closed. Sometimes they would start to slide shut like the curtains on a stage, only to lock up and open again as another customer came in. Sue made her obligatory greeting when a customer arrived (*Welcome to CVS!*) and the store's motto when a customer exited (*Stay healthy!*), whether they purchased an item or not. She had to say it. Aaron would surreptitiously approach like some prankish little brother, listening in on her interactions. That, or he'd poll customers while they shopped. He was always on the hunt for something to carp about.

"Are we done?" Sue asked.

"Done with what?"

"Talking?"

"No," Ex said, and he immediately felt guilty for the lousy state of their relationship. He tried to start the banter up again. "Tell me about this deactivation pad." He patted the flat, black square in front of the register.

"Why? So I can make it easier for you to steal?"

"Hey, hey, *hey*. Keep it down, huh?"

"I'm not your gun moll, Exley."

"Nobody asked you to be. I'm trying to talk. You asked me to talk."

"I asked if you were done talking. I just wanted to know if I should stand here staring at you or if I should get on with my day."

"Why are you being like this?"

"Ex, really?" Sue raised her eyebrows and huffed while rolling up the receipt paper. "We've barely hung out this summer."

"I've been busy."

"You have not."

"I have."

"I call your house and your mom tells me you're out. I ask 'Who with?' and she tells me nobody. Just yourself. How am I supposed to read that?"

Ex resented her making a problem where there wasn't any. He thought she was down—a loyal friend, stalwart, even if they didn't communicate regularly. Emptiness is what he felt. Felt it in his gut.

"Y'know. I really don't need this."

"Don't blame me for this, Ex. It's not my fault for bringing it up. But I'm not gonna play nice for the five minutes you spend talking to me on your break if you're ignoring me every second of every other day."

She watched him turn his body from the counter, saw his vacant eyes staring at the charcoal carpet tiles. His lean frame seemed to shrivel to a stick figure. His vulnerability made even her feel uncomfortable. The sensor doors opened. *Welcome to CVS!*

"Listen. I know your head's all fucked up about Emilia. I get that, I do. But don't take what we have for granted."

"I don't," he said. "I don't mean to, anyway. I've been in my own head, is all."

"I get it."

An elderly woman with coarse, blue hair pushed a personal two-wheeled shopping cart through the entrance. The doors closed. *Welcome to CVS!* The doors opened, and a gang of middle-schoolers who had only come in to cool down, ogle issues of *Maxim* and *FHM*, and chase each other up and down the aisles, exited. *Stay healthy!*

"So we good?"

"We're good," Sue conceded. "But you're gonna make the effort, right?"

"No doubt. What about the powwow? You wanna go?"

"I thought you said it was summer camp, that it was stupid."

"A lot of it is," he said. "I wasn't bullshitting you about the tug o'war. But I'm thinking about going anyway."

"Well, if you do, I'll definitely come along."

"Alright, cool." He rapped his knuckles and walked down Skin Care. He turned back to Sue: *Stay healthy!*

EXLEY WAS IN THE STOCKROOM pulling shorts because Vitamins & Supplements was down to one bottle of probiotics. He carefully slid an entire row of cardboard boxes off the steel-framed racks with pressed wood shelving, but he recklessly stacked them on the floor. The bottom box in the stack became crushed, its sides buckling outward. The stockroom was cavernous, and the floor-to-ceiling shelves projected a feeling of isolation. So Exley was somewhat unnerved to suddenly hear rustling behind his bending body.

"We need to talk, Ex."

It was Aaron with his hands in his pants pockets, attempting to pass for professional. This vainglorious version was far from the nitpicky and contemptible boss they all knew and loathed, the man you could find slumped against the dumpster as his girlfriend threatens to break up with him. The unfamiliar strut was due to the person he had with him: a middle-aged man with a Shenandoah beard and a black nylon jacket. He looked like the member of a bowling team. He held a two-way radio in his hand, presumably for radioing some corporate ghost.

"This is our Loss Prevention Supervisor," Aaron said. "Mike."

"Okay." Exley went about the job of opening boxes and cradling probiotic bottles in his arm.

"Let's go to my office to talk. Leave that."

Exley considered. He thought about dashing. He saw himself striding down the aisles only to be stalled by the slow-sliding sensor doors. And, of course, there was his personal information, the countless times he wrote it on the reams of paperwork he was told to fill out when he was hired. Or what about bald-faced refusal? He could simply answer, *No. Let's not go to your office to talk*, and keep on with his retail wage labor. He decided against both these moves, though. Instead, he answered with an existential *Whatever*.

Aaron and Mike escorted Exley to Aaron's office. They sandwiched him in between them—a perp walk for his fellow employees. Mike's black nylon jacket rustled against Ex's elbow. The closeness of the procession was overblown. The way they kept contact, it was as though they intuited he might run.

Aaron's office was windowless, the stockroom in miniature. A motionless Newton's cradle adorned his particleboard desk. Along with the numberless clock and the desk pad calendar with nothing but doodlings on it, the office overflowed with wannabe executive décor. Aaron sat in an ergonomic, mesh-backed chair that swiveled and rolled, but it was best suited for a gamer, not a retail store manager. Mike gestured for Exley to sit, which he did, and Mike pulled his chair close enough for their knees to touch.

"Shrink is a problem for us here, Exley," Aaron started. "It's a constant problem. And, frankly, our shrink has gone up since I hired you."

He couldn't stand this guy. The way he leaned forward with his elbows on his desk. The back and forth waving of his hands—he looked like he was passing and catching an invisible ball. The stiffness of his dress shirt, the way his neck didn't fill out his collar. He looked like a fool, an incompetent.

"The simple fact, Ex, is that shrink has gone up—it's increased. Since we've hired you," Aaron repeated.

No fewer than half a dozen Dust-Off canisters were on the top of Aaron's four-drawer file cabinet. They were arranged so the red stick nozzles all pointed the same way. Zike used to huff those, he thought.

"So, what? I'm losing too many items in the stockroom? Boxes of merch fall behind the racks all the time. And that's not just me."

"Okay," Mike interrupted. "That's enough, Aaron." He turned his chair, intruding even further into Ex's personal space. "We're talking about shoplifting and theft issues, Exley. Internal theft."

Ex didn't look at the Loss Prevention Supervisor. He didn't look at the store manager. His eyes stayed on the Dust-Off canisters.

"We know you've been stealing from the store," Aaron added.

"What did I steal?" Ex asked. "That low-res CCTV you've got is on the fritz. Everybody knows that."

Mike glared at Aaron, who fidgeted in his chair.

"One of your coworkers saw you place some socks down your pants," Aaron said.

Socks, Exley thought. *All this for a pair of fucking diabetic tube socks.*

"Who?"

"That's no concern of yours," Mike said. "What matters here is that the theft fits a pattern. We've examined your shift schedule. We've noted the windows when items are being lifted.

Everything's matching up on our side. All we're doing here—giving you the opportunity for—is to come clean."

"We're not sure how long you've been doing this," Aaron said. His interjections bristled Mike. "But the numbers don't lie."

"What else have you stolen?" Mike asked.

"Nothing."

"You know I don't believe you," Mike said. "I don't believe that for a second."

"Okay."

"So what else?"

"Nothing."

"Alright, Ex," Aaron said. "That's it then. Your final paycheck will be prorated, and we'll mail it to you. You're not allowed back on the store premises—not even as a customer." Exley stood up, moved his chair back to create a path out of the office.

"We need to search your locker, too, Exley."

"Nah. Forget that," he said, untucking his shirt. "I'm gone." Exley opened the office door to leave but turned when Aaron called for him to stop. He didn't look Aaron in the face—he wouldn't give him that. He focused on the Dust-Off canisters.

"For protocol," Aaron said. "I need to make this clear: you're terminated."

"You mean I'm fired."

"Yes. Fired."

Sue was checking out a customer as Exley stalked toward the point-of-sale. She gingerly bagged a purchase of reading glasses while mouthing, *What happened?* Ex shook his head and exited through the sensor doors—a lesser god.

26

M AY 1996.
Norval walked the path of corrugated scrap patio slabs to
Orrin's cabin. It was Saturday, not long after noon. Norval circled
around the back and found his brother sitting on a stepladder at
his worktable.

There was a half-eaten whitebread pickle sandwich at his
elbow, no plate. Lunch was secondary to mapping out the pattern of twine and bric-a-brac for the making of wind chimes.
Orrin tweaked and tinkered with the placement of wallet chains
and window pins, of doorknobs, of puddingstone and arrowheads. See, he didn't care for creating anything actually musical.
No minor pentatonic scale in mind. No significant vibrations.
These weren't chimes so much as showpieces. Orrin jokingly
referred to them as *clangs* instead of *chimes*. But everyone he
gave them to insisted on calling them chimes. And they'd later
describe how pleasant the chiming was, ostensibly to protect
Orrin from any harsh criticisms. Meanwhile, Orrin smoothed
his thumb over the deburred hole of a copper tube, with no

intention whatsoever of using it to produce a melodious sound.

Norval cupped his hand over Orrin's shoulder.

"Who's that one for?"

"I got nobody in mind," Orrin said without looking up. He always recognized his brother's gangly approach. "Any taker."

"Looks good, little brother. Looks good. Hanny'd have your head for those arrowheads, though."

"Maybe this one'll be for her then." Orrin laughed at his own joke and raised up off the stepladder. He looked at Norval, his disheveled clothes and sweat-smeared face. "Shit, Norv. You been at the bar?"

"No, I ain't been at the bar," Norval said, his hand falling from Orrin's shoulder.

"You look like you been. Look like you been sleeping under it."

"You're like Hanny with the third degree, you know that?"

"Hell, I don't care what you do." Orrin turned a blackened gold ring off his middle finger. He pinched it and rubbed it along his bottom eyelid, hoping the tarnish would cure a stye. "I'm just trying to know who it is I'm talking to."

"You're talking to me: Norv: your older brother."

"I mean is it shit-faced Norv or sober Norv?"

"I'm sober, brother. Dry as an old dishrag, as dirt. Trust me. I am seeing things clear as day today."

Orrin took a few short steps, overturned two produce crates, and motioned for Norval to join him. They sat there in the middle of Orrin's yard in the middle of the Ramapo Mountains like two thinkers or two woodcutters. And they didn't speak for several minutes. Orrin tore bites of his sandwich and sucked getaway pickle slices into his mouth.

"You been going out?" Norval asked, pointing to Orrin's muzzleloader that hung from a sling on a tree nail.

"Hunting?" Orrin answered with a mouthful. He made a fist in front of his mouth and swallowed. "Not so much. Still readying. You?"

"Nah. Haven't had the time or the interest. Hanny's always hollering at me about clearing the mudroom, though. All my gear's in there. She stubbed her toe the other morning. I didn't hear the end of it."

"Yeap." Orrin kept eating.

"I mean I boiled and waxed my traps a couple weeks ago, but I wouldn't count that as much."

"Well, y'know," Orrin choked on a clump of bread that had become like paste between his teeth. "You gonna have to do that all again. Cleanse 'em again, I mean. Those human stenches will hop right back on there, and you won't catch a cold or a caterpillar with 'em like that."

"Well, brother, alright now. Let's remember I'm not as serious at it as you be."

"Now that's it right there." He spit what was still on his tongue—some white matter—onto the ground. "Just 'cause I give you a tip don't mean you got to run the other way. Why not open yourself to the idea of improving?"

"What—you think I'm like Daddy? There's no doing shot practice with soda cans and stacked dice for me. I'm just a regular nimrod."

"So you say, so you say. Never know, though. Do ya?"

"I'm too old now, Orrin. Hell. You need to know what you're good at by my age. Got to know what your specialty is."

"And, you—what's your specialty, Norv?"

"Mine's not yet revealed itself." He chuckled. "I was speaking more generally. People, y'know. Not myself exactly."

It got quiet again. The brothers did this often: spoke falteringly about the nothingness of everything. The hunting they hadn't done. The women Orrin hadn't slept with. Unresolved problems. But, for Orrin, this time felt different, forced. He sat with the feeling, trying to figure it without asking Norval directly.

"You still salt your gunpowder?" Norval asked. "So's that the quarry won't spoil?"

"I do," Orrin affirmed. He was trying hard now to figure Norval's angle.

"You don't think that's the least bit, uh, superstitious?"

"I do or I don't. Either way I'm doing it."

"You don't think that's just some silly old stunt? Our da told it to us like his da told it to him, and so on. You don't think?"

"I don't see the harm."

"You don't see the harm," Norval repeated dismissively. The spring sun—the way it saturated the open space, Orrin's yard— it rendered everything sepia. Plants were explosively budding in those instants. It was all unseen, though—unseen by the naked eye.

"You alright, Norv?"

"I'm alright. I wanted to ask you, though. You remember when we was younger, how we'd trap and sell those rattlers to Van Saun Zoo?"

"I remember."

"We got good money on that."

"Don't forget the pharmaceutical companies," Orrin added. "We made *real* good money on that."

"I forgot about that!"

"You put some rattlers in a shoebox, drive down 17 with them sitting shotgun, and unload at Hoffman-La Roche. The security at the gate would wave us right in, knew our vehicles. Then they'd do whatever they did with them."

"They'd milk the venom."

"I guess you could say those snakes did right by us."

"You ever seen somebody milking 'em?" Norval asked, excited now. "Those pharmacists would hold 'em at the head—gloved, sure. But I'll be damned if they didn't look like some Pentecostal snake handlers."

"Where'd you see that?"

"TV one time."

Orrin fetched them two drinking jars, the outsides painted black, though. "This some distilled spirits?" Norval asked. It could've been anything; Orrin had a knack, or an interest, in making silly nostrums. Just pulverizing ingredients into a paste and adding splashes of Poland Spring. "Olde English cans, poured out," Orrin said. They sat and fell into a torpid state. Two scraggle-bearded men in sepia tone, awash in tan and oak bark and smears of tawny light. They looked more Frederic Remington than George Catlin. More cowboy than Indian, depending. Fur-trappers in plaid flannel. Huntsmen in hiking boots and gingham undershirts. Drifters diminished by their wooded and sawdust surroundings. Brothers having a drink.

"You're not old, Norv."

"How's that now?"

"Earlier. You said you were too old to know what you're good at, your specialty. A man in his forties isn't old, though. Not how I see it."

"Maybe off this mountain it's not old, Orrin. But look around here. Elders are few and far between. Look at us two, two bastards. Parentless. I should be so lucky to make it to fifty."

"And what do you think that's about?"

"You know, Orrin. We know what it's about. And everyone else knows, too. They either just don't want to hear it or don't care."

Orrin had never heard his brother speak this way: political, agitated even. Orrin knew what was in the dirt, in the water, and Norval did, too. Norval knew about the mines. The vile legends. But he never talked about such things. Norval couldn't spell disenfranchised, but he sure felt it. Talking about it—that was new, that was different, that was disconcerting.

"Maybe it's better, luckier, that way—cutting out early," Norval said after a minute.

"I wouldn't agree with you on that one." Orrin waited for Norval to say something. Norval just sipped his beer, though, staring off at the forest, considering its enchantments. There were no dryads, no offer of wood nymphs. It didn't conceal a refuge. It was full of wandering robbers, boorish plunderers. Norval knew the forests were no longer theirs, nor the mountains and streams. It all belonged to strangers who claimed it, not only through contracts, but also through the waste they strewed. The way a mangy dog yellows all over your possessions and looks at you, snout-high, like: *Mine.*

"Norv?"

"Too late for the mines and too early for extinction, y'know?"

"Not really."

"Endangered, I guess. Well. They're both basically the same, right?—endangered species and extinct ones? Not living either way," Norval said.

"I'm not sure I follow, brother."

Orrin rubbed his ring along his bottom eyelid. He stood up from his crate, adjusted his pants, his underwear that was climbing his groin, and resettled. He stretched his legs out in front of him and crossed them at the ankles.

"You sure doing a lot of thinking today, Norv. That's different of you."

"Yea-up."

"Everything good with Hanny? She know you here?"

"We ain't been good in forever, Orrin. You know that. She can't understand my not working."

"It's not like you don't try."

"Shit, little brother. You know I ain't tried in years."

"I see you try."

"I try to be a good da, to Zike, to Exley. Supportive. But we see how that's working out."

"Better than our da."

"Not by much." Norval waited with a buried desire for Orrin to say *No*, to say that he had it wrong—that he *was* an adequate parent, and present, a guidepost for the boys.

"Well…"

"Look at Zike. What's he doing? What's he up to? I don't know where the boy is half the time. When I do catch hold of him, he's in a state—blotto, stoned, or worse." Norval shook his head, looked into his jar. "It's bad, but, honestly, I used to enjoy seeing him go off on Hanny, or be rude to her, give her a hard time. Because I thought that meant he was on board with me. That I edged her in some way. That the boy liked me. Thought I could understand him. But that ain't it, because now I feel—and this is backwards thinking, I know it—that he does have a fondness for her. I see it in how he showers her with hatred. Me, though? I get nothing from him. He don't start anything with me, never. But he don't say *hello* or *goodbye* or *How 'bout you help me get my moeder off my back, Da? How do you do it, Da? How have you not blown your brains out after all these years, Da?* I get nothing! It's just nothing from him! My first born!"

"Zike's a teenager," Orrin said. "You can't know a thing for certain about a teenager. You don't need to have kids to know that."

"Maybe."

"What about Exley?"

"What about him?"

"He's a tender youth. There's adoration there—for you, for Hannah. I've seen it."

"It's just the same, though, Orrin. What do my sons have to look forward to? Where are they headed? Where are we? It's just ruins. Graveyards."

"I'm not denying it's ruins, Norv. If you want me to debate you on that, I ain't gonna. That's plain to see. We keep coming back to the same place—we meet *here*. We're eye-to-eye, mostly, on these points, Norv. But you got to buck up. See this," Orrin said, circling his yard and all his erratic collectings. "This ain't my property any more than it is the vermin, but it is *my* studio. See."

"I know, little brother," Norv said softly, soothingly. "You done good with it."

"Ford. O'Connor. Trespassers." Orrin numbered them on his hand. "They all been dumping on us, yes. I know that hell, know it well. *But...*" He leaned in low, looking to meet Norval's eyes. "But I take all they shit, and I turn it. I turn it on them, Norv.

That's the best, and that's the most, I can do. And I sleep, Norv. I sleep good and heavy."

"You got that, Orrin. You do. And I respect that. I admire that about you." Norval rushed his words. "But think back to—what was it, '82?—the Peters Mine fire. You remember it."

"I do," Orrin nodded solemnly.

"Recall how, me and you, we walked to the mine. Watched it burning."

"I remember it. Cotton was there, crazed. I thought he was under possession from the flames the way he was galloping around."

"Right, right," Norval said. "And you was carrying that old minnow bucket—you had it full of scrap from the Ford plant. You'd just gotten back and gotten wind of the fire. So we went to see it for ourselves."

"That's right!" Orrin said, excited. "Shit. That was a scrapper's paradise in those days. We picked that plant apart like buzzards on carrion." Norval shook his head, anxious to get back to his point. "Not so much now, what with that hotel they building sky-high. Who gonna wanna stay there? A hotel in the middle of Mahwah."

"Right," Norval said. "But that fire in the mine. You know what I was thinking? You know what I saw in that fire?"

"It burned for weeks, didn't it?" Orrin said. "What'd you see in it?"

"I saw those flames curling out the mouth of the mine—just

pushing out like a baby being born—and I thought of all that death, man. All the death in that image, Orrin. You feel me?"

"You gonna get all Hannah-type spiritual on me?"

"No, little brother. I'm talking about something real, hard." Norval pounded a fist into his palm. "I'm talking about all that death—the worst of it. All those years of mining, all that dumping they've done in those holes. The blackest black death. All-encompassing fire. I still got that chemicalized smoke smell in my nose, Orrin. Still got it."

"Shit's fucked, Norv. I know that. I know it. Like you said, we all know it. We know what this life in these hills is. But," Orrin paused, "I know you don't want to hear it. But you need to find some peace, Norv." Norval closed his eyes and shook his head *no no no no no.* "I know. You don't want to hear it. And you gonna do what you gonna do. You been thinking your own way since I was born, since I knowed you. You probably were thinking your way before me, too. I can't go to Ma or Da about that, though. They're gone. Gone already. Didn't even make it to be elders, really. Which, I guess, does a good job proving your point about us going extinct. Don't it?"

An hour had passed. Norval became withdrawn. He debarked and whittled a branch. Orrin went back to his business of patterning the chimes, but he spent much time organizing items in the yard. He often hesitated, his mind faltering and forgetting what he meant to do in the next moment. He'd been rattled by Norval's words. He kept thinking about what to say and whether to say it to his big brother. He couldn't come up with anything coherent, so he simply continued to putz. Placing a wood plane and then a sliding bevel on the hooks of his shed wall, he sliced his finger open. Once the bleeding slowed, he wrapped electrical tape around it. Norval stood up and wiped wood shavings from his lap.

"I'm gonna be heading out."

"Yea-up," Orrin said.

"I came here about a tarp. Forgot to mention it."

"A tarp."

"Uh-huh. You got one I could use?"

Orrin ambled to the lean-to coming off his cabin and disappeared behind shadows and mosquito netting and a tattered Ramapough Lenape "Keepers of the Pass" flag, hung vertically. He reached to the rafters and yanked on the corner of a blue tarp. He kept pulling and pulling until he had the whole thing in a heap at his feet, and then he dragged it over to Norval.

"It's twelve by fourteen, I think."

"That's plenty," Norval said.

"Have at it then."

"Help me fold it up?"

The brothers DeGroat took up two corners each. They spread the tarp and flapped it out, freeing it of dust and last autumn's leaf shreds and stems. They folded the tarp once and walked it in until the brothers met, bringing all four corners together. Their fingers touched. The tarp was folded smaller and smaller until it was a manageable square.

Norval left hugging the tarp to his chest. Orrin watched him go. Norval's hand went up in the air before following the trail into the woods, less like a wave than a semaphore.

ORRIN SPENT THE REST OF HIS DAY SCRAPPING. He trekked to Cannon Mine because he'd excavated some unique parts and pieces there in recent weeks. Cannon Mine was 2000 feet deep and seventeen levels, not including unlucky level thirteen. And all its contents seemed to get swallowed and submerged deeper and deeper from the surface with each passing day, which, Orrin thought, only made the dig that much more fulfilling. To bumble in the dark with nothing more than a pocket flashlight and scour for usable scrap required backbone and gall both. Being able to brag about this—even if it were only to himself—was endlessly satisfying.

The scrap he found that day was of a type. Long pieces. Wooden planks. Lengthy, chewed up legs of metal. He tied them all together with sisal rope and hauled them out. It took hours—exhausting work, but worth it. Through all his laboring, though, his time spent with Norval that afternoon stayed with him. Replaying their conversation in his head—a hazy recollection of sentence fragments and facial expressions—caused him serious consternation. By nightfall, he was organizing his haul on the mangle press worktable, aligning the pieces like the pickets on a privacy fence. But he was also feeling more and more certain—intuiting even—that something was awry.

Still, he continued working.

The assembly phase required only the most primitive of tools—claw hammer, deck nails, drill, and spur point and spade bit. There was no preplanning—Orrin, typically, afforded time for free play. He'd add and subtract, jumble, reshape, and alter base materials until a form he was happy with began to appear. And his junk sculptures were just that: *junk*. So there was no fear of missteps or goofs. He would simply deconstruct whatever he'd done to that point and commence a soft demo so the interchangeable parts would be spared.

Orrin held his hairy chin in his hand and appraised the array of stuff. He hocked a wad of phlegm onto the ground and spread it underfoot. He started by collaging reclaimed wood, crisscrossing and stacking pieces three boards high. Once a basic frame was outlined, he hammered, and he didn't mind if the wood split along the grain. He could always go back later and repair with wood glue. There was a slab of red oak, several sticks of cheap, purple-painted pine, two panels of knotty pine, hollow, pickled ash ceiling beams, a few pieces of primed crown molding, and a matching set of polyurethane trim and millwork. Nothing was sanded; nothing was straight. Rainfall had warped boards and careless handling had done severe damage.

After nailing all these disparate planks together, Orrin began to attach other accessories and discarded artifacts. There were a set of drawer pulls; rectangular tin plates you'd see in the corners of fences advertising the business name of the builder; door panels; a yield sign. There was an uncurled rebar cage, a pegboard, a concave piece of tin iron that wasn't to be confused with the section of zinc roof. Hardback book covers. Asphalt shingles. Filched EPA signs, the first of which had just begun to appear around the Wanaque Reservoir.

Everything was layered and crisscrossed, intersecting and overlapped. The aesthetic was established through rough-hewn, chewed up edges. Lead paint peeled in places. The sculpture, as a whole, creaked. Over the course of four hours, Orrin successfully completed the piece. He coated the finished assembly with tempera—a swill of berry pigments and egg yolk. Still wet, he stood the sculpture against his worktable, displaying it for no one. Some of the tempera dripped down, so he blotted the drips with a mechanic rag, leaving an imprint not unlike the gills of a mushroom. The end result had the dimensions of a pallet— that is to say, a square—not dissimilar from the steel plates utility workers set down after excavating a hole in the roadway, or the aluminum planks gravediggers set down after the plot is dug, awaiting the arrival of the casket, and then the start of the funeral ceremony.

ORRIN HEATED A CAN OF BAKED BEANS on the stovetop in his cabin, and he ate from the can with a fork while still standing over the stove. His bedraggled clothes, unkempt hair, and littered kitchen—it may as well have been a hobo jungle. Too, his thoughts were those of a man with little at stake. But, unlike most evenings, a single, murky thought—the thought of Norval's strange visit—kept intruding on him. He finished his baked beans, dropped the can into the sink, sat in his chair, and gnashed his teeth. For some minutes, he stared at the tower of diner matchbooks on the kerosene heater. Eyelids closed, and he drowsed. A vision swelled at the very front of his skull, his brain, his consciousness. He saw Peters Mine spitting flames from its entranceway. And the flames lapped and lapped and lapped. His body gave a jerk, and he hurried out of the cabin and into the darkling wilderness.

Orrin paced himself, careful of his footing, and breathed through his nose. His throat dried because of it, but it was what it was. He spat repeatedly and cleared branches from his path. Growing up, Orrin was the detached son. While Norval battered pots and pans beneath their moeder's floral muumuu as she prepared dinner, Orrin would be off somewhere alone—like in a garret, a self-imposed solitary confinement. He'd entertain himself with the queerest diversions: braiding the ribbon bookmark of a hymnal; biting his nails to nubbins and collecting the keratin in a locket; transforming their ma's porcelain dolls into kachina figurines. And this sort of behavior, his family thought, is what made him into the person he'd become: stoic; incapable of sustaining romantic relationships; dispassionate. Or, perhaps, it's just what he'd always been.

So as he neared Peters Mine, the foreboding was palpable, but he was as prepared as a private eye to stumble upon something ghastly. His mind was all lapping flames. Wingbeats could be heard overhead, and the leaves and rock fragments crunched underfoot. Passing a boulder wall, it was as if he saw the scene before he actually did: the clothes folded neatly at the crotch of the white oak; the pallet that had traced a path through the Ford scrap, pushing it all to the sides, forming a lane; the crumpled blue tarp centered in the adit. His consciousness was several steps ahead of him. But then material reality caught up.

He knew what he'd find, but he didn't know the details. Didn't know it would be so stagy. Didn't know the symmetry of the scene. He couldn't have guessed the tarp he and Norval had just hours earlier spread and folded would be so crumpled. There was a slight wind, and it caused the tarp to crinkle as if there were something moving beneath it. Orrin stood over the body and could see the shiniest spots were the wetness of blood. The right thing to do, he thought, would be to check for a pulse, but when he reached his hand down and flapped over an edge of the tarp, he saw there was no need.

Orrin stepped away from his brother's body, away from the mine and the lapping flames he saw in his mind. He looked off onto the valley-cleft and listened for the crosscurrents of the riverbed, but his mind was buzzing and he couldn't hear a thing. He jammed his index fingers into his ears and tried to scrape away the tinnitus as though it were earwax. He turned back to the body but didn't allow his eyes to settle on it. Not wanting anyone else to find it, he picked up the blued handgun. Children play near the mine, venture into it. *This is the responsible thing to do* went through his head. But that sentiment was only meant to drown out the thought of pawning it for cash.

Walking away from the body again, retracing his path through the woods, he resurrected their conversation as accurately as he could. He spent the next fourteen or so hours trying to recall their back-and-forth. If he could hear it again, he'd be able to know whether or not there was something he missed. But he failed to do this. He couldn't trace the causality of their statements, the subtleties and subtexts of their words. The only word that kept coming back to him was *Zike*. And so Zike was the person he sought out. Not Hannah, and absolutely not the park rangers.

THE FOLLOWING DAY, SUNDAY, was spent searching for his nephew. He rehearsed what he'd say: *Come with me, Zike. You need to see what you did to your da.* Or, *Your da's gone, Zike. No telling what pushed him to it, but he did it.* Or, *Had you any idea he would do this?—suicide?* Or, *I need you to come see about your da, Zike.* He'd tell him, *Zike. You need to come see your da, see what this world did to him. See what the world has done to us.* But, ultimately, it came out nothing like any of that.

Orrin nearly exhausted himself trying to find Zike. He wheezed and appeared to be the victim of an attack by a stickerbush. His underwear bunched from one too many big, lunging steps. Finally, he spotted Zike and his friends, the Van Dunk kids, across a glade. They loomed over a busted-up dirt bike. Zike was moving his body parts, attempting to pinpoint locations of hurt. He trudged a few steps closer, and then he whistled in their direction.

"Zike, I been looking for you," he started.

HYDROLOGY

The world is structured vertically, and all of civilization is downstream. Snowheaps melt in spring. Summer rain saturates the soil, there is flooding, and the runoff runs the ridge of the watershed. Brooks: streams: rivulets: runnels: becks: rills: bourns: tributaries: feeders—until convergence in big R I V E R. The water navigates what ancient glaciers made—gravel and rock and silt and sand—and fills underground aquifers and seeps into reservoirs. Treatment plants pock the banks. But what of the slag of the Ramapo ironworks? What of the sludge that Ford Motors dumped? Where is it carried, pumped, leached? How does it trickle down hillsides and contaminate the water and the soil? How does it poison, invisibly, on such a microscopic level? What's the science? Where does filtration fail? How do you catch something that can't be seen? How can the EPA be trusted? When does the poisoning—that is to say, the death—begin, end?

27

PATTING HIS POCKETS, EXLEY *MOTHERFUCKERED!* at the realization of his forgotten keys. He banged his fists on the front door and brought the two open wires together to ring the bell. There was no answer. It was nothing to fret about, though; they always kept a spare key in the nestbox on the side of the skinning shed. Still, he found the mental lapse bothersome, something like a flaw that reflected badly on him as a person. And, having just been axed, he wasn't in the mood.

The smell of sliced London broil in a frying pan full of butter issued from the kitchen. It was a smell he associated with autumn, with late afternoon naps after the first weeks of school, with the faintly echoing booms and blares he sometimes heard from the Mahwah High School marching band practicing their halftime performance for the upcoming football game. And it was the smell of his moeder—not just her cooking, but her. She didn't skimp on the butter, often lopping an unseemly chunk into the pan, always allowing it to sizzle, bubble, and brown before adding the steak.

Hannah had a chair pulled up to the oven, and she reached over the stovetop to flip the steak slices with a fork. Her arm was dangerously close to the grate, and the burning butter splattered her face. She winced. The move was made all the more perilous by the telephone wedged between her shoulder and her jaw, the coiled cord of which was pulled taut and umbilicaled around her neck.

"I got to go now, Elsie," she said into the receiver. "My son's here, and he's looking at me like I need to be punished…Okay, Els…Bye-bye."

Exley dragged his moeder's chair by the back legs and rungs; it squeaked across the linoleum.

"What're you doing sitting like that, Ma?"

"I was feeling lazy. Let me be." Hannah began to scooch her chair back to where it was. Exley grabbed the back.

"It takes like two minutes to fry up that steak. You can't stand for two minutes?"

"Oh, let me be I said."

"Why didn't you answer?" Ex asked. "I was knocking and ringing the bell."

"Like I said, I'm feeling lazy. That's all. Don't hold it against me now. Why you making all that noise anyways?"

"Forgot my key," he said. "I don't just knock on the door of my own house for no reason."

"Okay, with the attitude," Hannah said. She stood up and lifted the frying pan, but she started coughing and had to set it back down on the stove. Her eyes teared and reddened. She braced herself on the counter.

"You okay, Ma? You wanna do a treatment?" He started for the pantry, but she waved him off. She took a drink of water and regained her voice.

"You want some of this?" she asked, tilting the frying pan for him to see.

"Nah, I'm good."

"You look malnourished, child. Sit down and eat with me."

Hannah took a plate from the dish rack and set a place for Exley at the table. He reluctantly sat down with his arms at his sides as she pushed slices of steak from the pan to his plate, allowing the drippings of fat and butter to dress his meal.

"Do we have any bread?" he asked.

"Toast! I nearly forgot."

"I got it, Ma."

"It's done already. Just get it out the toaster." Ex used a serrated knife to retrieve the toast. "Unplug the machine, for heaven's sake, Exley!" He ignored her and put a slice of toast on each of their plates. After salting and peppering, Ex took an inordinate mouthful of steak. He squinted at the synthetic buffalo skull on the hutch, staring down its hollow eye cavities. He noticed the opaque outline of hot glue around the colorful beads and feather quills.

"You haven't been seeing your uncle, have you?"

"Who?"

"*You.*"

"No," Exley said, struggling to swallow a hunk of crust. "I mean who've I been seeing?"

"Your uncle, Exley. Orrin. For heaven's sake," she let her fork and knife both fall to the sides of her plate. "You've only got one."

"Oh, oh."

"Elsie said she saw you coming from the direction of his cabin."

"I saw him, like weeks ago."

"So she's right."

"I guess so. But who cares?"

"Have you been visiting him?" Hannah gnawed on a strand of gristle.

"Not on a routine basis or anything." His moeder continued to gnaw. "What does it—*why* does it even matter?"

Hannah shrugged.

"I don't know why you're so against him."

"Well, for one," Hannah said, "he doesn't *do* anything."

"Yes he does. He's got his hobbies, his art."

"His art?"

"His sculptures or whatever."

"I've always called them his crafts, which irritated your da, but—I mean, c'mon."

Exley watched the butter seep through the crannies of his toast. It was impossible to edge out his moeder in a debate.

He felt helpless, like her capacity to manipulate situations always left him feeling defeated and needing to apologize for something. For even bringing a contentious issue to the table in the first place.

"Have you been sleeping well?"

"Not *well*," he said. He didn't want to blame her or her coughing fits. "Why?"

"Your eyes," she pointed at them with her fork, "they've got dark circles underneath."

"That's not from lack of sleep." He knew, with that, he'd already said too much. He should've just accepted sleeplessness as his excuse. But he couldn't allow her to be right, especially when she wasn't.

"What's it from then?"

"It's bruising."

"Bruising?"

He was purposely laconic. By withholding information, he forced her to ask more questions. And the more questions she asked, the more empowered he felt, the more he wrested control from her.

"I got elbowed in the nose and…" he whistled while swiping his fingers below his eyes.

"How did you get elbowed?"

"Basketball game."

"When were you playing ball? You haven't played in months. I thought your knee was still bothering you."

"It's been feeling better," he said. "Gussie invited me to play in one of his men's league games. They were a man short."

"So he asked *you?*" she asked, incredulous.

"What?"

"You're not a *man.*"

"He said it wasn't a problem."

"Hmph."

"What, Ma?"

She got up from the table and doddered to the hutch. An Atlantic City souvenir ashtray with an image of the ocean, hotels, and boardwalk contained a bundle of dried sage. Hannah lit a match and burned the herb. She lifted a synthetic eagle feather from her shelf of gewgaws. The feather was coiled with hemp and leather and included plastic beads and a tassel coming off its end. All of its component parts had been acquired from Rag Shop, years ago, before they had gone out of business.

Hannah began to fan the sage smoke in her son's direction, eventually swooping the feather over his body, circling the crown of his head and cascading down his shoulders.

"Would you cut that shit out, please?"

"It will help you heal," she said.

"No it won't. It's gonna make me sneeze or gag or both."

She continued for another minute but stopped short of servicing his entire body. She wasn't about to exert the energy to crouch.

"I don't know why you're so resistant to what you don't even know, don't even understand."

"I understand enough to know that won't do anything."

"You don't know anything, Exley. So frosty—all the time with you." She set the feather back on the hutch and returned to the table. Exley pushed his plate forward and crossed his arms. His plate nudged Hannah's death ledger. "Mind that, please," she said. "I could apply some sassafras juice with a matchstick, soothe that soreness."

"No thank you."

"Or boil some water and vinegar. That vinegar vapor will put you right to ease. You'll see."

Hannah had a medicine cabinet stocked full of folk remedies and relics. Expiration dates were of no concern to her. These treatments were time-tested, she swore. And anyone would be a fool to turn them away.

"I'm good, Ma. I just need some sleep."

"You said it wasn't sleep."

"Recover, I mean. I need time to recover."

The death ledger doubled as a repository for recent documents and pressing paperwork. Hannah flipped some of its pages and pinched a paper with trifold envelope creases and Mahwah Public Schools letterhead.

"Explain this to me," she said.

Ex skimmed the letter—the "To the parents/guardians of Exley DeGroat" greeting; the bolded, italicized, *and* underlined "failure to receive summer school credits"; the "must repeat junior year" closing.

"Yea-up." He folded the letter and put it back between the pages of the death ledger. "It didn't work out."

"What do you mean 'didn't work out?'"

"The teacher had it in for me."

"Exley."

"He did, Ma."

"Well," she said, flattening her muumuu over her knees, "it is what it is. You repeat the year. You do it right this time. Right?"

He was relieved she wasn't making a bigger deal of it. "Don't worry about it, Ma. I'll be fine."

"I don't blame you, Ex. You've had a hard run lately." He nodded and got up to leave the kitchen. "Like with poor Emilia. Anything to report with that?"

He felt the way Gussie must've felt when Exley asked the same question. It was a rot in his stomach, his guts crumbling inward—compacting smaller and smaller—until it felt like his vacant body would keel over. And then all he'd do was *cry cry cry*, ending with a soft whimper.

"Nothing good, Ma. Gussie isn't talking about it much."

"I hope that poor girl stays with us," Hannah said. "She so young, just so young. Y'know, a little one—a boy, though—Jace Conklin, he was a child that got terribly ill when I was just seven or eight. And I can remember the feeling, the feeling that fell over the entire tribe. It was devastating. You'd think we'd come together—and we did, we did that as a community in the days after—but on the day of, the day he left us, everyone just stayed shuttered in their homes. Nobody was out. I can remember how eerie it felt. I can remember wanting to go out and play and my moeder telling me, *Not today, Hanny. Not today.*

"Back then, many people would still keep their dead in the home for viewings. And I remember it, clearly, walking up the staircase into the Conklin residence, walking just ahead of my moeder—her hands were on my shoulders and sort of massaging me. Everyone processed into the back room where Jace had passed. My ma led me along. And in that bedroom—it was dimmed, the curtains pulled closed—I saw Jace tucked into bed, the sheets pulled to his chin but his arms hanging over the top and at his sides like a paperclip or something. And I looked upon his face, all covered in black.

"This was back when folks still painted faces—they called it gloaming. They'd rub black ash all over the dead's face, masking it. It was a tradition, y'know—I see it in all its spookiness now, I do. But back then, that's just the way it was done. I had nightmares that night, though. Think I probably had them for many a night after. I remember my ma and da—your grandparents—taking turns sitting at my bedside, probably praying for me to fall to sleep."

"Ma. Stop."

"What?"

"Why you telling me all this?"

"It's your history, our history."

"It's fucking morbid, Ma."

"Language, Exley." She banged her palm on the table a single time, firmly. "And death ain't something to shy from. Looking back, I think it was good they took me to see Jace."

Standing in the doorway as if he was waiting to be excused, Ex looked at the figure of his moeder sitting at the table. He'd seen her so few places but there in the past year—seeing her with her tuberous legs, coarse hair, and feeble respiratory system. *When had she become so old?*

"Do you have work tomorrow?" she asked. "I still need you to pick up those folding tables from Zike and Elsie for the powwow."

"No. No work," he said.

"I thought you did." Hannah turned in her chair to scan the calendar. "Do I have your schedule wrong again?"

"I quit."

"What do you mean you quit? Exley, we need that extra cash."

"I know, Ma."

"And what about Zike, and Libby, and the other people who depend on you for their supplies, their necessities? Damnit, Exley. Really?"

"Sorry."

"I don't know, Exley. I just don't. This, this, this…" she looked to the ceiling. "This makes me think something bad is gonna happen for you, or us."

"I said I'm sorry, Ma. Don't get into the hoodoo now. Alright?"

"Alright." She closed her eyes and the lids fluttered. Her hands moved all around in front of her like she was swatting away a swarm of gnats, dismissing him. "Go to bed, Exley. *And...*," she said, sounding harder, "that toilet is clogged again. Take care of it."

"Gross, Ma. Why's that on me?"

"You're in no position, Exley. You know how much a plumber cost to come out here?"

"Is it full of shit?" he asked, puckering his face. "How long's it been sitting there clogged like that?"

"Don't be ridiculous. There's only wee-wee in there."

She still did this, referred to urine as *wee-wee*. Exley hated it. He hated it because it made him feel like he was still three-years-old. This from a woman who once attended classes to become a medical assistant. One would think she wouldn't be so peevish about piss and shit. Or, perhaps, she was intentionally doing it. To keep him small, to keep him baby, to keep him hers.

"I need those folding tables. You go pick those up tomorrow!" she shouted as Ex left the kitchen. "You should've done it weeks ago!"

28

Elsie was sitting outside her and Zike's trailer in a woven turquoise and green lawn chair. She sniffed her fingers and then continued to strip glossy spearmint leaves from their stems. As the sun shone differently depending on the tree canopy overhead, she rotated the herb buckets on the steps of the trailer. Her lawn chair was rickety with the monofilament webbing frayed where it curved around the aluminum frame. She bent her feet underneath the chair. Elsie was so short she could swing her legs back and forth without making a rut in the ground.

Pulling up in the Ford Escort, Exley hopped out holding a rainbow of steel-hooked bungee cords.

"Hi Elsie."

"Oh, hey Exley!" She set down a clump of spearmint on a napkin beside her and gave Exley a big hug, really clutching him. She was so small, though—her turned cheek met with his sternum. "Your mama said you'd be coming by."

"Yeap," he said as their bodies separated. "Gotta get those folding tables, if you've got 'em."

"We have them, we do," she said. "But sit—talk to me for a minute. How've you been?"

"Not bad," he said. He noticed her legs, how blemished they were with mosquito bites scratched to scabbed gashes. "How 'bout you guys?"

"You know how it is, Exley." There was a plain pair of gray sweatpants hanging over the back of her chair. She took the sweatpants, stretched them across her lap, and then punched her fist through a hole in one of the knees. "How ridiculous?" she said.

"Those look like they've about had it."

"They've *had it* several times over. But...*your brother...*" She blew air out of her mouth, and her lips—which were always so tight and wet in a way that Exley could never get enough of—vibrated. "He insists on this pair of pants." She began sewing the hole, closing the tear so Zike's clothes could be stitched together the same as his body.

"He won't get new ones?"

"Nope," Elsie said, angling the needle through the paper-thin fabric. "He says these are the only pair that work for him, that are comfortable."

"Oh," Ex said, again staring at her legs—what he could glimpse between the sweatpants. Her hair wasn't as pixie-short as it used to be; now it was neck-length. But she still wore barrettes on both sides of her head like a child. Exley liked it, but he liked the pixie cut more. He used to keep a picture of her looking like that in his nightstand. It was a disposable camera photo of her and Zike in high school. They were tangled in each other's arms, acting immature and zany—both sticking their tongues out. Her warped features didn't bother Exley at all. If anything, he thought, it made her even more attractive. Her looks and personality were both on display in the image. And so he kept it between the pages of an old address book. And he folded the photo in half, trying as best he could to eliminate his brother from the shot.

"I'm a sucker, Ex. I know it."

"You're just nice," he said. "Sometimes too nice."

"I'm sorry, but I am. A sucker and a nice person both, I guess. One in the same, right?" Ex heard the pinging of metal against metal—Zike hammering, he thought. Elsie kept him where he was, though. "You know how he is."

"I do."

"And—I hate to say it—but it's always so so *so* much worse when he's been drinking."

"And he's been drinking?"

"He's been drinking."

"Since what time?"

"Early, I'd say." She squinted into the sunlight, figuring the time that way. "I know he had a beer at breakfast, and he's been in the shed working on his bike for hours now. His cooler in there with him."

"His bike?"

"He's been trying to bring it back to life. That's what he told me. He's even had me chauffeur him around a bit—for parts. It's good for him in that respect, I suppose. But I much rather see him regain interest in me, in getting himself better, in getting off the drinking. I'm sorry…"

"What?"

"I shouldn't be dumping all this on you. It's not your problem."

"I don't mind. I like to help."

"No, it's not your problem. Usually I would talk to Hannah about this stuff. But, in light of how she's been feeling, I didn't want to bother her about it."

"How she's feeling?"

"With her coughing, her lungs and all," Elsie clarified.

"Right."

"She gets so upset when I give her bad news about him. She keeps right on believing he's going to improve, get better. I tell her, *No way he's getting better until he seeks out some help. AA or something*. But, your mama, she don't like to hear about her sons struggling."

"Some of her sons," Ex said, trying to elicit pity from Elsie, thinking—stupidly—it might make him more attractive to her.

"Your mama loves you, Exley."

That's not what he wanted to hear, and it made his guts gurgle. The adult, "auntie" tone she took peeved him. He stood up and craned his neck around the trailer.

"So Zike's in the shed?"

"He is. Go on and see him. He'll be happy to see you, I'm sure. He's in a mood."

THE SHED WAS BEHIND THE TRAILER and roughly forty feet off— one of those barn-looking sheds with a gambrel roof that you can order at Home Depot and have them install for free, unless— of course—the address reads "Stag Hill." Zike hired some local hands to erect the structure while he served as gofer to the crew. They had it up in an afternoon.

Exley opened the door and entered the confined space. It was cluttered with the inherited cabinets Zike got after their da died. Zike was wearing an old Iron Maiden t-shirt with the sleeves cut off and cuts down the sides to accommodate his larger body. He hovered awkwardly over his 4-stroke Honda, trying to hammer out a dent on the skid plate. Sweat beaded across his forehead and dripped from his brow.

"Do you need to have these doors closed?"

"What?" Zike asked. "It's hot?"

"Unbearable, bro." Ex opened the door as far as it would go and propped it with a cinderblock. "Better light for you, too." Shafts of sun lit the workspace.

Exley could read the labels of the items and tools on the cabinet shelves, all of it willed to Zike through some obsolete right of primogeniture. Cans of turpentine and varnish aged to antiques. WD40 in an unfamiliar typeface. Wood glue with the nozzle crusted shut. Cobalt steel utility knife replacement blades.

Tubing cutter with an easy-grip feed knob. Bonded rubber repair kit. All of it American-made. The interior of the shed was like the set of some 1960s television program. The cabinets and their contents carried no sentiment whatsoever for Exley—it was junk and it was shit. Evidence that his da did fix things every now and then.

"This is the last of the gauze, bro," he said, handing Zike three rolls from his pockets. The bungee cords were slung around his neck now.

"Check this out." Zike unrolled a poster from a cardboard cylinder. "You remember this?" It was one that Zike used to have hanging in his bedroom: a motocross rider doing a coffin in midair. Something about the camera angle made it seem more acrobatic and gravity defying than it actually was. Not to say it wasn't impressive, but Exley had become disillusioned with those sorts of stunts years ago.

"Dope," Ex said. "I kinda remember it. Was it above your headboard?"

"Yea-up, brother!" Zike was visibly amped at the find. "You know it. You know it." He looked over the image, beholding it as though it possessed some sacred quality, and his fingers felt at the chalky residue of double-sided tape at the corners.

"Like I said," Ex continued, "this is the last of the gauze for a while—or, forever, really."

"What you mean?"

"I got shitcanned."

"No!" Zike said, genuinely dismayed. "What happened, li'l bro?"

"What do you think happened? I got caught." Zike didn't say anything, considering—maybe—that Exley was about to blame him for the firing. He burped and Exley caught a whiff of the sickly beer smell on his brother's breath.

"Anyway," Ex said, "I came for the folding tables for Ma."

"*Stop*. Just stop, li'l bro. Slow it down. I'm *so* sorry. That fucking manager of yours. He's a fucking manager at CVS. Thinks he's pope. Thinks he's king. Who's he?"

"It's cool, Zike. I'll find something else."

"That gets me, though. Y'know? It gets me."

"Are those them?" Ex asked, pointing at three folding tables standing upright at the back of the shed. They were blocking a small window and were covered with a shear blouse of cobwebs.

"Yea-up. That's them. You taking them today?"

"That's why I'm here. Didn't you hear me say that?"

"*Alright, alright, alright,*" Zike said, closing his eyes, quieting the scene.

"Move out, Zike. I can get them myself."

"Okay. But let me get the bike out first."

"I'll move the bike," Ex said. "You just move out."

Zike grabbed a can from the cooler and hobbled out of the shed using a pilfered mini-golf putter as a cane. He heard a racket—something falling—inside the shed. "Easy in there!" he yelled to Ex. "That wasn't the bike, was it?" Exley didn't answer, he just replaced the pair of loppers that had fallen. As he moved the folding tables—shifting them one at a time, using his body to leverage them—light beamed through the back window. The shed, in turn, became a bit less of a crypt.

"You been ballin'?"

Ex lined up the folding tables outside the shed, still in upright positions. The cobwebs contained silk-spun yellowjackets and beetles.

"Actually, I have. I played with Gussie and his work buddies." Ex wiped at the cobwebs with his hands. "You got a hose?"

"Watering can." Zike pointed to the trailer steps where Elsie's herb buckets were.

"That'll do."

Elsie was still sitting in her lawn chair, spacing out or maybe picking up fragments of the conversation.

"Can I borrow this?" Exley asked.

"Go ahead," she said. "You need help carrying those to the car?"

"I got it."

"I'll come help," she insisted.

"How'd that go?" Zike asked as Exley watered down the folding tables, wiping the cobwebs as he went. They tangled in his fingers, clumping, and he violently shook them free.

"How'd what go?"

"The basketball. With Gussie."

"It went well. I was on."

Ex didn't say anything about Harry Adams. What would be the use, he figured. What good would come from letting his twenty-five-year-old brother know he threw down with some dickhead from his high school days? Zike, Ex assumed, held tight to the belief that he'd all but vaporized in the minds of his former schoolmates. There was no need to let on otherwise. *Let that be Zike's truth*, he figured. *Let him be vapors.*

"If you were on," Zike said, "then you need to *get on*—as in, on this motherfucking bike and see how it's running."

"Not a chance."

"C'mon. For me, li'l bro. I sure as hell can't ride it. I'm all full of holes. Swiss cheese me."

Elsie hissed at his joke. It wasn't his laughing at his own misfortunes that bothered her; it was that she didn't believe it. It wasn't self-deprecation—it was self-loathing. He never would've made the joke sober.

"I can't," Ex said, nodding his head to Elsie. He grabbed one end of a folding table, and she grabbed the other. They walked the table to the Escort and heaved it onto the roof. They repeated this for the two remaining folding tables—working in concert, not saying a word.

He and Elsie bungeed the folding tables to the roof, passing an additional rope back and forth over the car and through its open doors to secure it. Despite moving to Stag Hill in her teens, Elsie was still as hardnosed and thrifty and rugged as any lifelong resident tribeswoman. She was muscly, too. Exley could see it: in the space where her neck met her shoulders—on each rope throw it would tighten; and in her calves when she let herself down from the foot of the open car door—the muscles would flex.

"Exley," she said as she hit the ground. "You're doing your mama so much good with these little errands. It adds up, y'know?"

"I guess."

"Will we see you at the powwow?"

"I wasn't gonna go," he said. "I really don't like going. But I think I will."

Just then, Zike rolled his dirt bike out from behind the trailer. He was barely holding it up, and the mini-golf putter was under his arm. Ex ran to help.

"You talking about the powwow?" he asked. "Shit, Els. Tell this youngblood who's the all-time leader in tug o'war. Go 'head: tell 'em."

"Tug o'war's a team game, honey."

"But, Elsie—c'mon now." The boyish expressions he was making with his fleshy and scarred face were disturbing, even to the ones who loved him. "Who wins it for the team? Who's got those ribbons as proof of it? C'mon now."

"Let it go, won't you?" Elsie said. "You're not winning this year, right?" Exley saw regret instantly spread across her face. She tried to amend it: "Not to say you couldn't, but you know where you'll be—with your hand going numb in the cooler, pulling out beer after beer."

"That's nice, Elsie," Zike said, his voice suddenly much softer. "That's real nice—in front of my little brother and everything."

"I'm sorry, Zike. But since when do you conceal anything from Exley? He's here, isn't he? Seeing everything the way it is, for what it is. And where are you?"

"Uh. Here. Obviously."

"No, Zike," she said. "You're drunk. You're fucking drunk." Exley had never heard Elsie swear. "And you know what?—I don't mind taking care of you, Zike. I don't. But, at some point, you've got to take care of yourself, too. It's got to be the both of us."

"How do I not take care of yourself—" Zike stumbled. "Of *my*self?"

"Your hygiene, for one."

Zike's eyes widened to perfect ovals in his head, showing so much white. He jerked back, and his thick mass of hair shifted.

"There it is," he said, clinically. "Right there. You seen it, Ex. *There it is.*"

Elsie became quiet before slinking back to her lawn chair and her herbs. She layered basil leaves, one on top of the other. Zike glowered at her, even after she'd made herself invisible.

"So how 'bout that ride?" Zike asked.

"I can't, bro. You know I never really rode that much—mostly ATVs, if anything."

"You know how," Zike declared. "And if you're well enough to run up and down the basketball court, you're well enough to get on this." He slapped the burning-blue Blessed Virgin on the seat fairing.

"I'm gonna pass." Ex jangled his car keys.

"You know Da used to ride, right?" The question was equivalent to Zike blockading Exley's path to the driver's seat of the Escort with nothing but the bulk of his body. "He had that Triumph. Ma made him sell it off before you were born. Said the money could go to Gerber or diapers or whatever the hell they needed for their *wittle bwaby.*"

"I knew that," Ex said. "I know he used to ride. Not trails, though."

"No, not trails." Zike took a moment to lift his t-shirt and check the fluid level in his colostomy bag. "You know what Da told me one time?"

"What, Zike?"

"He told me if he was ever gonna off himself he'd ride his Triumph into a rock wall he knew about. Some wall by the on-ramp to 17. He told me he'd have to turn right, accelerate, and *kaboom!* Simple as that. He said there was enough road there for him to get good speed. Said there'd be no question of survival. He told me the state troopers could have fun picking up his pieces."

"Oh?" Ex's expression was neutral. He and Zike didn't talk about their da's suicide, not to each other. They never had.

"Apparently that was all bullshit, though, right?" Zike guffawed.

"Don't talk to him like that, Zike," Elsie shouted. "About those things."

Zike didn't turn around, but he leaned on his putter and said: "Stop sounding like a wife!" Elsie shook her head and continued to sew the hole in his sweatpants. "So you gonna ride, or what?"

"I'm really not up for it."

"Ex, look. I geared up a couple teeth on the rear sprockets. I invested in the spark arrestor. And, check it," he said, pointing. "I added a larger fuel tank so you can ride as long as you want, getting as lost as you want."

"I wonder who drove you to get all those parts," Elsie mused.

"Ignore her," Zike said to Exley. "Do it for your big brother. I can't take the pleasure in riding it, but you can. Exley," he said, turning serious, "do it for me."

"Why you being so dramatic?" Ex asked. "You're showing your drunkenness." He looked over at Elsie to see if she heard what he had said. She hadn't.

"Just ride the bike."

Exley walked to the Escort and slid his keys onto the dash, slamming the door after him.

"One ride," he said, sternly. "A quick one."

EVEN WITHOUT ANY SAFETY GEAR ON—no helmet, either—Ex felt armored. Skid plates and radiator guards protected the dirt bike from minor damages. And he, in a way, was an extension of the bike: an appendage. Zike had selected him as a crash test dummy just as he'd selected the skid plates. The care and the fastidiousness with which Zike resurrected his most expensive toy equated to a kind of honor bestowed onto Exley, the rider. The fraternal bond throbbed.

Still, Exley was awkward and clumsy on there—his long, spindly legs as inflexible as a ladder. He wasn't much of a rider— that much was true—but he and his brother both knew he had a knack for just about anything if it had the whiff of a challenge.

Following a nameless trail, Ex went along slowly at first. He didn't know the turns and the curves of the backwoods like his brother had. Zike could ride blind—in fact, he once did on a dare. The trail was rutted, but Ex could feel the adjustments Zike had made to the bike—they made for a softer suspension. His knees brushed against climbing tearthumb weeds strangling out the brush. There was a white trail blaze nailed to a treetrunk in his peripheral, and then a dead muskrat—its teeth frozen in a snivel— sprawled in the clear path ahead. He must've scurried up from the gulch, Ex thought. He managed to safely swerve around it, but his stomach dropped at the keeling of his body and the bike.

And then he smiled.

The ride was easy, and he was comfortable with it. Control. His hands bridled the waffle grips as he leaned in, lifting himself higher off the seat. Long stretches of the trail were without interruption—no ditches or gullies. No pebble or boulder could throw him. The wind just cracked off his back and shoulders in large chunks like onionskin. Nothing bothered him.

But then—as he slowed at the turn that would bring him back to the start, back to Zike and Elsie and their ten-wide trailer painted in the colors of an Easter dress—his eyes caught and settled on a pile of rocks that weren't rocks. Rocks that were paint sludge petrified. And he *knew* they were sludge—he wasn't fooled into thinking, *Oh, rocks*—because they were gouged. Probably from other riders, their reckless speeds and wild disregard. Exley could see the feathered colors—the rangoon red, the diamond blue, the flame orange: a rainbow. He was instantly racked with worry.

Behind him, he saw the knobby tires churning up dirt, mud roosting in a mohawk. And he thought of all the times his brother came home from riding with Lenny Van Dunk. Coming home late, after dark, a plate made for him on the stove covered in saran wrap. His ma berating: *Why are you so late? How does somebody even ride in the dark? You're gonna get yourself killed—wrap yourself right around a tree. That food is cold and will taste like rubber after you nuke it.* He remembered their da not moving from his chair, or asleep already, or not there at all. He saw himself, floor-sitting, playing *Operation*—tweezing the "Writer's Cramp" pencil bone from the wrist of the lithographed patient. How he watched his brother from below—Zike's stature: mythic—crossing the kitchen for his plate, covered from the feet up in thick manure-like mud. He remembered the buzz of the tweezers touching the metal sides of the cavity on the game and how it made him shiver. How the dark, fresher mud on Zike's boots contrasted with the light brown mud at his knees, cracking. His brother would wait for the microwave to beep, drumming on the countertops. Exley would pick at the rough circles of sap on the soles of his feet—tacky like the double-sided tape residue on Zike's posters. Sap that wouldn't wash away for days, that had to be picked from his feet by fingernail or nail file. Sap from the one-off sugar maple he played barefoot beneath in the early afternoon while his moeder watched soaps on the couch in a shuddering half-sleep. First, collecting twigs. Then, collecting whirligigs, and getting a handful and leaning over the porch railing and letting them fall, flickering like stained-glass light through the narthex. He thought of Zike noisily removing his reheated plate from the microwave, whumping to his bedroom, and throwing his sullied jeans onto the floor. And he thought about how he'd see Zike in the same pair of jeans—unwashed, unbeaten, mud un-flaked off—the following morning before he left for school.

Sickness. Sickness was his next thought. A flash of Zike's scathed mother-naked body. Body of boils. Body of pus. *Body of us*—Exley made the rhyme. Zike tilting back the cheval-glass and leaning forward, falling. He saw shattered glass and that pattern replicated on body after body after Ramapough body. *How many times had Zike fallen?* Those feathered colors. Those paint sludge rocks. The thwack of a hammer to a chisel and the peel and carve of the chisel on rock. The poison air that it emitted. The toxic slick that it seeped—into dirt, into river, into mouths. Exley slowed to a wobble. He saw the trail ahead of him. He saw himself in front of his brother's cheval-glass mirror. He saw Zike waiting for him to pull in, desperately wanting to know how well the ride went.

SWATCHES

[*As noted in* Color Codes, a Ford Paint Cross-Reference]

You got your dark moss green, your aspen red, your nightmist blue. You got your seafoam green, your silver moss, your meadowlark yellow. You got boxwood green, lunar green, willow green. Rangoon red, raven black, fawn tan. You got colonial white. You got your diamond blue, your brittany blue, your wedgewood blue. Woodsmoke gray. Silver smoke gray. Sandshell beige. Maize yellow and moonrise gray. You got candyapple red, and you've got copper brown. Springtime yellow. Thanks vermilion. Anti-establish mint. Freudian gilt. Inca gold. And chalk pink. And gunmetal gray. And you can't forget your indian turquoise, your indian fire. Flame orange.

29

EXLEY SAW THE WATER FOUNTAIN in a dream: Zike's water fountain. CVS was Mahwah High School; aisle was hallway. And the water fountain was under repair: a wrinkled, black trash bag was masking-taped over it like a gothic gown. Exley walked down the aisle, which was longer than any aisle in any CVS in any incarnation of America. Exley entered Aaron's office and watched a CCTV monitor. It showed a simple shower stall. Mold climbed the square tiles and grime filled the grooves of grout. The showerhead sprinkled a cone of discolored water—brownish, as if someone had unscrewed a fire hydrant cap. A man entered the shower, all brawn and water-darkened body hair. The hair on his head was thick and the water beaded off it, glistening. Exley was seeing the man's back—no chest or tummy, no face, no genitalia. There was nothing vulgar about the man's nakedness. It was a solid specimen, firm and of good health. The man soaped himself, and the suds fell in clumps like Spanish moss off a bald cypress. He raised one arm and then the other, rigorously scrubbing his pits as if they were matted with fast-setting concrete. He kept at it, grinding his washrag back and forth. Exley began to believe he would scrub until he bled, until he scraped out his lymph nodes.

Leaning in closer to the screen, so that the image of the man began to pixelate and blur, Exley abruptly jumped back as the man began a slow turn toward the surveillance camera. Exley watched the man's feet pivot, his hips swivel, the revelation of his mesomorph chest. Finally, the face. Zike's face. *It's Zike face*, Exley muttered. Unscarred, impeccable, unpolluted. And, after he wiped the soapsuds from his wincing eyes and let the water rinse off the rest, he opened them for the camera—which is to say, for Exley—and he simpered. Surprised by the expression, Exley averted his gaze, scanning the body downward until he settled on his brother's groin. And there was nothing there but a smooth, hard plastic mound substituting for skin and scrotum and manhood.

Exley ran out of the office and hopped onto Zike's 4-stroke Honda, zooming through the CVS sensor doors. His handlebars quivered as he rode along the ridgetop of Houvenkopf Mountain, and so he tightened his grip. The front end of the dirt bike began to buck. He came to a barricade of felled trees and metal—nature and industry, and he closed his eyes at the feeling of the bike taking flight, the feeling of his body separating from the bike, and the feeling of his face furrowing the ground.

The smell of standing water was in his nostrils: beaver feces, mosquito larvae, and paint thinner. He was facedown in dirt with a mouthful of it. He spit, his tongue lashing this way and that—but he couldn't get it all out. He clawed at his mouth, scooping the harder chunks from his inner cheeks and scraping the smaller bits from his tongue. The dirt kept falling out in crumbs. And he started to choke. He got to his feet and began hocking dirt wads from the back of his throat. He coughed, gagged. From out of the woods, his da approached him to help. Norval crouched before his son, clapped his hand over Exley's injured knee, and began to speak to him. But Exley couldn't hear the words. His da was muted and seemed oblivious to his voicelessness, which, for Exley, made it that much more frustrating. He was still coughing, crying too. He sobbed, and dirt drew deeper and deeper down his throat with each insuck.

His da babbled on about what Exley could never know. So, dismayed, Exley slumped. His head fell, and he looked over his body. He was horrified at what he saw: a porous body—holes going straight through him. Each hole a culvert pipe for a tributary of sewage. He turned to his da for solace, but Norval had become a mannequin positioned into a crouch. A strong wind would topple him. Exley's coughing intensified. Dirt spewed out in uncontrollable streams. He coughed and he coughed, coughed until his dry, barking cough became his moeder's hacking cough, and then he woke up.

HE CLOSED THE BEDROOM DOOR that had been left ajar, and, in doing so, muffled his moeder's coughing. He wiped the corners of his mouth and smelled his breath—it was rife with stale saliva. His tongue was so dry it felt like it was forking. Exley sat on the edge of his bed, the room so dark it was almost beyond eyesight adjustment—it was like a pit. So dry. So dark. *So what now?* he thought, sort of anesthetized in a twilight state, his dreams slipping from short-term memory.

Exley opened the vanity mirror in the bathroom, removed the toothpaste and his brush. His own reflection startled him as he closed the vanity. He opened it again—the shelves were stocked with deodorant sticks and perfume bottles and floss and tweezers and tubes of zit cream edged and flattened and nearly empty and cotton rounds and Q-tips and his moeder's SMTWTFS pill organizer. He closed the vanity again—*his face.* Opened it—*the shelves.* Closed it—his face. Opened, shelves. Closed. The faster he did it, the less real he seemed. The less his face was his face.

He wasn't forceful with his brushing, but the hard bristles on his overused brush pierced. Hannah's gums had receded so far you could see a row of triangles when she smiled wide. Exley didn't want that, so he brushed softly in small circles. Foam filled his mouth, but he refused to spit until the tops were done. Stubborn child. He kept the tap running, and the drain—clogged with hair—caused the water level to gradually rise in the basin.

He looked into the vanity mirror and saw what lay beneath his face. He could, essentially, skin himself from scalp to sternum. Exley, skinless. Only a bone-white skull. He bared his teeth while brushing, while forcing mint-flavored floss between molars, and he saw a skeleton jaw hinging from his ears. He pulled the flesh from his eyes, a *snag*, revealing orbital bones and the roundness of his eyeballs. He held his red hair back from the hairline and saw a cranial vault, a fully formed and impressively fused skull. And it freaked him. It was seeing something he shouldn't—the future, or a father naked.

Suddenly superstitious, he released his face from such scrutiny, from such prophesying, from remembering that he had to die. He should have forced himself back to sleep, but instead Exley puggled the toilet with a wire coat hanger as his moeder had asked him to do the day before. He poured in half a jug of Drano, despite the label explicitly stating: DO NOT USE IN TOILET. He left it there to sit, to work, and then he left the house, more asleep than awake.

HE VAGARIED THROUGH THE WOODS and decided to make the tree rim his destination. The ball was safely hidden behind the gorse bush. It really was a remote location, isolated. No hiking trails crisscrossed anywhere near the meeting of those two glens. And no Ramapough kids had any interest in shooting hoops there, what with the Tribal Community Center courts always available. On clear nights, a full moon would act like floodlights, and Exley could understand why his da called the hideaway the sacred hoop.

"There he goes, Hanny. Our son's off to the sacred hoop to work on his jumpshot," he would say.

"That's not what that means, Norv. Way to teach the boy disregard for his own culture."

"Culture," his da would huff.

The rim sat crooked on the beech tree, so Exley jumped and tried to right it. *I should get a net for this thing*, he thought. He often missed the *thwap* of his swishes. A net would make the whole exercise more satisfying, less like he's just lofting a rubber ball in the air in the middle of the woods.

On one such shot—*All net!* is what he would have said to an opponent if there was one: a net or an opponent—the ball bounced off into a tall patch of spotted knapweed. The wind whirled and brushed the thistly, purple flowers against Exley's arms as he bent to retrieve the ball and irritated his skin. He dribbled the ball off a gnarly root. *Fucking sacred hoop*, he muttered to himself. And, because he was audibly speaking to himself, he wasn't sure if he really did hear the shifting and rustling of footsteps on the slope.

He spaced his feet for a foul shot—his right toes aligned with what passed for the front of the rim.

Hey there.

Exley turned and saw a figure scuttering down the gradient of the glen. His first thought was Unky Orrin, but this wasn't anyone familiar. Disregarding the words he swore he heard, he considered, *Maybe a black bear cub.* He cocked the basketball back behind his head like pegging the creature would kill it. But he let it drop at his feet, realizing the ungainly man before him.

"My name's Lest," the man said, walking toward Exley with his hand extended. "Lester Brodsky. I work at the college." He wore a black button-down and brown suspenders with two stripes of mustard yellow running vertically. His watch strangled his greeting wrist, fat pushing out both sides of the band.

"You work these hours?" Exley asked.

"Well now," the man said, suddenly comfortable. "Let's just say my wife bemoans not knowing where my work ends and my leisure begins."

He spoke with a New York accent. His long, black hair was greased and trained behind his ears. His eyes were black, too, dilated-like. Possum-like. His sideburns were silver-white, while his mustache was bushy and black with shoots of that same silver. Trollish body type. Hannah once told her children that if you hit a troll between the eyes with a pebble it would pule and crawl back to its brush pile.

"You a scientist?" Exley asked. The man carried an Abney level and a field book and had rockpicks in his belt loops. "A geologist or something?"

"Good guess. Ecologist," the stranger corrected, proudly.

"Oh, alright."

"I'm not one of those men in hazmat suits, if that's what you're thinking," he added. "You know the ones—with power washers, dousing boulders. That sort of thing. I'm not one of those. I'm not EPA."

"Clearly," Ex said.

It felt awkward for Exley, spooky: standing in his supposedly sacrosanct place next to a stranger. And at such an hour. If he could be sure the stranger actually existed and he wasn't still dreaming, he might've been alarmed.

"Are you a member of the Ramapough Lunaape Nation?"

Other than his moeder and tribal leaders speaking at organized events, Exley had never heard anybody refer to him and his people that way. It was such a formal way of putting it, but it sounded smooth and ingratiating coming out of the stranger's mouth.

"Yeap," Ex confirmed. "I'm Ramapough."

Sensing there was no threat, Exley continued to shoot around. He felt embarrassed when a shot fell short, despite the stranger not giving any indication he cared or was keeping count of made field goals versus missed.

"And you live on the mountain?"

"Yeap," Exley said, lifting his chin in the direction of home. "Stag Hill." He got close to the rim and easily put the ball through the hoop. His biddy ball coach called that *getting a feel for it*.

"If you don't mind me asking, why are you out here so late?"

"Sleep problems."

He finally sank a jumper, but the contentment that came

with doing so was diminished as the ball bounced erratically off another tree root.

"What kind of problems?"

"Can't sleep."

"Yes," Lest said, "obviously—can't sleep. But do you know the cause?"

"The cause?" Ex spun the ball backwards between his hands, blurring the black ribs. "I don't know. My ma's coughing?"

"Your mother has a bad cough?"

"That's what I said." Exley turned to face Lest and held the ball on his hip. "What are you getting at? Why does this matter? Why you talking to me?"

"Ford," Lest said, ignoring Exley's questions. "The sludge. You know about all that? Your family does?"

"Of course," Ex sneered. "We do leave our homes, y'know."

"Of course," he said. "And the EPA—have they been in communication with you?"

"I don't know."

"Well has anybody ever come to your door? Shown you their findings? Had you give blood?"

"We're not too keen on giving our blood over to the government," Exley said, reciting what he'd heard his ma say many times herself.

"But they've been in touch?" Lest pushed.

"No. I don't think so," Ex answered haltingly. "Sometimes. They ring the bell now and again. Ask questions." He was in a wide stance and dribbled between his legs. "Mostly they do their thing. They're just sort of there. In the background."

"You know a lot of sick people—I'm sorry," Lest said, plucking out his suspenders. "What's your name?"

"Exley."

"Lexi?"

"Exley, *Exley.*"

"You know a lot of sick people, Exley? Are there a lot of people with chronic or terminal illnesses—on Stag Hill?"

"Yea-up." An image of Gussie cradling Emilia in his arms—not as a newborn though, but as her four-year-old self, with arms and legs dangling lifelessly—flared in his consciousness.

"And you know why that is?" Lest asked. "Those rates, those high incidences?"

"Mud."

"Mud, yes. Mud, definitely," he agreed. "But air, too. And water. The toxins, the heavy metals are pervasive."

"Kinda hard to have fun in the backyard knowing all this," he poked. Exley was comfortable being flippant. The stranger reminded him of Unky Orrin. Lester Brodsky was Unky Orrin in white man form, a paleface familiar. A haint. Something unreal. He didn't mind fucking with him a bit.

"And what's your take?" Lest asked. "Is it all just bad luck? Bad luck that this is what's befallen your tribe?"

Exley took a shot. It went through the rim, deflected off the treetrunk, and rebounded right to him. A flawless shot like that established his dominion.

"Shitty, fucking terrible luck. That's what I'd call it."

"It's not luck, though." Lest seethed a bit, casting down his eyes and toeing the ground. "You need to know that—it's not luck. There's *intent*."

"And nobody cares." Exley shrugged, the ball balanced in his upturned palm. "*No-bo-dy*."

"I know it, I do," Lest agreed. "But it doesn't have to always be that way. That can change." He became roused by his own words. "You know what I do? I walk with my head down. You wouldn't know it from my physique, I know," he patted his belly, "but I walk *a lot*. In the dark. I walk at these hours—the ungodly ones— and sleep through the afternoon. I like the disorientation, the fog of it all. My wife, she hates it. It's a passion. I study the issues of this land—your people's land—one square unit at a time. I've found pig iron more times than I can tell. Each time it's a thrill. And these trees—*Christ*. Some of these trees, you know, they're relatively new. This land's been stripped and pillaged before. The ironworks...those blast furnaces needed to feed, and feed they did. They fed on the trees." Lest outstretched his arms, presenting the forest as a vast economy. "Just marvel at it!"

Exley dribbled the ball, spun it in his hands—feeling the smoothness of it against his skin. He heard what Lest was saying but gave an impression of apathy.

"And nobody cares, you say," Lest continued. "I care. I've been walking with my head down around these mountains for a long time. And listen," he said, intensifying his gaze. "It might be in your backyard now, but it's gonna be coming out of their taps soon enough." He pointed, accurately, in the direction of Rio Vista. "Then we'll see who matters."

"I guess," Exley said. He drove at the basket and gracefully put in a reverse layup.

"Alright," the stranger announced, turning to go on his way. He picked up a black rock from the ground. "Chert," he said. "A sedimentary rock." Exley wasn't paying any mind; he was bent, dribbling the ball inches from the ground. But he started listening when he heard *your people*.

"Your people—going way back now—used it to make stone tools, to spark fire—tinderboxes and whatnot." Lest formed his hand and fingers into a gun. "Flintlock firearms, that too."

"Oh, yeah?" Ex asked coolly, not wanting to let on that he was actually interested.

"Nobody rolled over, you know. Your people fought back. And I mean from the start, through the middle, and up to the now, the present calamities and traumas."

Lest felt like he had lost what little of Exley's attention he had.

"Listen to me rambling on."

Exley stared back at Lest. The stranger clawed back up the slope of the glen and walked off with his head down—an apparition.

Trekking back home, sweaty, Exley found a clump of hair—human hair, he was pretty sure—in a hole of a fallen tree. The brittle trunk crumbled inward as he reached to grab it. Bushy and matted, like a tuft—it resembled steel wool, the SOS wire sponge on the windowsill above the sink in his moeder's kitchen. He examined it, delicately placed it back in its hole, and smeared clean his hands on the front of his shirt.

It usually goes like this:

When he returns from his nighttime wanderings, Exley is heedful of noise. He never wants to interrupt the near-drone of cricket chirps and the rasp of chorus frogs, so he gently closes the screen door and tightens his whole body to muffle the mechanical crank of the doorknob.

He'll peek in the kitchen. On the countertop, he'll see the component parts of the nebulizer soaking in the sudsy stew bowl of tap water, Palmolive, and white vinegar. The facemask will jut from the bowl with bubbles still fresh on its suctioning edge. The nebulizer will still be on the table in the alcove because his moeder sees no reason to return it to the pantry. She might need it again in the morning, after all.

He'll see the fan oscillating back and forth and the Medicaid statements flittering on the corkboard. He'll see the previous day's newspaper folded open to the crossword and notice the ink on the tip of his moeder's Bic has coagulated. He'll usually skim the ACROSS clues for easy ones, ones she might've missed. If the throb of exhaustion isn't too irrepressible, he'll skim the DOWNS, too.

He'll usually look in the living room and see his moeder on the couch, fetal. And that position will make her seem young, maybe the age of when she would've cozied with *her* moeder. He'll think, *Why didn't they take more pictures back then?* And, he'll answer himself: *Because taking a picture was an ordeal—complicated, expensive, reserved for special occasions.* He'll go into his bedroom and collapse, aslant—it usually looks like he's giving his mattress an embrace. And he'll sleep—hard.

And it *was* like that—the usual sequence was in place—but only until he peeked into the kitchen. He didn't see the typical still life. He saw his moeder collapsed on the linoleum floor, close to the pantry where she stores the nebulizer. Her afghan was partially spread over her, so she looked less like a body and more like an amorphous blob. He went to her, leaned over her, and then dropped to his knees.

Her face was slack, like sleeping, and he listened and looked for breathing. Her chest didn't seem to heave, but he couldn't rightly tell with her lungs buried so deeply beneath the afghan, her muumuu, and her flesh. Exley pressed two fingers to her neck—first in one spot, then another—but he couldn't find a pulse or couldn't figure out how to properly check for one. His mind was steel wool being pulled apart.

9-1-1. He jumped up and grabbed the telephone off the wall. The ringing angered him. *Why would the emergency number ring at all? Shouldn't a hand be on the receiver, picking up even before a vibration of sound was felt?* All the 9-1-1 calls they'd made prior to this one whooshed through his thoughts. The calls they made to report harassment, and trespassing, and mischief in the night. The unresponsive Mahwah Police Department: they never even made an effort. *What's your emergency?*

Exley stated all the words that needed to be said: *my ma, kitchen floor, unconscious, not breathing, found her, DeGroat Drive, Stag Hill.*

Hanging up the phone, he felt listless and alone. He didn't know if it was just the standard tone of the dispatcher or her not caring, but she did little to comfort him. Would a medical emergency—rather than a complaint about paintballs pelting their windows—elicit the proper response? All she'd said was they'd send an ambulance immediately. *Had she even said "immediately"?* He replayed the conversation in his head, standing several steps back from his moeder's body. That made him feel like a bad son. He should be closer, he thought. He should be hugging her and kissing her and telling her how much he loves her. He shouldn't be thinking. He thought about how he shouldn't be thinking. Emotion should take over. Adrenaline. Hysteria. He tried to summon the appropriate reaction, but the more he thought about what that might be, the worse he felt.

Standing alone in the kitchen. But he wasn't. He had to remind himself that his moeder's body—even in the state it was—was still present, still with him. He hovered over her and—as he used to do when he was young, attempting to rile her from a deep sleep—repeated: *Ma Ma Ma Ma Ma Ma Ma Ma Ma Ma Ma.* And doing that made him feel young, immature though. Like it was silly to do that. So he backed away, crinkling his face together, especially around the eyes, because he wanted to conjure tears. That would be an appropriate reaction. Tears for the paramedics to see. Wailing. He could wail. He could demonstrate panic.

The wait was surreal. The stillness begged for a disruption— the wail of a siren, the slice of blue and red lights. Everything, everything was so still—the room, him, her body. What else could he be doing to accelerate time, to preserve life? He considered: *Should I turn her over, thump her chest? Should I put my mouth to hers and exhale all I've got in my lungs? Should I pray?* He fidgeted, and then he staggered down the hall to the bathroom.

Exley lifted the lid on the toilet bowl only to see shredded wisps of white with some markings of brown: still clogged. All his coat hanger poking and puggling had been for naught. He could smell the honeysweet odor of the Drano, the gel coating the pipe interior. He shut the lid again, forgetting he had to piss. Exley braced the sides of the sink and stared at himself in the vanity mirror. There it was again: his skull.

He couldn't wait. The empty promise of the 9-1-1 dispatcher— that ambulance might never arrive. He picked up the phone and dialed Zike's number. All the while, his moeder's body (*Yes, yes,* he reminded himself: *that is still a body*) rested in its heap. Elsie answered, her voice husky and slumberous.

"Exley? Is that you?"

"That's right—it's me," he said. His voice was calm but only in an unnatural, stilted way. "Where's Zike?"

"He's sleeping."

An image of Elsie asleep on the couch came to him. Meanwhile, Zike in the bedroom, alone with his carbuncles and pus and funk under loose linens, untouched.

"Ma is unconscious on the kitchen floor."

"Oh my God—*what?*"

"I came in, and she was like that," Exley said. "Like that," he repeated, looking over his shoulder at her.

"What are you doing, Exley?" She was accusing him. "Don't call us! Call 9-1-1!"

"I did!" he shouted, and the volume of his voice shattered the stillness of the scene. "I'm calling you guys because who knows when the ambulance will show."

"Okay," Elsie said. "Okay, okay." Her voice drifted, maybe saying something to Zike in the other room. "What can we do? What do you need us to do?"

"I think I need to get her to the hospital myself. I need to get her in the car."

"You want us to meet you there?" she asked. "What hospital are you taking her?"

"I need you here," Ex said. "How'm I gonna get her in the car?"

"Okay," Elsie said, "I'm coming, I'm coming. Stay calm."

When Exley heard *coming*, he hung up the phone.

Exley was active now—he could feel his heartbeat, the sweat sting of his armpits. Everything in the kitchen had a swirling sensation. He lifted one of his moeder's arms and felt the weight of her. *How?* How was he going to move her? He'd heard stories of people raising wrecked cars overhead and barreling through doors to rescue children from infernos, so why couldn't he lift his moeder's body onto his shoulders? It seemed like such a simple act.

Thinking ahead, he ran outside to move the Escort closer to the house. He'd move it right next to the stairs, as close as could be. But he forgot to grab the keys and had to double back. As he ran down the porch steps he saw Val across the lot. She was standing at the bottom of her steps, and he detected a shift in her shoulders and knees, like she was taking a step forward. The baggy t-shirt and sweatpants that were her pajamas sagged off her. Unlike the other times they had crossed paths at this hour, she didn't slouch back into her home. She seemed alert and willing.

"Help me?" Exley asked.

Val didn't verbalize an answer. She didn't nod or gesture in any way. But she stepped forward and hustled over to where Exley stood.

"Wait here," he said.

Exley quickly reversed the car to the steps, riding up the bottom one and splitting the wood. He heard it snap. Dirt clouds emerged in a funnel shape from the back tires and looked like shadows against the black night. He jumped out of the car and ran back in the house. Val was already in the kitchen, lifting Hannah. She had her hooked under the arms. Exley saw his moeder's face straight on—her jowls drooped and there was no arch to her eyebrows.

"I found her like this," Exley said, gathering up other parts of his moeder's body. "She was like this, on the floor, when I got home." Val didn't acknowledge what he was saying, she only began to heft Hannah's body toward the hallway.

"Lift there," she instructed, not to Exley but to Rhetta Galindez. Exley hadn't even seen her come in. "Bend your knees for leverage," Val told her. "It's like dead weight." Intoning the word *dead* weakened Exley's muscles.

"I've got it," Rhetta said. "Don't worry—I've got it. I've got her."

Together, they carried Hannah DeGroat's body out to the car. Val was effective in cushioning Hannah's bobbling head with her mitten-like hands so that it wouldn't bang the doorjambs of the Escort.

"Do you want me to come?" Val asked Exley as he put the key into the ignition. The dinging from the dashboard that signaled the still-open driver's side door was incessant. It disrupted and made dissonant the music of the crickets and the chorus frogs.

"That's okay," Exley said.

"We'll come," Rhetta asserted.

"No," Exley said. "Really, I'm good. Elsie is going to meet me."

"Where are you gonna take her?" Val asked.

"Good Samaritan?"

"Okay." Val grabbed Rhetta by the wrist, letting her know she shouldn't insist on going along. "Be safe," she told Exley.

Be safe stayed in his mind. It was a mantra to repeat, but it was too short. Those two syllables only caused him to speed faster down Stag Hill Road. The darkness of the night had given a bit. Closer to morning now, blacks turned to blues and appeared almost bioluminescent. The surface of Silver Lake shimmered the same as it did under the moon, reflecting distorted images that couldn't be deciphered from a moving car. And everything in the wilderness around him oozed and dripped. Viscous—like the Drano gel he emptied into the toilet bowl so many hours ago. *How many hours—two, three, four?* The clock on the dashboard read 4:12, but that time was unreliable from a weak car battery and Exley's neglect in keeping up with Daylight Savings. The leaves of the forest trees coalesced and dripped to perfect little points. Rock edges and boulders were blunted and softened into loops like lariats.

Exley regretted not allowing Val or Rhetta or both to come along. He looked between the driver and passenger seats, and— above the lid of the console—he could see the mass of his moeder, her muumuu bunched at her waist, revealing her beige underwear. Her thigh jiggled as he crossed a portion of unpaved road. Her body shifted on the turns and bounced as he negotiated the deep ruts. Val could've stabilized her. Rhetta could've patted his hand on the steering wheel. She could've said something, like, *Almost there, youngblood. Almost there.*

His arm hung out the window, and he rapped his knuckles on the door exterior. He squinted through the thickets as he neared the location of the abandoned gristmill. He looked for the giant askew waterwheel. It wasn't just where his cuz had camped out. When he was a kid, it was nothing less than a legendary castle.

Two rectangle headlights flashed in his rearview mirror. His first thought, as always, was trouble. But then he thought maybe Rhetta had defied Val and had decided to follow. The car honked its horn three times in quick succession, holding on the last honk and disturbing the tranquility of the hour. It sounded like so many former cars, cars full of teenagers in hot pursuit of a remote neighborhood. Honking for nothing other than to demonstrate a lack of humility, or humanity. Exley pulled over to the shoulder, and the following car did as well, spotlighting him with the highbeams until the driver clicked them off. It wasn't Rhetta running toward him, though. It was Elsie.

As she approached, Elsie looked, not at Exley, but at Hannah's body in the backseat.

"Christ," she said and cupped her hand over her mouth. "Let me in."

"Come around," Exley said, reaching across the passenger's seat to open the door.

Exley watched Elsie mutter to herself as she walked in front of the car. His headlights blanched her small body. She nervously spun her wedding ring in place on her finger.

"How is she?" she asked, plopping down into the seat. But she shouted, "Drive, drive, *drive*," before Exley could answer. Elsie hit the domelight as Exley pulled off the shoulder and continued down the road. His ears popped at a steep switchback.

"Was she coughing much in the night?"

"Not any more than usual."

"Ambulance never came?" She reached into the backseat and placed her hand on Hannah's shoulder.

"I couldn't wait," Exley said. "I didn't want to chance it."

Elsie hoisted her body and bent her twig-like legs underneath her butt. "You did the right thing."

Exley resented her praise. He resented it because that's not what he needed. For her to think he needed to hear words like that meant she must think he was weak, desperate for approval or recognition. It meant she would never see him as anything but a helpless child.

They emerged from the woods and whizzed by the industrial park. Bulldozers and excavators were lined up next to a pile of gravel, awaiting the start of the workday. Another, larger pile was nearby: the remnants of a building foundation—cinderblocks with bent rods of rebar violently angling every which way.

Highway patrolmen hid in recessed areas off 287 with boxy radar guns pointed at oncoming traffic. Exley knew all the locations, and he also knew it was too early for them to be there. Still, he fantasized about an encounter. He thought about the flashing lights, being pulled over and asked for his license and registration. And he rehearsed what he'd say and how he'd say it. Like speeding with a woman in labor, shuttling an unresponsive person to the hospital meant traffic laws didn't apply. It would allow for him to speak to a cop in a way he'd always wanted to. In a way that nobody besides Lenny Van Dunk had the guts to. He accelerated in the left lane.

Elsie pointed a bony finger at the windshield. Exley followed the motion from the soft skin under her chin, to the cilia on her wrist, to her flawless, off-white nail. There was a mound of roadkill cozied to the Jersey barrier, a deer with its belly flapped open to expose its squished organs. Exley figured that was what Elsie was pointing at. And then there was an insuck of breath—gravelly and hoarse—and a sputter and hacking cough. Exley's hands stayed gripped to the steering wheel, but his torso spun to look into the backseat. His moeder suffered back to consciousness, her face straining and each desperate cough barely finding its way out of her lungs. The neckline of her muumuu had been stretched and hung low on her chest, almost to a nipple. Elsie climbed over the console, lithe and solicitous. She used her body to prop Hannah's upright. Hannah's eyes opened and landed on her son's form. Exley saw the wakefulness in her eyes but knew she wasn't seeing him.

"Keep driving!" Elsie shouted at Exley, her hand flat against the cleft at the bottom of Hannah's neck.

30

EXLEY SLEPT LIKE A STARCHED SUIT in a deep, vinyl chair for the next however many hours. A recording of a woman's voice played over the hospital intercom at 8AM: the recitation of a prayer. As he rested in a shallow sleep, drifting in and out of nightmarish visions and a slideshow of Elsie poses that made him hard against his own thigh, he acknowledged the tinny prayer, and it seemed to go on repeatedly. They were praying the rosary.

His body was stiff when a nurse came into the waiting area and told him he could see his moeder. He expected his joints to audibly creak as he stepped, but instead they just ached. His palms were sweaty, and his face was similarly filmed. When he wiped his forehead, a glistening smear remained on the back of his hand. He was oily—like Zike in the cauldron pool. Elsie had left hours earlier with the promise of returning soon, with Roy Rogers and his big brother. *I'm good*, Exley told her drowsily. *Take your time. No rush coming back.* But now, steps from seeing his moeder in a state, he really wanted a western platter and company.

She was reclined—gowned and tubed and outfitted with

all the necessary breathing apparatuses—he expected all that. He expected her to be bedraggled and starved and discolored. Expected a chaotic spirit of gas and no sign of a solidified bodily form. She was all that. But what he didn't expect was a restive and angry patient, unmanageable even. The nurse grabbed a tan pitcher of ice water to refill and raised her eyebrows at Exley.

"She's no better," Hannah said—not to Exley, not to anyone.

"Ma." Exley sat half on the bed, mindful of the coils and loops falling and following from the IV trolley. "How are you, Ma? No better than what?" His voice was unnaturally subdued, somewhere between babytalk and church manners.

"The doctors," Hannah said, her voice scratchy.

"What happened to your head?" he asked. A purple bulb protruded from beneath her hairline, a bump speckled with bruising.

"She must've gotten that from the fall," the nurse said as she set down the pitcher.

"*Must've gotten that from the fall,*" Hannah mocked.

"Ma," Exley said, his ordinary voice returning. He turned to the nurse, shaking his head apologetically. "I didn't notice it when I brought her in."

"Maybe it hadn't appeared yet," the nurse said.

"Maybe." Exley moved in to touch it. Hannah jerked.

"Try not to move, ma'am."

"I'll do what I please, thank you."

The nurse raised her eyebrows again and left the room.

"How are you feeling?" Exley asked her. "What did the doctors say?"

"*What did the doctors say?* The doctors said what they always say."

Exley stood up and adjusted himself. His skin felt so filthy. He wanted to pour the pitcher of ice water over his head. He didn't sit back down.

"That doesn't make sense, Ma. 'What they always say'—what does that even mean? Why did you pass out last night?"

Hannah put her hands at her sides and ever so slightly lifted herself from the hospital bed. She moved the tubes on her lap to her legs and back to her lap. He'd seen her do these same movements before—the endless moving of crochet hooks and unspooled yarn and her incomplete afghan.

"Ma?"

"All I remember is waking up, heading to the kitchen for a treatment, and that's it."

"That's it?"

"Well I was coughing hard."

"Harder than usual?"

"Hard as always, Exley. You didn't hear it?"

"I was out. Walking," he said. "I found you on the floor, y'know. I thought you were gone."

"Yea-up, well," she looked off at the curtain partition in the windowless room. "Thank you for getting help. That was smart of you to call Elsie."

"Elsie only got there after I'd moved you to the car. Val Mann and Rhetta Galindez got you in the car."

"Really?" she said. The coughing started up again. Hannah seemed to be communicating to Exley through her eyes, but he had no idea what the message was. The nurse poked her head back in the room and said, "Less talking."

Once the coughing fit subsided, Hannah patted the mattress and Exley sat.

"They should be coming back soon—," Ex said. "Elsie and Zike."

Hannah nodded.

"I need you to help with something else, Exley."

"But, Ma," he interrupted. "What did the doctors say?"

"Lungs, Exley. It's always lungs. My lungs are shot. Now listen…" She spoke softly but deliberately. One word was communicated at a time. "I need you to fetch the ledger for me. It's in the pantry same as the nebulizer. I've got it wrapped in baking parchment—those pages have gotten so brittle this summer, the way the sun just slices through the kitchen window. It hits right on my things."

"I'm not doing that, Ma."

"You are, Exley. I'm asking for your help."

"The death ledger?"

"You know I've never called it that. That's all you and your brother."

"Call it that or not, Ma, everybody knows what it is—what

its purpose is. Did the doctors tell you anything?" He was trying not to say *dying*.

"No, they haven't said much of anything."

"Then you've got no reason to think that way—it's extreme. They would know if something was seriously wrong—wrong on that level."

"I *know*, Exley," she said solemnly. "I know. They don't know me like I know me. I've been living in this body all these years. Just as you've been living in yours. Just as your brother lives in his. Doctors only know as much as their books tell them. You know that. I've taught you enough for you to know that."

31

Unky Orrin was welding when Exley went looking for him later that afternoon. Exley didn't find him in the yard and, exhausted as he was, resented having to walk back to the front of the cabin. Orrin, as it turned out, had his gear dangerously hooked up in the living room of his hovel. Exley entered with the pack of diabetic tube socks under his arm. Orrin was in the middle of a project and was about to attach a steel cylinder to the base metal. Exley, again, couldn't discern what it was yet. Orrin held an electrode in his strong hand and secured it into his screw holder. He lowered his mask with a nod of his head.

"Gimme a minute," he said, his voice muffled behind the visor of his mask. "I'm just finishing this up."

Exley chafed at having to wait—the piece was nowhere near completion, clearly, and he wanted his uncle to somehow intuit he was arriving with bad news.

Sparks flew and Exley backed away, receding into the kitchen area. He tossed the tube socks onto the cruddy floral-printed couch and watched Orrin prop his rod pinky-to-thumb and roll his wrist—it was a graceful, even artful, motion. The crackle and spit that sounded as Orrin carried the bead along the joint, pushing the puddle, was mesmerizing. His weld pool was imperfect, but it wasn't in Orrin's personality to worry about impurities—he welcomed them the same he would a waifish beauty or a stray hound that happened into his yard.

Exley watched his uncle work. Orrin seemed to have the luxury of obliviousness, never involved or attached enough to be affected. He was only immersed in his work, his art. And Exley envied that. He knew he wouldn't be allowed to shoot baskets forevermore. He envied Orrin's freedoms—from beard growth to joblessness to handicraft.

The welding equipment obscured the usual furnishings: it was a takeover. A tube of electrodes coated with lime flux leaned against the arm of the couch. There was an acetylene tank with blackened brass fittings standing beside an argon and carbon dioxide tank of shielding gas. Stretched out on a bath towel like chef's knives on an unrolled carry pouch were a flint, tin snips, and C-clamps. The kerosene heater altar was tainted with metal burrs.

Orrin had a copper-plated ground clamp pinched onto the chamfered edge of his worktable, which was, before today, his kitchen table. He had dragged it into the living room, nicking plaster from the doorframe in the process. He had a box fan on the floor inside the door for ventilation, but it wasn't turned on.

A piece of sheet metal pocked with rosette welds was under his feet like a mat, and wire wheels for grinding off spatter BBs and slag rested on fiberglass and felt blankets unfolded like throws on the back of the couch.

Ex recognized the cylinder Unky Orrin was welding was meant to resemble a stovepipe hat. Orrin stepped back, admired his work, and unplugged his portable high freq TIG from the wall outlet. Methodically, he slouched in his folding chair, unsnapped his cowhide apron, and slid off his goatskin leather gloves. Ashen white splotches covered his brown complexion, the skin-peel of a flash burn.

"Did I ever tell you about tensile strength?"

"No," Exley answered. "And don't."

"You want that MIG?" Orrin kicked a different welding machine that was next to the couch. "I'm gonna use it to tack weld some steel boxes in place, but then I'm done with it. Gone." He waved the holder clamp around loosely, as if to tantalize Exley with the offer. He poked the nozzle at the air in front of him. "Got some extra filler rods, too—all yours."

Exley shook his head *no* and asked, "Why are you doing this inside?"

"There was a downpour earlier. You missed it?"

"I did…"

"I didn't want to stop working. Was in a rhythm, y'know, hitting on all cylinders and whatnot. So I moved everything in here."

"You got a fire extinguisher in here?"

Orrin groaned.

"Doesn't seem safe, Unky."

"What's *safe*?"

Orrin coughed and hocked up a glob of mucus. He spat it into a whiskey glass and set it back on the floor.

"Inhalation of fumes aren't gonna help that," Exley said. "Why don't you run that fan?"

"The white noise—" Orrin trembled his hand in front of his face. "It disturbs my process."

Exley cleared a space for himself on the couch. He pinched one of Orrin's Pall Malls and tamped it against his thigh.

"What're you doing here anyway?" Orrin asked. "You look like shit shat out."

"Ma's in the hospital."

Unky Orrin scooted his chair back at Ex's statement. It was a goofy movement and made Exley regret speaking as bluntly as he had.

"What happened?" Orrin asked, genuine in his concern.

Exley didn't want to tell it again, but that's why he had come here—for the talking. He couldn't go to Gussie with it, not with Meal so sick. Zike and Elsie would be making their way to Good Samaritan to do their shift at Hannah's bedside, to deal with her attitude—good luck with that. Sue, sure, but he felt the pull of blood. He was drawn to Unky Orrin's cabin. He sided with his moeder on plenty, but on Orrin, he felt she had it wrong.

"I was out, walking, and got back home and found her on the kitchen floor."

"Hurt?"

"Out. Unconscious."

"You were out walking?" Orrin asked with his lip curled. His gums were diseased, discolored like a mutt's.

"Yea-up. I do that. You know that."

"I know, I know, I know," Orrin said as he shook his head, a confused look on his face. "What time was this—that you found her like that?"

"I don't know, late—two or three in the morning," Ex estimated. "Four maybe. It's all been so surreal. What's the exact time matter?"

"Well I was out and about myself last night." Orrin got up and began to pace, counting hours off on his fingers. "I might've been near you. Could've helped you."

"Don't beat yourself up. I did fine."

"I didn't hear any ambulances barreling through here last night."

"That shocks you?"

"You called 9-1-1, didn't you?"

"I did," Ex said, whiny. "Lot of good it did me, though."

"So what'd you do?"

"What do you think I did, Unky?"

"Well, fuck's sake, youngblood!—I don't know why you can't tell me the full details from beginning to end. Why you're giving this slow drip of information. Just lay it all out there, huh? This is my sister-in-law we're talking about." Orrin looked mad, what with the skin-peel on his forearms and still wearing the welder's mask. He pointed at the ceiling with both hands, looking like he was reprimanding gods.

"I got home," Exley explained. "She was on the kitchen floor, unconscious or knocked out or whatever. She'd been coughing. It was her lungs. She couldn't get air, I guess. So she collapsed. That's how I found her. Looked like she was heading to do a nebulizer treatment."

"Okay, alright," Orrin nodded and rubbed his hands together. "Okay, that's more like it. That's more like it."

"Can I finish?"

"Finish—go 'head. Finish." Unky Orrin returned to the folding chair, crossed one leg over the other knee, and leaned forward. He bit his dirty nails.

"I called 9-1-1, assumed they wouldn't get there fast enough— or at all, and so knew I had to get her to the ER myself."

"How'd you manage to lift her?"

"No, *listen*," Exley said, enjoying telling the story now. Orrin's eagerness to hear it made Exley feel as though he was in possession of something precious and powerful. "I pulled the car up close to the house—right up to the steps. And, out of nowhere, Val was there, and then Rhetta, too. And they helped me get Ma into the Escort. And I got her to Good Samaritan quick as hell."

"Wait—hold on now." Orrin blew out. "Val helped you? Val Mann?"

"She was out on her porch steps like she do, and I guess she figured something wasn't right with me. She probably picked up on my panic."

"Val Mann," Orrin repeated. He blew out again and inadvertently whistled.

"Like I said, Rhetta came out, too."

"So is your ma alright? What they say?"

"She's awake, conscious. I didn't talk to any doctors. All she told me was that it's her lungs. She's been going on doctor visits a lot lately—Elsie's been bringing her. She don't tell me nothing about it, though. I just assumed it was whatever. She told me *lungs* this morning. *Lungs.* Whatever that means. She's thinking the worst, of course. Wanted me to fetch her the death ledger so she could fill in her own name from a hospital bed. I told her to forget about that—I'm not doing it." Orrin was quiet, piecing together everything Exley was saying. "If she's awake, though, I don't think it can be that bad, right?"

"How long she lose consciousness?"

Exley tried to calculate in his head, but he had nothing to go on. "I don't know," he said. "Not long, I don't think. She woke up in the car on the ride to the hospital. She was super fucking disoriented."

Unky Orrin stood up again and stared at the altar on the kerosene heater. He might've been looking at the pale corydalis, which was wilting and browning at the petal edges.

"Maybe I should go visit her?" Orrin said, still staring at the altar. "What you think?"

"*Shit*—," Exley said, bewildered. "I don't know."

"How serious we talking?"

"I told you what I know, what I think. She's awake now. I think she'll be alright."

"She breathing on her own?"

"I guess?"

Orrin broke his focus on the altar. He looked at Exley, and the visor on his welder's mask caught the afternoon sun.

"Damn, youngblood. You need to ask doctors questions— you need to press them. You don't know that?"

"What the fuck, Unky?" Exley said. "I do now. *Alright?* Next time I'm there, I'll press." Exley pulled on the cigarette and blew the smoke out, but there was nothing relaxing about it. His leg jittered and the springs in the floral-printed couch squeaked. "Y'know what? I *don't* think you should go visit. I think that's a bad idea, if I'm being honest."

"Why you say that now?"

"I don't know if you noticed, but my moeder's not too fond of you."

"You can check the sarcasm, nephew. I know she's not *fond of me*, as you put it. But she still family. That's still my brother's wife."

"You know she hates that I come here?"

"I could've figured," Orrin said. He coughed and hocked up something thick and bitter in his mouth. His cheeks bulged as he scrambled around trying to find a whiskey glass in which to spit it.

"Why is that? Why does she hate you so much?"

Orrin found a whiskey glass behind the MIG welder. He plopped the glob of spit into it, and a viscous string of saliva trailed behind, still stuck to the tip of his tongue. He wiped his mouth and swirled the whiskey glass as if it were a wine.

"She's got some good reasons, she does," Orrin admitted.

"I don't know. She goes at you hard anytime even a whiff of you comes up."

"Well, see…" he struggled. "Your ma's…This is hard for me to talk about. Hard for me to talk about to *you*."

"Now I'm expecting something, Unky," Exley said. "Just speak."

"Alright, well," Orrin started, "it goes back to your da's passing." Exley's face changed, went empty. He leaned back on the couch and his shoulders shrunk inward. "You were too young at the time. *What were you?* You were seven, right?" Exley nodded. "That's young for all that, too young. It is." Orrin sat down on the couch beside his nephew, on the middle cushion. They both looked forward, though Orrin tucked his chin near his right shoulder when asking a question. "What do you remember about Zike at the time?"

"I don't know. Not much, I guess."

"Let's just say your brother was wayward."

"What you mean?"

"*Wayward*—he was fucking up. He wouldn't listen to a damn thing Hanny told him. Norval neither. Well, it was really only your ma, I guess. Your da tried not to get too involved. He was more of the mind that Zike would do better in a year or two. I gotta say I agreed with that. But your ma was all over Zike. She rode him hard. Anyway, when your da passed—what do you remember about that?"

Exley bit his bottom lip.

"Some. Not much. I remember my ma picking the plastic off the telephone cord in the kitchen. She was waiting for someone to call, and she was making a lot of calls herself. She picked through the plastic and got to the wires."

"Okay, okay," Orrin said. "Well, the thing is, there was a hell of a lot more to it than that. There was a lot of drama amongst the family in the days that followed." Orrin tucked his chin to his shoulder. Exley could see the white of his uncle's eye. "I found him. I found your da the day before. Saturday, right? And then I screwed everything up. I went and told your brother about the whereabouts. I actually took him there the following day, that Sunday."

Outside the window, Exley saw the black-knot fungus on the chokecherry tree. It was like tar, like petrified feces. Nature was scatological—it was all shit and piss and people hiked through it lost in wonder, like fools. The galls didn't look the same as when he'd noticed them earlier in the summer. They were green and soft then—a velvety growth. Now the galls had blackened and hardened, and the branches the galls seized upon were crippled, gone arthritic. The leaves of those branches were wilted, and, soon, they'd die.

Orrin clenched his teeth.

"I suppose, all these years, your ma has been protecting you from me, from knowing I did what I did. Hell, that's a favor she did for me, in that case. It explains why you still talk with me, visit me. See, that's the crux of it. That's why your ma hates me so much, for telling your brother about your da. For sending him up there like a lamb to the slaughter. That's a major part of it."

"Why did you?" Exley asked, his eyes fixed on the black-knot.

"I talked to your da earlier that day—not Sunday, but Saturday—the day he did it. And he had gone on about Zike and how rough it'd been lately, what a hard time he'd been giving your parents. And so I guess I sort of thought I could set Zike straight. If I could put that responsibility on him, he'd get in line. Of course it didn't work out that way. The opposite actually.

"And then, when this all came out—that I'd talked to Norv earlier that day, found him first and all—your ma got on me about that. That I'd talked to him, had a hunch something was wrong, and didn't do anything about it. Let me tell you, though. I can't tell you the number of times I've asked myself why I scrapped at Cannon Mine instead of Peters that day. Hanny started screaming at me about how I let Norv go through with it. She called me an accomplice. *Accomplice! Accomplice!* She kept shouting that, crying the whole time, of course. It was a mess."

"Stupid," Exley mumbled. "That was stupid. Of you. To try to arrange it like that. To want it to be Zike to deal with it, to see it."

"I know," Orrin said. "And there's more, too. In hindsight, I know. I know I shouldn't have handled it how I did. I wasn't thinking. Or I *was* thinking, and I was certain I was doing the right things."

"What more is there?" Ex asked.

"Right. Well. Another reason she has to hate me is for taking the gun."

"What gun?" As soon as Exley asked the question, the answer—clear and obvious as it was—came to him, and he wished he could withdraw the question, suck it back up into his mouth and swallow. He realized the design of his question. He knew what Orrin would have to say.

"The handgun your da did himself with."

The weight of the gall on the branch of the chokecherry tree seemed immense. The branch would bow soon, so soon—any second now—and snap.

"I took the weapon, the handgun," Orrin continued, "not for any, for any…I took it—I just wanted a remembrance. And I sure as hell didn't want some kid playing at the mine and picking it up. Hanny thought—your ma thought—she thought I made a mockery of Norv by doing that, made light of it, the situation. And the situation was fucked—'scuse my language. I seen your da there, in the mine—all I seen was offal. She accused me of trying to keep it a secret, trying to cover up what I knew, how me and him had talked that day before he went off to do it. She said by going to get Zike—and, right, I didn't find your brother until the next day—she said I left your da there to rot. And, I admit, I was stupid in the moment—not thinking right, not wording right. I told her 'I scrap' when she asked why I took the handgun. And you know that set her off, rightly. She said I was scum, said 'Pawn it then! Pawn it, you scum!'

"I just wanted a remembrance, youngblood. I wanted something to remember my brother by. You hear me?" Orrin shifted on the couch, turning his body to Exley, looking at him directly for the first time since he'd sat down. The lower lids of his eyes were glistening, and Exley saw that.

"You're old enough now—and you're getting harder," Orrin said. "Before you're stone, it's only right you got told the truth of it. This is like we talked about last time. This is what I was trying to get at. This is why you should care about your people, us. Your da couldn't see it. But he felt it. We'd talked, and I *know* he felt it. He felt it so deep that he whilomed himself over it. Y'know, your da was feeling sick himself around that time."

"I don't get it," Ex said.

"What's not to get?"

"I just don't understand how it's so major. For one, I've never known you to get hung up on anything. But on this, you are." Exley calculated on his fingers. "You took a gun. Okay. And you showed Zike what nobody would want to see, but still."

"You're right. You know, for the most part, I'm guiltless. Guilt's a crock. I believe that. But on this—on this, I lost my family over it. *All of it.* In one rude gesture. All except you, y'see?"

"But for Ma to disown you over it? Doesn't seem fair."

"It's fair," Orrin said. "It's appropriate. This is family we're talking about, betrayal. I was wrong. And, on this, I'm on the side of guilt."

Unky Orrin coughed into his fist and cleared his throat. He got up and went into the kitchen and was out of sight. Dishes rattled as he slammed a cabinet door, and Exley could hear him spit into the sink and run the water.

"I lost my job," Exley said as Orrin reentered. The visor on the welder's mask fell forward, so Orrin pushed it back up. There were beads of water in his beard and his eyes were bloodshot.

"Lost your job?" Orrin asked. "You mean you got fired?"

"Yea-up," Ex said. "Terminated."

"How does somebody get fired from Rite Aid?"

"CVS," Ex corrected. "How do you think?" Exley grabbed the pack of diabetic tube socks from under his butt. His sitting had squeezed them in between the couch cushions. He tossed them at Orrin who failed to catch them but picked them up off the floor. "Fired for stealing socks for you!"

"Oh, don't give me that now. That's on you."

"Who was I stealing for? Who begged me for socks?"

"You just let them accuse you and cut you loose?"

"They knew what I had taken."

"They have proof?"

"What proof? They knew the exact item I stole—*those!*" Exley pointed at the socks.

"Oh you did yourself in, youngblood. You let them get you."

"Whatever," Exley sneered.

"Now listen here. Ain't nobody can talk to you or me—or any of us, for that matter—about stealing. This is something I know a bit about, so listen." Orrin reassumed his position in the folding chair and gesticulated in a way that resembled a psychotic break. "I used to steal chickens."

"*Chickens.*"

"Chickens—yes, chickens. Listen now. We all used to scavenge the deepest, hellish levels of the mines—it wasn't just me. Everybody, before you were born, used to try to get a piece of the pie. We all dug for copper," Orrin said, tapping the wrist of his weak hand where he wore a twined copper wire to beat back the rheumatism. "We dug for that and tons else—anything that you could squeeze value from. That's stealing, ain't it?"

Exley shrugged, apathetically.

"That's stealing. But that don't automatically mean it's wrong. Who put it there? Who put all that metal and copper there for the taking? No one can talk righteously is what I'm saying, nephew. Not nobody."

"Did I say I felt bad about it? I don't. Trust me."

"You got caught nimming. It's nothing. They think that merchandise is sacred," Orrin went on. "What's sacred? Don't talk to me about sacred either. Our shrines are cemeteries. How's that for sacred? You got caught. Don't get hung up on it, though. You'll find some other crumby job soon as you go looking for one. Be more careful when you steal from that place."

"Anyway," Exley said, getting up to leave.

"Hold up a sec." Orrin gestured for Exley to sit again. He left the room only to return seconds later with a toolbox. It rattled the way toolboxes do. Orrin set it down on his folding chair and crouched in front of it, his broad back facing Exley and obscuring what he was doing. He pivoted while in the crouching position and presented his nephew with a gun wrapped in a red mechanic rag.

"You're owed this," Unky Orrin said. "I owe it to you. You're the most family to me. And it's more yours than mine, really. The less I have the better."

Exley had held weapons before, but this gun seemed heavier than any of those. He turned it over, examining it—the red mechanic rag was like swaddling clothes. He thought it looked like a cowboy gun, like it would go *pow pow pow*.

"It's a blued Ruger Blackhawk handgun," Orrin said. "And it could jump a deer back five yards—that was always your da's brag about it. Never got more than a grouse with it, though."

Unky Orrin adjusted his pants and snapped his apron back on. He plugged the welder back into the wall and set the polarity. The amperage dial clicked as he adjusted it. He slid on his goatskin leather gloves and filed a rod tip.

"Your da worked acetylene," Orrin told Exley, who was making for the door. "Amateur that he was. He didn't have the hands I have—*the touch*, we used to call it. But he could flicker that acetylene feather when he needed a quick weld done, he could. If he tried to do this," Orrin eyed the steel cylinder piece on the worktable, "he'd end up with arc strikes all over the place. All his welds were porous." Orrin nodded his head and the mask visor fell over his face. "But I miss my brother everyday," he said, muffled. "I miss family."

The electrode ignited, the crackle and spit signaled to Exley it was finally time to leave the cabin. Orrin stopped momentarily to shout, "Your ma will be alright, I think. Hanny's tough." And then he returned to his weld.

Sparks flew at Exley's back as he left.

PART 3

VERSIONS & VARIANTS (CONT'D)

I am a Romopock. I am a Ramapock. I am a Ramapo. I am a Ramapough. I am an aborigine. I am a kidnapper. I am a non-foreigner. I am a gypsy. I am the Wolf, the Turtle, the Deer. I am the RMI. I am clansfolk. I am a lowlife. I am a miney. I am a treasured invention. I am racially polluted. I am a squirrel-eater. I am a horse-thief. I am a car-thief. I am inbred. I am hillfolk. I am a mountain nigger. I am a marginal man. I am a Van Dunk. I am a Von Doonk. I am a Van Donck. I am a Van Donk. I am a De Freese. I am a De Freece. I am a De Vries. I am a de Fries. I am a De Freaze. I am an Emanuel. I am a Mayne. I am a Man. I am a Mann. I am a Galindez. I am a Milligan. I am a Suffern. I am a Conklin. I am a De Groat. I am a De Groot. I am a Degroot. I am a Degrote. I am an exonym. I am an endonym. I am a hippie Indian. I am a yuppie Indian. I am settler Dutch. I am a buffalo nickel. I am a flesheater. I am a black landowner. I am the dispossessed. I am a specimen. I am bad genes. I am torsion in the blood. I am a lazar. I am a degenerate race. I am between two fires.

32

THE POWWOW TOOK PLACE on the last weekend of August. For the first time, it was to be a two-day event by virtue of additional funding from the Cultural Studies program at Ramapo College. In return, students were welcomed and permitted to take notes and record video of the gathering. Some tribe members grumbled about it, others number-crunched, and still others didn't care one way or the other.

Fortunately, there was a break from the humidity. People said what people say as they arrived and greeted each other, remarking on the change in the weather—either how *beautiful* or *gorgeous* the day was, and how *lucky* or *blessed* they were to have it. The clear skies were preferable to cloud coverage, but the open field that was the fairgrounds would heat up something sweaty and musty by late morning. The fairgrounds were still littered with trash from a carnival the County put on two weekends before. Teen volunteers were slow to sweep up.

Tents were pitched and staked, often with hooked rebar. Ropes were double-knotted so that the canvas was pulled taut in case winds picked up in the evening. Vendors tended to their booths, unpacking crates and coolers and carrying out all the necessary preparations. There was already zeppole dough steeping in deep fryers. Columns of kabobs—skewered steak and chicken—were placed across grill racks. A vortex of pink fiber, the makings of cotton candy in the kettle. Roasted corn on the cob with husk handles. The M.C. tinkered with his PA system—the mic was hot and the feedback screeched and echoed across the open space. Everybody on set-up duty collectively groaned.

Other than the specialty junk food provided by vendors, the powwow was a potlatch. Tribe members brought homemade main courses, sides, and desserts, offering them freely. The Head Staff at the Tribal Community Center had done enough research to know it was about communal sharing and atonement, and that the wealthiest were obligated to give the most. Because they didn't have any singular success among them—no corpulent moneymaker who commuted to Manhattan every morning—they didn't press anyone to give more than they could. There was always plenty, and people typically brought Tupperwares with them for leftovers.

Lib had her baby laid out on a picnic blanket behind a row of port-a-johns. She was flanked by propane tanks and a minivan. Two teenagers unloaded aluminum food pans and Sterno cans from the bucket seats inside the sliding door. They politely ignored Lib, who was on her knees wiping the baby's butt with a dry napkin.

"What the hell was your sister eating?" she asked the twins. They didn't hear her. The twins were taking turns throwing rocks at the port-a-johns, and they high-fived each other after every hollow-sounding direct hit. "*Shit!*" Lib said, folding the napkin over. "Her poop is bright green."

She fastened a clean diaper onto the baby and walked with the messed one into a port-a-john. She held the door open with her foot and pumped soap into her hands. A rock pelted the exterior wall. "Stop that!" she shouted at the twins. "Go watch your sister on the blanket. Make sure she don't crawl off."

The twins ran off and flopped onto their bellies next to the baby. Lib preened in the square of mirrored glass glued to the port-a-john wall. She sucked her bottom lip over her teeth and jutted her chin, trying unsuccessfully to pluck a chin hair. She squeaked lipgloss off her front teeth.

"*Boo!*" Zike shouted as Lib let the spring-loaded door flap shut. "What's the word, lady?"

"Zike," Lib said, struggling not to look him up and down. "What's up? How are you?"

"Oh, I am *fantastic*," he said, gripping her elbow in place of a hug. She felt the coolness of his clunky skull rings, and she could smell the booze on his breath. Zike's colostomy bag and scars and open sores were, for the most part, hidden from sight. His long-sleeve Champion sweatshirt and gray sweatpants were so baggy he might as well have been wearing a toga. The blandness of the outfit along with the hood he wore to hide the carbuncles on his neck made a monk of him. His loose and unlaced Lugz boots were the only part of his wardrobe that proved otherwise.

"I'm glad," she said. *His face has changed so much*, she thought. The features had fissured, and the angles had hardened. The contours of skin over bone had petrified. She began to walk away, back to the picnic blanket where her kids were. But Zike followed, keeping pace with the aid of his mini-golf putter cane and despite his bowlegged strut. Dark swaths of sweat spread over his clothes like continents.

"How's your ma doing?" Lib asked.

"She's hanging in there," Zike said. "She's, she's…what's it called?"

"What?"

"Y'know—laying up in bed all day, getting better. Fuck."

"Resting?" Lib tried. "Relaxing?"

"No, no," Zike waved her answers away. "Shut up for a second."

Lib inhaled and looked at her kids. The twins were pretending to eat the baby's toes. Zike was walking so slowly. She wondered why she was being so nice, why she slowed her steps for him.

"What the fuck did the doctor call it?" Zike mused. He snapped, but his fat, enflamed fingertips didn't produce a sound. "*Convalescing!* She's convalescing."

"I don't even know what that means."

"*Uh duh der der*," Zike sputtered. "Read a book sometime, Libby."

"You're a real charmer, Zike. Y'know that?"

"She's supposed to do rehab," Zike continued, "but insurance won't cover it, and she refuses to pay out of pocket."

"Go play," Lib told the twins, making room for herself on the blanket. She sat down, cross-legged, and lifted the baby into the cozy space between her thighs. Zike leaned on his cane, looming over her, a giant.

"Remember when Lenny left the War Dance competition to get a handjob in the woods?" Zike asked. Lib looked up from her baby and scrunched her face at him.

"All those glory days of yours, the tug o'war and all that shit, and that's what you reminisce on?"

"Alright, alright," Zike said. "Miss Maturity over here."

Lib spread and straightened the picnic blanket. The twins had moved on to untightening the valves on the propane tanks.

"I'm just saying, is all," Zike continued, "he got his while he was here."

"I don't want to talk about that," Lib told him. "Not anything like that. *Stop that*—" The twins jumped back and dashed off. "You two wanna blow up the whole powwow?"

Lib walked over to the propane tanks, stooped—still holding the baby on her hip—and secured the valves.

"These two are just as bad as you and Lenny were."

"Maybe so," Zike said, "if by that you mean we had fun."

"That's not what I mean by that." Lib bent her knees and hoisted the baby higher. She was wearing denim cutoff booty shorts and the frayed edges tickled her thighs. She still had a fair amount of baby weight hanging from her tummy, but it didn't bother her. She pushed it out, with pride, as she shifted all her weight onto one leg and tilted her head at Zike.

"You look good," she said.

"Shut the fuck up, Libby."

She grimaced, embarrassed: "I'm just sayin'."

"How many damn kids you plan on having?" Zike asked, pointing at the twins.

"Why?" Lib snapped. "You gonna be their daddy?"

Zike's face did something—crumpled a little. He watched the twins: they were collecting twigs and throwing them into a pile. They had a modest campfire tipi going. Lib saw she was losing him, his mind blanking or flooding.

"Where's Elsie?" she asked.

"Visiting with Ma. She'll be around later."

As MORE VENDORS ARRIVED, THEIR TENTS and tables completed the circumference of the powwow. The circle was roped off with yellow-braided cord. The host drum was off to the side of the entrance. The gateway to the space was three long tree branches twined together at the top—corn stalks running along the branches, too—forming a triangle structure. A halved black barrel, like a bull's eye, was at the center of the circle. It was set between two cinder blocks and was smoking. There was a monitoring well inconveniently dug within this circle, so they positioned haybales to conceal it—just like evergreen sprigs and sprays concealed the new celltower in Rio Vista. It was so no dancers or competitors or even spectators, for that matter, tripped over the obstruction, hurting themselves or damaging it. The EPA, they all quipped, would *not* be happy.

There, beneath one of these tents, was Exley—unhappy as anyone, or so he put off. Actually, though, he wasn't as bothered by sitting at the folding table as he seemed. He was beside Sue— the legs of their folding chairs touched, something like inanimate footsies—and all this foldable furniture was a reminder to him that he could leave whenever he pleased. Nobody was keeping him there, not even his moeder. He wouldn't be so unmannerly as to leave, not with her in the condition she was in, but—if, for some unforeseen reason, he needed to—he would.

Exley's backpack was hanging by its straps off the back of his chair as though his chair were wearing it. In it was the blued Ruger Blackhawk handgun—the hand-me-down, the family heirloom—wrapped in the red mechanic rag in which Unky Orrin had presented it to him but now also in a pair of boxer shorts for added protection. Exley wanted to maintain the condition it was currently in—he didn't want it to scratch or abrade. He was contented to have had the conversation with Unky Orrin, and he understood why his moeder considered him scum. He *was* scum. But so was his da, and it could also be said for most anybody he knew. And the dying yellow grass of the fairgrounds was scum, too, toxic from its top layer to its deepest core. Scum was everything and everyone. And here Exley was at the annual scum powwow. And you couldn't just skim off the scum. The scum was there to stay.

The Grand Entry would begin soon, and old man Cotton staggered—already drunk—toward where Exley and Sue were sitting. He leaned onto the folding table, setting the fingers on each of his hands abnormally wide. *So* wide, something like the spokes on a wheel. He wiped the milk-white saliva from his mouth corners and dabbed the air before his face, readying himself to edify.

"*Powwow*," he said—looking left, looking right, "is from *pau wau*, meaning 'he who dreams.' There now."

Cotton gave two rapid claps and staggered off again.

"Who was that?" Sue asked, a little disconcerted but still giggling.

"Just Cotton."

"Cotton?"

"Cottonmouth," Exley said.

"Friend of yours?"

"I wouldn't go that far."

"But, like, you are related to all these people in some way?"

"Related, like blood? Not necessarily, not really. Family's here, sure, but more friends and neighbors and just people who've been around forever."

"I'm not trying to say…"

"I know," Exley said.

Sue tore a sheet of paper towel off the roll and sopped up the water Cotton had spilled. His oafish hands had knocked over a Dixie cup. The folding table was full of them, though not all of them were full. Ex and Sue had them arranged close together like a honeycomb. On the ground next to their chairs were four or five Poland Spring 24-packs of bottled water. And behind those were two coolers crammed so tight with icebags from Krauszer's that the lids wouldn't close. Exley had removed the cardboard base from one of the water cases and scrawled FREE ICE WATER on it. Sue bent the sign so it could hang over the front of the table without falling.

"Does your mom always give away water here?" Sue asked, wringing out the soaked paper towel.

"Always," Ex answered. "For as long as I remember anyway."

"What's with it?" she asked. "Anything behind it?"

"There's *always* something behind what my moeder does."

"So what is it?"

"It's a story my da told her years ago." Exley reached behind to push the lid shut on one of the coolers, even though—as he already knew—it wouldn't. "My da met a guy, a real Indian." Sue's eyes widened. "You know what I mean, an Indian from the plains or something. He came out this way on some sort of business or something, I don't know. And he told my da about a long, desolate highway in North Dakota—*no*, wait. South Dakota. It was South Dakota. And the highway had nothing on either side of it but sand and rock, sand and rock: endless in every direction.

And every mile or so, there would be a roadside sign—nothing fancy, just a wooden stake and a placard. They advertised FREE ICE WATER. Then another would come, and then another. With slight variations. *Straight ahead* and *Just ahead* and *It's waiting for you*. They had the whole oasis thing going on. And—this guy told my da—if you followed the signs all the way to the destination, sure enough, there was a no frills stand there, a shack, giving out free ice water. Just that simple. So my ma loved that story, so she started giving out free ice water at the powwows."

"That's cool," Sue said, "that your mom's got a reason behind it and all. I bet the guy spinning cotton candy onto a stick doesn't have a story like that."

Sue lifted her hair from her neck and let it fall, the move forcing her to sit up straight—shoulders rolled back and back arched: it got him. Exley thought about her unclothed, naked of everything but her forearm splint, which she was still wearing but as an accessory now. Something unique, like a wallet chain or a nose ring.

Exley chiseled chips of ice off the block with a flat-head screwdriver and dropped them into the Dixie cups. Sue followed his pattern, pouring water into the cups. They did this until all the cups were full.

FLAGS. THE US FLAG. THE STATE OF NEW JERSEY FLAG. The Ramapough Lenape flag: its red, yellow, white, and black spaces, and the turtle splayed at its center, pinched between two dreamcatchers. They were all carried in like pickets during the Grand Entry, and Chief walked in the eagle staff. Chief had been ejected from the bleachers of no fewer than thirty-seven Little League baseball games, and he boasted of the fact. *Those umps are biased against us*, he'd say if somebody asked him about it.

The flags kept Exley's attention even more than the indecipherable shouting of the M.C., even more than the steady beating of the host drum. He stood on his chair and held Sue's hand so she could stand on hers as well—she wanted to see, and a crowd of people in front of their table was blocking her view.

Head Man and Head Woman led the way, and the M.C. announced everyone thereafter. This was only meant to be a tease, a glimpse of what was to come. The dancers circled the fairgrounds—their groups interspersed with veterans in button-covered trucker hats—moving in short, shuffling steps in rhythm with the drum. There were Grass Dancers—not in moccasins, but sneakers—with bells on their ankles, orbiting hula-hoops wrapped in fur. Buckskin Dancers followed the sun, while the next group, War Dancers, went counterclockwise. There was much feather dancing and crow-hopping, and the Fancy Dancers wore belt cuffs and armbands and bustles like windblown roadkill. The Fancy Dancers had the most complicated footwork, and—it was known—moonlighted as breakdancers in local B-boy competitions.

Sue was stirred by the regalia. The tribe was short on tanned hides, but the number of items purchased at A.C. Moore was expansive, an honest-to-goodness spree. They found synthetic substitutes for everything: elk teeth, claws, porcupine quills. Horsehair fringe could be purchased on the internet for pennies. Pigments weren't applied by way of bark and berries and clay, but, for the most part, through Crayola washable paint kits. The quality of the materials did little to diminish the splendor of it, though. Sue's eyes lit up at the bone hairpipe breastplates, the broadcloths and breechcloths, the sashes, shawls, chokers, and rhinestone chains. Bountiful wampum, ribbons, plumes. *Birds of prey*, she thought. Exley wondered what she was thinking, whether she thought she was just watching a show.

"I like it!" she shouted into Exley's ear.

He nodded his head. *Good*, he mouthed. He sat back down and slugged a Dixie cup, biting down on its waxy brim afterwards.

The host drum resonated across the fairgrounds, the thud of it seemingly overhead at all times, ricocheting. The rawhide head was purchased at a slaughterhouse in Elizabeth only days earlier, replacing the old one that had a tear. The Head Staff had to hurry along the assembly of it, but it got done. Tension casings were turned, tightened. Now the Ramapough Wishy-Washy Drum Group sat in a circle around the drum—some with dogwood sticks; others opted just for blanks from Robbie's Music on Route 17. They were cheap, wrapped with electrical or medical tape. The kids—running wild, running amok—got giddy at the vocables the drummers belted out.

Val and Rhetta, increasingly visible since the Hannah episode, were among those sitting at the drum—right up front, not in the second row with the other women. Val momentarily broke her beat to chase off an old geezer who had a beercan in his hand and was getting too damn close to the drum. Desecration of that magnitude wouldn't be tolerated. The other drummers guffawed as Val stomped her feet, menacing the drunk.

THE FIRST DANCE BEGAN. Exley and Sue shouted into each other's ears, remarking on the individual performance of a youngblood who was enrolled in classes at the Passaic County Community College Wanaque campus, the darling of the tribe elders. He was what Zike should've been. Sue parodied a swoon. *Muscles*, she panted. "He's all bulk," Exley told her, crushing an empty Dixie cup. "He probably can't even lift his arms above his head." The kid had a bandolier over each shoulder, yarn drops falling from his hips. The garters had a double-row of sleigh bells that jingled at his every spastic turn. His hair was in two braids, and the rigid plaiting at the tips bounced off his clavicle. So much braided hair at the powwow. People who never wore braids did so at the powwow. Exley thought it looked like endless rope, like a people roped together—an entire people kidnapped, held hostage.

The dancer's arms and legs bent at perfect angles, articulating and moving as a mannequin's would. Sue bobbed her head, taken up by the drumming and the music of the sleigh bells—maybe even the muscles. Sure, Exley conceded, the performance was unrivaled. But it was all for nothing. No cash prizes were offered for the dancing contests. Winners only received comically heaped plates of second helpings of food. It was all like that for Exley—the powwow: it was hollow, empty. He didn't feel a connection the way it seemed Sue, an outsider, did. The powwow had only been established fifteen or so years ago, anyway. Hell, they'd only been recognized as a tribe by the State a couple of years before that. The collectivity of the powwow felt real to Exley, the communal effort. But the dancing and the drumming and the food felt as inauthentic as the synthetic buffalo skull on his moeder's hutch.

LATER IN THE AFTERNOON, a semi-sober Zike and weary Elsie stopped by Exley and Sue's folding table. The lids on the coolers were closing now, the icebags having ripped and the contents having avalanched into the chest. Exley watched Zike hobble toward him, arm-linked with Elsie, his cane divoting the dirt.

To Exley, Zike was different now. He was no longer only the fleshy ghost, slobbering and secreting all over himself. No longer the teenage screwup who bore the responsibility for his stasis. Here was big brother Zike bludgeoned, returning from a battlefield. Unfairly punished by the blunt force trauma of his progenitor's naked corpse. A poisoned well. Exley wasn't sure how, if at all, to put what he'd learned about their da's death to Zike. Unky Orrin had exposed Zike to their da's corpse. It had been exhibited to him. And there was malice in the mix. The revelation of how it all went down was still so fresh for Exley, and maybe Zike would prefer the secret be kept. Maybe Zike had convinced himself to believe Unky Orrin was right in what he'd done. But that was wrong. Orrin *was* wrong. Feeling guilt for what he'd done was appropriate. What he had done *did* matter. It was cold and uncalled for. Zike was only a kid. Exley wanted to have a word, to commiserate, to tell Zike, *Hey, we can share the weight of this. It's as much mine as it is yours. Our da. He's our da. Ours together.* But as he watched Zike approach, shrouded in a sweatsuit sweat-soaked and darkened like a raincloud, he couldn't yet conceptualize having that conversation. Even as brothers, they could only share so much. Zike had seen their da dead in the mine. Exley had not.

"*Howdy howgh*, kids," Zike said in a baritone, allowing his bodyweight to fall against the folding table.

"How's it going over here with you two?" Elsie smiled at Sue. "Business booming?"

"Oh yeah," Sue said, "profits are up, up, *up*."

"Through the roof," Exley deadpanned.

"Well that's gonna ruin Hannah's day then," Elsie said. "You know she likes the profit margins low, nonexistent."

They paused to hear the M.C.'s voice announce the start of the footraces—the 40-yard dash would be first.

"Get going, Ex. That's all you."

"Right. Thanks, Zike."

"What, li'l bro? You're the picture of good health. Look at that knee. Go on, now."

"Yeah, Ex," Sue teased. Ex was embarrassed by her teaming-up with Zike.

"I'll pass."

"C'mon," Zike continued, clanging his mini-golf putter against the legs of the table. "Take a Dixie cup with you. Clutch it to your chest like an amulet. For luck."

"Okay, okay," Elsie said, shifting into protectress mode. "Let Exley be. Zike, you're not as funny as you think you are." Zike failed to get a word in. "Your ma, Ex—she said stay out as late as you want tonight. She doesn't want your good time ruined thinking you've got to get back and take care of her."

"My good time?"

"I'm gonna be going back there later," Elsie continued. "Really. Hang out. If not here, go somewhere else." She smiled at Sue again.

They all turned their attention to the footrace. One of the participant's sneakers came loose and flew off his heel into the air behind him. The crowd roared as the runner stopped mid-stride to pick up his Nike, tuck it into his elbow like a recovered football, and finish the contest with an awkward, uneven gallop. He played to the laughing crowd, spiking his shoe at the finish line before collapsing to the ground.

"Why don't the two of you go off for awhile?" Elsie said. "Me and Zike can man the table."

"That would be awesome," Sue said. "Thank you."

"We're good, we're good," Ex said, trying to stare Sue back into her chair. "Don't worry about it."

"No. Go, dummy." Zike caned Exley across his shoulders, the nape of his neck. "Go be young while you're still alive. Go, go."

Elsie and Zike replaced Sue and Exley at the table. Zike sat uncomfortably at the edge of the seat, legs spread and arms bowed—it was always best if he could manage not to let any parts of his body touch. The irregularities of the pose were softened by the extension of Elsie's hands onto his. His skull-ringed and gnarled hands cupped the grip of his cane, and she cupped her much smaller and smoother hands over that rugged terrain. She leaned over and whispered something to him. He shook his head, but then he smirked. Exley could see it—the smirk climbed the side of Zike's face. It might tear through his cheek and blow his hood back. There was a swelling of warmth, a sunburst—it was a slow explosion in Exley's chest.

Sue held Exley's hand as they wended through the fairgrounds. Their shoulders brushed against older folks, and then they squeezed through a group of raucous kids, none taller than their thighs. The attraction of their bodies, the static of their arm hairs seemed to pull them closer. Her fingers shaped into peg hooks, interlocking with his. They angled their way through the cheering crowd, voices hysterical as another footrace came to its end. Volunteers extended the tug o'war rope, hefting it into place. It thudded with the lifelessness of a knifed snake. The Whistle Man blew his loon-looking whistle over the heads of the drummers sitting at the host drum. Cotton entertained Lib's twins with a pocketful of buffalo nickels. And Exley diverted their path after spotting Unky Orrin up ahead, joyriding on some poor elder's jazzy scooter that he had managed to hijack.

In the interval between the footraces, the M.C. was going on about matriarchy, making jokes about how his wife runs the show. And the further Exley and Sue got from the fairgrounds, the clearer the M.C.'s amplified voice got. It echoed against the mountains. And then, some steps further, they were so far that the voice from the microphone muffled to a hum.

IN THE DARK SHADE OF THE TREES and a big and impressive boulder wall of gneiss, Exley and Sue leaned against each other, their bodies like two boards of knotty pine, gouged in spots, rubbly and bumpy. Sue ran her fingers through Ex's crimped, red hair. *You're like a wild carrot*, she told him, and he, unguarded for once, laughed.

"End of summer," Exley said, his chin resting on the top of her head. A stray hair stood straight up from her part and touched his lip, tickling it.

"I can't believe you have to repeat junior year."

"It doesn't matter."

"It does." She pushed one of her legs in between his, like prying open the teethy slit of a cowrie shell. "I'll miss you in my classes."

"You'll get over it." He was finding it difficult to keep up the act—the dismissiveness, the hardness.

"You won't miss me? Whose gonna hold my books for me?"

"Shut it." Ex pinched the skin behind her arm.

"Fucker."

Sue pushed her body off his. He backed up against the wall of gneiss. She leaned against him again, fitting her body into his backwards this time. Reached behind and wrapped his arms over her shoulders and around her neck as a scarf. She pressed, *pressing.* The din of the Jingle Dancer reached them. The Jingle Dance was about healing. It was about sending sickness elsewhere, skyward. Exley always thought of green-colored germs—microscopic creatures with cartoonish facial expressions—ascending beyond the tree canopy. He didn't know where he had gotten that vision, maybe his ma. But he thought of it then, even with Sue squeezing and smothering.

The Jingle Dancer's dress was the most dazzling of all the dancers—an audible and optical illusion of clinking metal cones. They were patterned in rows around the ankle-length skirt, and they clinked in rhythm with the beating of the host drum. The Jingle Dancer swished a feather fan, brushing back blood and coughs from the audience, from those too weak to attend the powwow, too. Sue spun around, still in Exley's arms, and he stooped to meet her mouth. They used to collect the lids of tobacco cans year-round in anticipation of the jingle dress, but, for some time now, Unky Orrin had been honored to curve his own metal scraps into the cones.

Healing. There was healing going on, almost as in a time-lapse. A bloody opening in the skin could close, suture itself and scab. The scab could be picked prematurely, leaving a rift of faint red.

There could be the clearing of airways, the pinking of lungs, the flaking off of sores. There was water washing over everything and everyone, a flood of healing. The deluge serenaded by the tinny, clattering music of the jingle dress—metal on metal. A fire bag hung from the Jingle Dancer's skirt that held a flint and a clump of moss. It was decorative—part of the regalia—but, if needed, could be used. Exley felt at Sue's waist, as if grasping for the leather drawstrings of a fire bag. He found her navel, and his fingers traced the fatty flesh there. And he felt good. And she felt good, he thought. Sue felt the long, brass ring that Exley wore around his neck—the one his ma had given him so many years ago to keep his nose from bleeding. She felt it hanging at the small of his back. Her limbs feathered over his, weightless. And they looked at each other, briefly, if for no other reason than to bear witness to what they were doing.

THE STEADY DRUMBEAT GREW LOUDER as they walked, hand-in-hand, back to the fairgrounds. Party poppers had been distributed among the children, and the boys and girls pulled the strings sending crimped confetti streamers into the air. The Jingle Dancer was going strong—her subtle footwork could've easily been mistaken for a standstill—but the metal cones on her skirt were singing and shimmering in the sunlight. Exley saw Zike and Elsie through the crowd. Elsie was pouring water into Dixie cups and Zike was watching her do it. But, behind them, up the hill where a maze of yellow caution tape designated parking spaces, Exley saw two expensive cars—an Audi and a Lexus—pull slowly to the crest.

Applause for the Jingle Dancer was resounding: everyone— elders and youngbloods and even the littlest, stroller-bound kids— hooted and hollered their support. Exley, not wanting to let go of Sue's hand, didn't join in. But his eyes went back to the two cars on the crest of the hill as both drivers began to obnoxiously blare their car horns. The honking soon got the attention of everyone at the powwow—they craned their necks and rose up on their toes to see beyond the peaked canvas tent tops.

Exley could see clearly what was happening. Bodies were leaning out the car windows and waving wildly. One slender torso even emerged through the Lexus moonroof. The horns continued honking—perplexing plenty of the tribe—until that noise subsided and the occupants of the cars clarified their message.

They brought their hands—shaped to sip water, shallowly cupped—up to their mouths and patted. Short, recurrent pats. They produced a low, monotonous sound that echoed against their patting hands: *whoa-oh-oh-oh-oh-oh*. War whoops.

Sue looked at Exley but didn't say anything as he let go of her hand. He negotiated his way through the crowd, rushing to his moeder's FREE ICE WATER table. He bumped it as he squeezed around, spilling the Dixie cups on that side of the table. *The fuck?* he heard Zike say, but he ignored his big brother and crouched behind him. Exley unzipped his backpack on the chair and reached his hand in, rustling for the handgun. He felt the red mechanic rag, the boxer shorts, and uncovered the weapon. He felt the cool steel of the handgun like a stinging burn on his fingertips.

"What the hell you doing?" Zike asked, struggling to turn his body, his carbuncled neck, to Exley behind him. "Don't you see what they doing up there? Punks." He spit.

Exley's mind had gone pitch black: a depthless space of staticky friction. But Zike's words, and his presence, woke him. He zipped the backpack and slung it over his shoulders. He hustled to join with a group of elders in full regalia trudging across the field to scatter the hecklers.

"Where you going?" Zike shouted to him. "Leave that alone!"

Exley caught up with the elders and surpassed them. His fists gripped the straps of his backpack, hiking the bag up high on his shoulders. The bottom of the bag, weighted with the blued handgun, bounced off a notch in his spine. He was bellicose and red. He pushed back his thatch of hair, out of his stinging face. As he got closer to the two cars, he yelled: *Ayyo!*

None of them looked at Ex. Nobody shouted back at him or gestured. They abruptly climbed back into their cars, settled into their seats, and the drivers shifted into gear. Exley saw his moeder behind the Audi, violently coughing and waving away the group. She put her fist to her mouth and limped to the side as the cars pulled away. Exley's anger was redirected onto Hannah. Her hair was wild, a reckless bonfire of fibers. The coughing continued, sandpaper coarse and choking, but—if not for that convulsion— she'd be a sleepwalker, somnolent in her muumuu and house slippers. A widow wandering a hillside, the spray of her coughs a black mourning veil. Her eyes watered from either crying or coughing.

"What the hell do you think you're doing, Ma?" She couldn't answer, still struggling to get her breath. "Get back home—to bed. I can't believe you're out here."

"Exley," she managed. "Exley." She put her hand on his arm, holding him.

"What, Ma?" he said, his anger subsiding. "You shouldn't be out here. I really don't think you should be out here. You walked all this way? Are you crazy?"

"Exley. It's Meal. Meal Milligan, Exley." His jaw clenched, his face turning stony. "She's passed, son." The elders mounted the hill. The stark simplicity of Hannah's clothes looked incongruous beside their regalia of feathered plumes and colorful beads and stiff buckskins. She turned to them, reporting the news not to respected authorities, but to neighbors, friends. She said it again. *Meal Milligan has passed.*

Word spread amongst the masses. And then there were no words. No more war whoops, but no jubilation either. No jingling metal. Old man Cotton coiled the tug o'war rope, collected it into a potato sack, and slung the sack over his shoulder. One of the college students in attendance had to be told to stop filming. Much of the crowd slowly dispersed, while others methodically packed up their wares and collapsed their tents. Exley stood on the hillside in his moeder's embrace.

33

GUSSIE DIDN'T KNOW WHERE TO GO. He drove to the Mattress Factory to pick up his paycheck. He parked in the front lot, not wanting to go anywhere close to the loading dock, not wanting to run the risk of seeing Theo, Dew, or Tone. He wanted to be unseen; he only wanted the money owed him—a slip of paper with a perforated edge that would remind him he was a provider, that he had provided.

He wiped his nose with his shirtsleeve and left a streak of snot like a slugtrail. The door chimed as he entered the showroom. Beds everywhere. Customers reclined on them—cozying, fetal. His mind zagged.

Kent, the sales manager, tried to offer condolences, but Gussie couldn't quite look up from the floor long enough to say thanks. Kent rifled through a stack of envelopes looking for Gussie's. He found it after two passes. Gussie got out of the store as fast as he could. He opened his car door and stripped to his undershirt— his California Kings team t-shirt. His armpits were sweating, and white flakes of deodorant clumped together, matting the hair.

He drove down Route 17, stone-faced in start-and-stop traffic. He didn't curse or tilt his head against the window glass or rage. He squirmed and lifted himself forward, sliding a tattered and furry and shredded tissue from his back pocket. He dabbed his nose, feeling the fibers pull apart, feeling the paper disintegrate. *Soft tissue*. Every time he and Ora and the doctors, the oncologist, spoke the phrase *soft tissue*, this is what Meal must've thought of. This: a torn-up tissue from her daddy's pocket. This raggedy paper product he handed her when she cried in agony at the pains shooting through her legs. Not of sarcomas or *sarx* or flesh or malignancies. But a reused and repocketed Kleenex. There was so much she would never know. Gussie nearly rear-ended the car in front of him.

The rearview mirror was adjusted so that it still reflected Meal's car seat. Its slack straps and buckle were twisted and crisscrossed, and their disarray emphasized emptiness. He wouldn't readjust the mirror, he wouldn't. He didn't care what was coming up behind him. Damn the approaching traffic, the tailgating cars. He didn't want to be aware of his surroundings. He wanted his daughter's body to be, to be in that car seat, to fill its void—her dangling legs and tucked-in arms. He wanted serious joy. Wanted to see Meal mouthing the words to a pop song on the radio. See her singing to an imaginary friend. *She's not sick. She's not gone. This hasn't happened.*

Gussie's car went diagonal, almost perpendicular to the traffic lanes in order to pull over to the shoulder. He barreled out of the car as if there were a fire inside—the dashboard engulfed, flames lapping against the inside of the windshield. He crossed his arms, hugging himself with a pained look on his face, his neck muscles strained into an old-growth, hardwood treetrunk. He needed to be alone even if he wasn't alone. He wasn't alone. Passing cars rubbernecked. Several honked—if not at him, then at the rubbernecking vehicles in front of them. One even screeched, stopping short, and the tires left skidmarks on the asphalt and burnt rubber wafting through the air.

He lifted his legs—first one, then the other—over the guardrail and into the shrubs, kicking at the accumulated roadside debris and litter. Into a thicket of vetches and a field of fetid pennycress. His steps sent off a flurry of moths. A tupelo tree was bowed groundward, bowing at Gussie, offering condolences. He wept.

Wellaway! Oh, to be orphaned or widowed instead—but no. There was nothing: no consolation, no words. Only a *non*-ness, a without. He would lead a privative existence from then on, a posthumous existence. Father to a whilomed child, now. *No no no no no.* What was left was to while away, wither some, to wait. He was bereaved of his daughter, bereft of his land. It all, for Gussie, had the feel of finality. *Whither to go?* He collapsed in a heap of man.

He thought of the morphine drip, the stiff cellophane-like pillow in her hospital bed. He wanted to go back there, to scavenge for hairs and hangnails, for any semblance of her. No: he didn't want to go back. He thought of his bedside chair pulled close enough to rest his chest beside her. How he brushed her hair back as he'd done when she were a baby in the dead of night, early AM hours, with his eyesight maladjusted and her body just the blur of a blessing. But in the hospital it was midafternoon, and there's no romance to 2PM. No one, least of all Emilia, should die on a sunny day. It was like the best days he'd spent with her—digging in the yard, tramping the woods, capering at a playground. He'd drive her to a nice one, one in Fardale, outfitted with an elaborate jungle gym. When she was two, she'd crouch and gather fistfuls of woodchips. As she got older, she learned to climb, fearless and full of risk. And Gussie would be stricken with terror at the gaps in the towers she might mistake for a slide, the tunnels that had ladder holes like trapdoors, the metal bars of the teeter-totter. At the right angle, death was always there. He was guilt-ridden— *why hadn't he better protected her?* He'd done so much wrong, he thought. Why did he push so hard when they potty-trained her? She'd withhold, and they would wait and wait and wait for her to break, but she wouldn't. She'd squirm uncomfortably, and they could feel her discomfort. Gussie recalled how she would pad her feet against his legs, beg to sit on his lap—something about the pressure would make the withholding easier. And he hated that. He'd push her off him. *Go pee*, he'd say. *Do your business already.* How he regretted it now.

Still on his knees, he rotated to face the highway. Traffic had started to move. He couldn't register the faces in the passing cars, and he was grateful for that. How could he face anyone? He'd peel his face right off his skull if he needed to, if that was what it would take. The mask of mourning wouldn't cut it. He could only tolerate pity and sympathy meals for so long. Gussie knew, going forward, it would be harder than ever not to die.

34

June 1998.

It had been almost two months since the diagnosis. Zike hadn't told Elsie yet, and that meant they hadn't had sex in that span either, which meant she had her suspicions. The absence of Zike's grab-assing made it obvious something was up. He'd also given up on driving to school with her. The discomfort he felt with his own body—the alienness of it—made him reluctant to even be in her presence. He didn't want to put himself at risk for a hand-hold or a casual cuddle. *Distance.* He needed to keep his distance from her, from the intimacy of others.

So Zike rode his partially repaired 4-stroke Honda to school. He left home early and would do a lap on Cannon Mine Trail. *It clears the head*, is what he told himself. But the more he repeated it, the more those *clears* piled up and crammed together and cluttered his head with a dyslexia of stress and nerves.

The day Zike got himself expelled from school was far from routine even before the fight. Helicopters hovered like hummingbirds overhead—there had been a house explosion in Ramsey. A gas leak, they'd find out later. Naturally, Zike looked up. He slowed at the hairpin turns, tentative, still very much in touch with the crash he had had two years before—the keloid scar on his chest: a caterpillar crawling between his pecs. He looked up, watching the sway of the helicopters, making the bold numbers on their sides—two, four, and seven: news channels. The unnatural looking up and looking down—sky to trail, trail to sky—irritated his neck, the nodules there, maroon red and shiny.

There was a black hawk up ahead, a fan of off-white on the tail feathers. Zike watched it soar over the canopy. His grip tightened at a rutted portion of the trail. And, having neglected gloves, the web of skin between his thumb and forefinger chafed something awful. He was happy to get off the trail, onto the open road, and ride the chipseal and then the smooth asphalt.

He arrived at school sweaty and bookless. The massiveness and the messiness of his body parted the cars in the parking lot—each vehicle seeming to dent or deconstruct at his passing. He saw a pickup he'd never seen before with a sticker on the cab window: *Buy a gun. Piss off a liberal.* He bumped the sideview mirror as he angled through. Everyone noticed him: he was broad-shouldered and brooding and malodorous. His hair was moussed and hardened into a devilock that split his face in two. Specks of dandruff fell on his black hoodie like confectioner's sugar. From the waist down, he was splattered, mud-caked at the cuffs of his pants. He was death metal walking.

Elsie would always wait for Zike outside the auditorium doors where they'd hang out until the first period bell. Zike would go to his locker first and retrieve his one-subject spiral notebook—the only item he carried to every class. With the arrival of June, classes were winding down, final exam prep was starting, and the lax attitude of the faculty and students—after nine months of the school year—finally matched up with Zike's slackering. Bodies were everywhere. Students slumped down to the floor in front of their lockers eating French toast sticks and stale bagels from the cafeteria. Some were even splayed, sleeping, on the checkered tile floor.

Zike opened his locker, which he always kept pre-set for convenience, and a landslide of deodorant sticks came tumbling out at his feet. He tried to slam the locker shut to prevent their falling, but he couldn't manage it. He only made himself look like a klutz, his knee rising to stem the flow of the Mennen Speed Sticks. He kicked some of them away from his space, sending them across the hall and finally heard the laughing.

The students—his peers—crowded around him in a semi-circle. Zike's jaw ached. He'd been clenching his teeth since he pulled into the parking lot. Now, though, he was clenching tightly enough to grind enamel away. He turned and looked at the crowd surrounding him, his vision divided by the devilock. Once a point of prideful nonconformity, he felt silly with it now. And then some stooge—some accomplice to the prank, somebody Zike didn't even know by name—stepped close enough to be confrontational, looked Zike in the eyes, and commented: *Stank-ass hill nig.*

Zike lunged, grabbed the kid by his collar, and spun him around. The kid's shocked expression failed to evoke mercy in Zike. Zike openhandedly walloped the kid's face. The smack was deep and resonant. Zike's palm was like a wad of stiffening plaster. Everybody *ohh*-ed at the sound.

He staggered the kid across the width of the hallway, crashing him into the lockers on the opposite side. Zike, unthinking, closed his fists and pounded the kid's face, the top of his head. The skull knotted above the eyebrow, and Zike kept at the knot with the promise of cleaving it. He didn't feel the bands of his skull rings cutting into his own knuckles, and he didn't feel the kid going limp. The downward motion of his fists, paradoxically, held the kid's body up.

The knot opened, and Zike pushed the kid mightily into the water fountain on the wall next to the lockers. His swelling face hit the porcelain, and the top and bottom teeth shuttled out and tinkled on the floor. The jaw dislocated and dangled like some animatronic skeleton skull. This kid—the one with the mouth on him, who had something to say—crumbled to the floor.

Outside the auditorium doors, Elsie overheard one girl say Zike's name to another, and she watched the two girls rush off, arm in arm, toward the senior wing of the building. Other students rushed along, too—some even running. She was most alarmed when the school police officer—a nearly retired

Mahwah detective who everyone called "Narc"—barreled down the corridor, noise and feedback and calamity coming out of his walkie-talkie. She followed the crowd.

The vice principal and the dean of discipline were dispersing students. Elsie had a clear view of her boyfriend. He was sitting on the floor against the lockers, his knees pulled to his chest. She saw his chest heaving and the dried mud on his boots and ankles splattered all the way up to his knees. Narc was standing over Zike with his fingertips grazing his shoulder, restraining him with just that. He spoke into his walkie-talkie, issuing directives to other administrators not yet on the scene. Zike's victim—bloodied and barely with it—had already been removed from the hall. A voice from the walkie-talkie indicated an ambulance was en route. Ms. Valentine, the guidance counselor, kept Elsie from getting anywhere close to Zike.

Janitors were already showing up with their castered buckets. They rolled up to the water fountain and remarked on the blood smear across the front of the basin. A trail of blood—first only some drops, then something that could be considered a puddle—stretched several feet along the lockers. They sloshed their mops for the following hour, glugging no less than two hydrogen peroxide bottles onto the bloodpool. The fumes filled the hall, and, between bells, students held binders and five-subject notebooks to their faces.

35

IN THE DAYS FOLLOWING MEAL'S FUNERAL, Exley couldn't shake certain sounds from his head. The squeaking wheels of the casket trolley. The cawing of a crow on the crosspiece of a telephone pole at the cemetery. But the loudest and most trenchant was Ora's quavering screams at the burial plot. It reverberated in the way a stone hitting a stop sign does. Exley heard the quaver as he watched Ora pass into the bathroom, or as she opened the refrigerator door for coldcuts, or as she swayed on the porch in grief.

Ora had asked Hannah if her and Gussie could move in temporarily: the damage done unto their home by daughter death and sinkhole was too much to live with. Hannah, of course, obliged them, though Gussie had yet to show, and Ora hadn't bothered to search him out. Ora relieved Elsie of her caretaking duties; she cherished the time with Hannah and her infirmity. Hannah seemed to become a surrogate for Ora, a daughter she might save. And every time Exley witnessed Ora in that mode— motherly, affectionate, fetching a glass of water or gliding an ice chip across his ma's neckline—an image of Meal's face flashed to mind. A shadow was superimposed over her face. Black ash. She was gloamed, entombed in contaminated earth. She was gone but still so close, so very near the surface.

THE HUMIDITY RETURNED the first week of school. With no AC, Mahwah High was sweltering like a blast furnace. Students relayed into the hall to make wet bandanas out of rolled-up paper towels at the water fountain. Teachers grumbled about the distraction, flipped the lights off—that old preschool trick—and reviewed syllabi in the dim. By the end of the week, a repulsive, adolescent funk had pervaded the building.

Exley sat in junior homeroom not talking to anyone, feeling and seeming like a pariah. The day was passing—not as periods—but as *moment, moment, moment.* He stared out the window at the signboard near the school's entrance, which read, *Make it a great year...or not. The choice is YOURS!* He carved his EX D initials into the curved edge of his desk, snapping off his pen tip and inking his fingers. He wiped the ink with the hem of his t-shirt, but the spots only grew cloudier, like bruises. While other kids copied homework, he concentrated on clearing Meal Milligan's closed casket from his mind. What would it be like, he thought, to have Gussie living with him? It would be a hollowed out version of the man, all angles and anguish. Not a roommate, available to ball or bullshit. Exley wasn't sure he'd even be able to look the man in the face for fear of seeing a semblance of Meal there.

The bell rang and Exley was first out the door. He hustled to the senior wing, one strap of his backpack slung over his shoulder. The weight was still there—the weight of the blued handgun. The red mechanic rag; the boxer shorts; and now a marble notebook and a prayer card with the name Emilia Milligan printed onto it. The card lacked holiness: no saint icons, Bible passages, or even prayers for that matter. It was no better than a lotto scratchoff. These simple items—meager objects—made him complete. He could up and hobo it to the other coast if so compelled. *What was it*—two items? Those two items, representing a dyad—his da and his Meal—would be mile markers, trail blazes. He could bounce back and forth between the two for the foreseeable future, forever.

Sue found Exley before he found her. She approached him from behind and gripped her hands around his waist. It made him tighten and wince.

"You alright?" she asked.

"I'm good, I'm good."

"You don't need to be good, Ex."

"Yea-up," he said. "But I'm good."

They walked down the senior wing toward her locker. Exley held her hand but only because he felt the need to make up for his flinching. Sue was trying, he could tell, to bring him back from where he'd been in recent days.

Sue's locker was in the neighborhood of Adams', and Exley

brimmed with dread seeing him up ahead. His hand went stiff in Sue's, and his feet dragged.

"I only need my pre-calc book, Ex."

He relented and allowed Sue to lead him by the hand as though leashed.

Sue's locker was pre-set, so it was a short spin of the dial and she was in. Adams clattered his shut and did a goon lean against it.

"Look at the lovebirds." He nudged Hitch.

"Fuck off," Sue told him. Exley was surprised by her scorn.

"DeGroat," Adams said, ignoring Sue, "how's the snot box?" He squeezed the bridge of his nose and made a creaky noise. "My brother says hi, DeGroat. He's sorry about the elbow to the nose. He is. He *really* is." A smile slithered across Adams' face. The men's league game seemed ages ago, and Adams invoking it ruptured time.

Exley arched his back and put his free arm through his other backpack strap. He tightened the tethers of each strap, one being long enough to reach into his mouth. And he gnawed on the end, which was only starting to fray. For a moment, he was the bigger man—sagacious, sighing heavily. Sue saw it in him, and he swelled with confidence.

"That's what your career's come to, huh, DeGroat? Playing old-timers ball? Next up," he thumped Hitch on the chest, cueing his lackey to laugh, "next up it'll be wheelchairs. Special Olympics, DeGroat?"

"Keep talkin', dude. Everything's a standup routine with you," Ex said, coolly. "No cameras here, though. Your daddy's not in the stands with his video camera recording your highlight reel. Like he was doing for your brother. Pathetic fuck."

Sue hooked Exley's arm, but his teeth freed the backpack tether and he wouldn't allow her to tug him away. The saliva on the strap touched him at the elbow, and it both invigorated and irritated him. He waited for Adams' comeback.

"Not as pathetic as that fucking brother of yours with his swamp dick."

Exley shoved Adams—two hands into the chest, and his fingers scratched at his collar. Sue grabbed Exley's shoulder, but he was rigid, immovable. The bell rang and nobody went to class. The throng established a ring, a clearing, and—for Exley—it all became dreamlike.

REALITY FUZZED. THE EDGES RIPPLED like riverwater, like gamma rays. Then those edges went soft and blurry like talcum in the eye. *Like, like, like* all of this was happening at once. A sort of tunnel vision in the tunnel of the senior wing. A mine adit, a mine shaft—posts and lintels. A passageway. Adams wasn't at the other end; Zike was. If he squinted, he could see Zike—a silhouette of his brother's body in the shape of a keyhole. A distance of years away, sure, but he felt the weight of Zike's entire mortified body sprawled over his shoulders like a ratty shawl. Time folded and creased; a fingernail sharpened the fold; razorblade sharp. His fists landed the same as his brother's had, as cobblestones on soil. Fists like ziploc bags of powdered formula. Puffs of smoke with every punch. Stage magic. *Poof!* Norval DeGroat vanishes! Lenny Van Dunk vanishes! Emilia Milligan vanishes! Disappear those people. Dispeople those woods. There was the momentum of Zike's muscular movements behind Exley's. Exley was a double; he had double vision. Adams was his older brother and Exley was his. Exley sensed his body sprouting sickness—carbuncles, skin grafts, and scarred flesh: springtime buds. His body became brutish, crude, and decomposed. It swelled with tension. He could contaminate Adams, contagion him. Silence his commentary, the insults. Exley was awash in slurs and aspersions, a welter of historical abuses. His brains went fizzing like when you yank the ballchain on the bare bulb in Unky Orrin's shack, and it goes dim, less dim, brightening, near-bright, and bright once and for all. He and Adams were him and Zike in the cauldron pool—algaeslick and flailing. Whatever words he was gabbling were serifed, so they could catch Adams' clothes, so they could cut his skin. He and Adams' antipodal positions, an arm's length apart. It was all too familiar. Just a pattern, a history unrevised. Told over and over again with fewer details and less passion. What was left to say or to show? The water fountain. It wasn't so far down the hall. The water fountain's whiteness. That's what white is. Whitest of the white, right there. His skin was blanched. Then it all, suddenly, went black again. Black and blued by a jaw jab. The blued handgun in the backpack still on his back, strapped to his shoulders.

He was strapped. He wanted to brandish it. *Brandish it.* Swing it by the trigger guard. Unzip the backpack, Exley. Step back. Unsling the backpack from your shoulder; unzip it. Unpack what you're packing. The heat. He was so hot it didn't matter. His sweat was cool dew. The handgun should've been tucked in his waistline; he could've lifted his shirt, flashed it. Instilled fear. It was bulletless, yeap, but no matter. There's always the butt of the gun—blunt force. Don't be the butt of the joke, Exley. *Want* to leave triangular lacerations. *Want* to skull fracture. Pistol-whip the sonofabitch, the sonofagun. Pistol-whip his bleeding pink inside-out eyelids. Pistol-whip him. (They used to call it buffaloing.) Go off, Exley. Go off the reservation. Go off on him. The blued Ruger Blackhawk handgun must go off. If only it had a bullet, if only. And then, suddenly, it's: *You're following in your brother's footsteps, son.* It's the vice principal's office. It's the guidance counselor sitting across from him. It's Aaron the manager and Mike the LPS guy all over again. Knees. Knees close together. Backpack between his feet; hands still gripping the straps. If they only knew what he had in there. It's: *Automatic twenty-one day suspension.* It's: *We can't be having this, son.* It's: *This is what we're going to do, son.* Don't call him "son." What was this judgment, this death sentence? Why was he sitting in this windowless office with the sallow light? Don't call him son. He's not your son.

36

EXLEY DIDN'T STOP TO SAY GOODBYE to Sue before leaving school. The vice principal told him to leave the premises right away—his suspension began immediately. So Exley sped out of the parking lot as fast as his ma's Ford Escort could. His body was still suffused with adrenaline, and then his muscles relaxed as he slouched in the driver's seat.

Out the window, the Tenax orange mesh fence at the roadside blurred to a solid streak of orange. It seemed to run the length of the Wanaque Reservoir—a grounded sun dragging along the earth's surface. There were no EPA officials working, but Ex counted the monitoring wells monitoring. He made a mental note of the new NO TRESPASSING sign fastened to the entrance gate. Unky Orrin would probably want it for his collection.

The Escort struggled up Stag Hill Road, sputtering even, and Exley could feel the engine failing. Once he reached level ground, he was good. And then it was the usual bumping and careening of the unpaved road. The unaxed wilderness was at its densest right before his arrival at the holler, and then it was the junkers and the pallets and Rhetta's wire-meshed chicken ark, the mere presence of each item a clear inconvenience to nature.

He spied Gussie in his garden, disheveled and dirty-faced. His hair was misshapen into a corn shock. Harvest-time had all but arrived, and Gussie had returned to the tangled vines of his raised beds to glean what he could. Exley didn't slow the car, acknowledging Gussie still wasn't right for conversation, still wanting to be unseen. Gussie was camouflaged within the trellises and poultry netting. He parsed the overgrowth, snipping with shears at what had rotted on the vine, seeing if he could extricate the okra stalks from the remorseless strangling of the zucchini plants. And behind the mechanical movements of Gussie's bent frame was the Milligan household visibly tilting into the sinkhole.

At the DeGroat home, Ora wasn't pacing the porch, and her car wasn't in their driveway either. Exley was pleased with that. Maybe she was out looking for her husband, unaware he was as close to home as he'd been in a week, his hands green from the gloveless uprooting of plants by their stems. Regardless, Exley was grateful to avoid whatever questions she might have and whatever quavering screams the sight of her might conjure for him.

It was quiet inside—no phone conversations, no soap actors overdoing it on the TV, no nebulizer. He passed the photo of his parents hanging in the hallway, the one with them in the hollow of the tree, their feet obscured by the lens flare. He peeked in on his moeder's room and saw her regally propped in bed on a mountain of pillows. Her mouth was agape until it chewed and her lips smacked in reaction to the creak of the door. She was certainly asleep—not dead or even dying—and her slumber put Exley even more at ease.

He entered the bathroom and opened the vanity mirror. He picked up the hair buzzer that had its kinked cord wrapped around itself. He unraveled it, and it fell like a ball-and-chain but didn't hit the floor or the sink edge. Exley swung it back up and held it for a second—it, too, had the weight of a weapon. He set the buzzer down on the sink and lifted his shirt off. He removed the attachment clip that was on the buzzer so he could achieve the closest shave possible—a prison shave or, perhaps, a monk shave. Someone once told him you cut off your hair to grieve the loss of a parent, only allowing it to grow back fully when the grief is gone. Exley decided it was time to grieve.

He ran his hand over his thatch of red hair, and it was hard to the touch—stiffened with beeswax gel hours before. His fingertips massaged the side of his head that was already shaved, feeling a mole that emerged from the bristles. He clicked on the buzzer, and it sizzled with electricity. The blades quivered. The back of his head went first, from the nape of his neck to the crown. Then he circled the buzzer around the side, riding the contours of his cranium. The stiff hairs fell to his shoulders and then to the basin. Red hair clumps contrasted with the porcelain white of the sink: it was like the sheddings of some nocturnal varmint.

He laughed, humorlessly, at his reflection. What he'd left was a forelock of hair, Kairos-like, that fell over his face like the excess end of a leather belt. He rubbed the back of his skull, and the prickles tingled his soft and sensitive palm. There was a mild knot and a nick where Adams had grappled. Exley folded back the forelock while clearing the shavings from the buzzer blade with a miniature brush. He clicked on the buzzer again, and gave a final pass at the forelock. It fell thick and stiff like a warped piece of plywood. That was it: Exley's noggin was bald.

After slipping his shirt back on, he checked on Hannah again—still asleep. In the kitchen, he stopped at the sink to smack tap water onto his face, allowed it to drip dry, and then he took the death ledger from the table and crammed it into his backpack. He started for the door—wanting to be out of there before Ora returned—but he doubled-back, wiggled loose the hutch drawer, and pocketed his da's plaited lanyard compass. Forget the handgun. If there was a family heirloom, the compass was it.

He was on foot now, the contents of his backpack bulging, the weight of the load being something he wasn't accustomed to. One foot in front of the other, though, and he headed through the woods in a literal sense—his head a full stride in front of his body.

Unky Orrin wasn't in or around his cabin. Exley cupped his hands around his eyes and looked into a smudged and streaky sash window. The disorder of the living space was enough to make someone suspect a break-in. Exley tried the knob but couldn't gain entrance. He circled the premises and came back to the front and settled on the junk sculpture with the yellow oil funnel antennae. The figure was bothersome to look at—it felt as though he were gut-pressed with barbs. Orrin had completed the piece, and its coal-black body had been properly striped with primer.

Watching the haunting figure and not his feet, Exley stubbed a blue propane torch. It had been abandoned in the yard like a baseball bat or a fallen tree branch, and it rolled unevenly away from him, the nozzle already attached. It was old, the Bernzomatic label was a palimpsest, worn and peeling and bearing the mark of Orrin's hand. It was just what Exley needed, so he angled it into his backpack and the nozzle stuck out where the zipper stopped. It looked as though he'd be radiating radio waves across the Ramapo valley. He hiked away but kept his eyes on the creepy or consecrated sculpture, seeing it for what it probably was intended to be—a life-size kachina doll, which Unky Orrin had once schooled him on. Even still, the sculpture troubled him like a jinx.

Exley tried to keep his head. He browsed off on a little-traveled trail before cutting through a denser course. His thinking was prosaic—tree there; rock underfoot; sky up. It was about positioning, establishing some set of abstract coordinates within himself and only knowable by him. The woods were blank and undefined, awash in their constituent colors. The forest just watercolor paints pooling on a metallic surface. A set of pastels each ground into the same, small spot.

Then he came to a clearing, and he ran. He ran wildly, vigorously, exhausting himself. His gut filled with nausea and it rose like a wooden block and lodged in his throat. *Sprinting*—he was sprinting. It was like the conditioning drills they ran the first week of the basketball season after tryouts. Baseline to foul line and back. Baseline to midcourt and back. Baseline to opposite foul line and back. Baseline to other baseline and back. A *suicide*, coaches across the country called it. The word settled in Exley's mind.

White oaks framed the mountain—they were scaffolding and fenceposts and gangly-limbed behemoths. Exley was in the area of Peters Mine now, approaching it from a direction he hadn't before. He knew he was near it because of the debris— the dented barrels, outdated car parts, and variegated sludge chunks. His chest heaved and his pulse raced as he began to regulate his breathing, slowing his steps. There was a steep incline, and he scaled it by leaning forward so his backpack wouldn't drag him down into a gulch. His sweat-slick hands grabbed at a boulder wall of gneiss, clasping at its convexities. After making it to even ground, he squatted and sized up the rock. It shimmered with specks of quartz, but Exley didn't know—hadn't been properly taught—what any of it meant. It was a rock, sparkly, with thin lines of white. It had moss-filled rifts. He knew nothing of the magnetism throbbing within the rock. Nothing of the iron ore that time had buried within it, nor did he care. He dug his da's plaited lanyard compass from his pocket. He didn't read it—didn't know how; he just began lashing it, lashing it against the rock, cracking the compass face. He lashed it until the glass was spiderweb shattered. Thus satisfied, he shoved it back into his pocket and kept climbing.

When he got to Peters Mine and was staring down the adit, he sensed there was no sun. He felt like he'd never been there before. *He was born with a knife in his brain*, his da was fond of saying whenever Exley tantrumed or fell over his own feet, and now it seemed that brain had either no understanding of anything or total understanding of everything.

He looked at the mine: it wanted fire.

Exley sat on a pallet and swung his backpack off his shoulder and onto his lap. He removed the blue propane torch, his marble notebook, the death ledger, Meal's prayer card, and the blued Ruger Blackhawk handgun. He leaned back and pulled the plaited lanyard compass from his pocket. Everything was spread around him on the planks of the pallet as though he had gone camping and taken some time alone to reorganize his rucksack.

The pages of the marble notebook pulled easily from the sewn binding leaving loose ends of string dangling. Exley tore the pages north to south and then into smaller and smaller sawtooth squares, to bits, and stacked them. Then, taking up the death ledger, he flipped pages and skimmed entries—all those evenly arranged columns titled with *DOBs* and *DODs* like stumpy, googly-eyed losers—until finally: *Norval DeGroat*, in his ma's looping script. The listed cause said not *suicide* but *self.* Exley massaged his fuzzy skull, which, with the open air swirling around it, seemed to emanate potential energy.

He flipped to the farthest, most recent—what would be the final—pages of the ledger. *Emilia Milligan* was penciled in (as though it weren't certain yet) preceded by *Hannah DeGroat*— premature and prognosticating—followed by gaps, slots of white space, negative space. Her name and date-of-birth were filled in, but there were blanks for cause- and date-of-death. And there was a yellow sticky note at the margin—a reminder to her son, for what he had to do. Exley wanted nothing to do with that. He wasn't ceremonial—that's what county clerks and funeral directors were for. *Fuck the gloaming*, he slurred under his breath. He briefly turned the ledger over, tented it on the pallet, took up Meal's prayer card, ripped it in half, and added it to the paper pile, the tinder. Then he clutched the death ledger close to his ribs and ripped its spine apart. The pile of paper grew higher.

Rising to his feet, Exley walked closer to the mine, slightly staggering, stood inside the adit, and held the handgun like a gun is held. He rewrapped the handgun in the red mechanic rag, replicating how miners used to walk into adits with handkerchiefs snuggled around knifeblades, or so he'd been told. It was to ward off whatever might lay in wait. Exley could sense his blood moving through his body the way water fills a hose. He became dizzy and disoriented. He was spinning off north. Exley was a youngblood—a strange, unsettled boy, Orrin once told Norval. *Strange*, because the ground was made of metal. And on the ground is where infant Exley played. Nothing could be done about that now. He inventoried his relations: he had a ma; he had a da for seven years; had a brother, an unky, and woodpile relations aplenty. But he had no relation to the earth. Who or what he belonged with, he didn't know. So he stopped his staring at the mine and chucked the handgun into the maw of it.

Exley carried as much of the paper pile as he could and dropped it a few feet into the mine. He added tree bark and dry grasses, too. He would provide fire. He opened the valve on the propane torch and triggered the flame. A young flame—sharp and blue— pierced the paper pile, blackened and burned the edges and the whole stack went up. It didn't take much at all.

And he fed the fire. He fed it and fed it. He believed the mine could be satiated, and he intended to satiate. He threw in armfuls of branches and twigs, dragged leaves to the base of the fire with the side of his sneaker. He heaved in a pallet—the one he had been sitting on—and the planks and galvanized nails of another. He shoveled in as much debris as he could find. He threw in sludge barrels still lined with linseed oil and polyurethane. Those dormant chemicals—the thinners, lacquers, and strippers—were all still very much combustible. They fed the fire. He visualized the drift of heavy metal molecules and ions, absent from sight but not from air. He flung in the lanyard compass. He wasn't bringing anything back.

The fire filled the adit. The mine was throwing up flames. Exley's face was flushed and perspiring. He backed away. He'd wait for nightfall. Maybe he'd watch it burn for weeks, for three weeks—the length of his suspension. He'd make no effort to call the fire department. Damn them. If anything, he'd stay on site to keep the fire from going out.

Exley thought he heard chimes as the fire burned—that rough clanging of Unky Orrin's creations, or maybe just the crackling of embers and snapping of branches. Smoke drifted in the direction of the money mansions in Fardale. They would see the tendrils from Rio Vista, and, eventually, the stench of the blaze—something like nail polish remover—would reach Cragmere.

Exley beheld the conflagration, the fire-flaught sky. Let it be a spectacle, he thought. Let the sky shift and alter the landscape. Let the guests on the highest floors of the Sheraton and even those living in Manhattan gawk at the horizon, at the manmade and unnatural disaster. Let the fire simmer for weeks on end. Let those people suck and sniff the fallout. Exley tensed at his thinking. But the tension in his chest, he was sure, was the indwelling ghost of his da. Exley watched the scrim of smoke rise over the mountain, and he felt materially better than he had.

ACKNOWLEDGEMENTS

A variety of texts helped shape the development of this novel: Leo Marx's *The Machine in the Garden: Technology and the Pastoral Ideal in America,* Louis Owens's *Other Destinies: Understanding the American Indian Novel,* Phaedra C. Pezzullo's *Toxic Tourism: Rhetorics of Pollution, Travel, and Environmental Justice,* Kevin Dann's *25 Walks in New Jersey,* Robert Steven Cohen's *The Ramapo Mountain People,* Maro Chermayeff and Micah Fink's *Mann v. Ford,* the reportage of Jan Barry, Mary Jo Layton, Alex Nussbaum, Tom Troncone, Lindy Washburn, Barbara Williams, and Thomas E. Franklin for the *Toxic Legacy* stories in *The Record,* and Alan Moore's *Saga of the Swamp Thing.*

Deep gratitude to those who supported the writing of the novel in ways intangible or material. Thanks to John Pietrowski at the Writers Theater of New Jersey for the shoptalk and the 1099s. Thanks to Nathan Oates for the early read and ongoing support. Jess Row for always answering my questions. To family who always ask how the writing is going. To Uncle Jeff for the correspondence of many years. Thanks to my parents for the support since inception. Thanks to Michelle for the generous time and for always being my first reader. To Joleen and Cecelia for adding emotional depth to my life and my work. Gratitude to the NEA for the boost to the bank account. To Jeremy Winter for proofing it. Eileen Holt for always reading the stuff. Thanks to Maria Scali for helping process everything. Thanks to Tricia Matthew for the encouragement. To my SPC-15 brothers whose real lives have never ceased to inspire fiction. Special thanks to Marc Estrin for having faith in the work and for the editorial patience to make it better. Thanks to Donna Bister for the assiduous work on making the book a book. Thanks to Two Clouds for the time spent at the Split Rock Sweetwater Prayer Camp, Chief Vincent Mann, and Chief Dwaine Perry for all you do to protect water, land, and people. And to all the Ramapoughs who continue to exist in spite of a hostile world. Another world is possible.

ABOUT THE AUTHOR

Joseph Rathgeber, a native of New Jersey, has received fellowships from the New Jersey State Council on the Arts for his poetry and the National Endowment for the Arts for his prose. He has previously published a story collection, *The Abridged Autobiography of Yousef R. and Other Stories,* and a book of hybrid poetry, *MJ.*

Fomite

About Fomite

A fomite is a medium capable of transmitting infectious organisms from one individual to another.

"The activity of art is based on the capacity of people to be infected by the feelings of others." Tolstoy, *What Is Art?*

Writing a review on Amazon, Good Reads, Shelfari, Library Thing or other social media sites for readers will help the progress of independent publishing. To submit a review, go to the book page on any of the sites and follow the links for reviews. Books from independent presses rely on reader to reader communications.

For more information or to order any of our books, visit
http://www.fomitepress.com/FOMITE/Our_Books.html

More Titles from Fomite...

Novels
Joshua Amses — *During This, Our Nadir*
Joshua Amses — *Ghats*
Joshua Amses — *Raven or Crow*
Joshua Amses — *The Moment Before an Injury*
Jaysinh Birjepatel — *Nothing Beside Remains*
Jaysinh Birjepatel — *The Good Muslim of Jackson Heights*
David Brizer — *Victor Rand*
Paula Closson Buck — *Summer on the Cold War Planet*
Dan Chodorkoff — *Loisaida*
David Adams Cleveland — *Time's Betrayal*
Jaimee Wriston Colbert — *Vanishing Acts*
Roger Coleman — *Skywreck Afternoons*
Marc Estrin — *Hyde*
Marc Estrin — *Kafka's Roach*
Marc Estrin — *Speckled Vanities*
Zdravka Evtimova — *In the Town of Joy and Peace*
Zdravka Evtimova — *Sinfonia Bulgarica*
Daniel Forbes — *Derail This Train Wreck*
Greg Guma — *Dons of Time*
Richard Hawley — *The Three Lives of Jonathan Force*
Lamar Herrin — *Father Figure*

Fomite

Michael Horner — *Damage Control*
Ron Jacobs — *All the Sinners Saints*
Ron Jacobs — *Short Order Frame Up*
Ron Jacobs — *The Co-conspirator's Tale*
Scott Archer Jones — *And Throw Away the Skins*
Scott Archer Jones — *A Rising Tide of People Swept Away*
Julie Justicz — *Degrees of Difficulty*
Maggie Kast — *A Free Unsullied Land*
Darrell Kastin — *Shadowboxing with Bukowski*
Coleen Kearon — *#triggerwarning*
Coleen Kearon — *Feminist on Fire*
Jan English Leary — *Thicker Than Blood*
Diane Lefer — *Confessions of a Carnivore*
Rob Lenihan — *Born Speaking Lies*
Douglas Milliken — *Our Shadow's Voice*
Colin Mitchell — *Roadman*
Ilan Mochari — *Zinsky the Obscure*
Peter Nash — *Parsimony*
Peter Nash — *The Perfection of Things*
George Ovitt — *Stillpoint*
George Ovitt — *Tribunal*
Gregory Papadoyiannis — *The Baby Jazz*
Pelham — *The Walking Poor*
Andy Potok — *My Father's Keeper*
Frederick Ramey — *Comes A Time*
Joseph Rathgeber — *Mixedbloods*
Kathryn Roberts — *Companion Plants*
Robert Rosenberg — *Isles of the Blind*
Fred Russell — *Rafi's World*
Ron Savage — *Voyeur in Tangier*
David Schein — *The Adoption*
Lynn Sloan — *Principles of Navigation*
L.E. Smith — *The Consequence of Gesture*
L.E. Smith — *Travers' Inferno*
L.E. Smith — *Untimely RIPped*
Bob Sommer — *A Great Fullness*
Tom Walker — *A Day in the Life*
Susan V. Weiss — *My God, What Have We Done?*
Peter M. Wheelwright — *As It Is On Earth*
Suzie Wizowaty — *The Return of Jason Green*

Fomite

Poetry

Fomite

Stories

Fomite

Fred Skolnik— *Americans and Other Stories*
Lynn Sloan — *This Far Is Not Far Enough*
L.E. Smith — *Views Cost Extra*
Caitlin Hamilton Summie — *To Lay To Rest Our Ghosts*
Susan Thomas — *Among Angelic Orders*
Tom Walker — *Signed Confessions*
Silas Dent Zobal — *The Inconvenience of the Wings*

Odd Birds

William Benton — *Eye Contact: Writing on Art*
Micheal Breiner — *the way none of this happened*
J. C. Ellefson — *Under the Influence: Shouting Out to Walt*
David Ross Gunn — *Cautionary Chronicles*
Andrei Guruianu and Teknari — *The Darkest City*
Gail Holst-Warhaft — *The Fall of Athens*
Roger Lebovitz — *A Guide to the Western Slopes and the Outlying Area*
Roger Lebovitz — *Twenty-two Instructions for Near Survival*
dug Nap— *Artsy Fartsy*
Delia Bell Robinson — *A Shirtwaist Story*
Peter Schumann — *Belligerent & Not So Belligerent Slogans from the Possibilitarian Arsenal*
Peter Schumann — *Bread & Sentences*
Peter Schumann — *Charlotte Salomon*
Peter Schumann — *Diagonal Man Theory & Praxis, Volumes One and Two*
Peter Schumann — *Faust 3*
Peter Schumann — *Planet Kasper, Volumes One and Two*
Peter Schumann — *We*

Plays

Stephen Goldberg — *Screwed and Other Plays*
Michele Markarian — *Unborn Children of America*

Essays

Robert Sommer — *Losing Francis: Essays on the Wars at Home*